Joyce Holms was born and educated in Glasgow. She has worked in a range of jobs, from teaching window-dressing and managing a hotel on the Island of Arran to working for an Edinburgh detective agency and running a B&B establishment in the Highlands. She lives in Edinburgh and her interests include hillwalking and garden design. She is married with two grown-up children.

Praise for Joyce Holm's previous Fizz and Buchanan mysteries

'THIN ICE proves that Holms is adroit at creating a diverting cocktail of suspense and humour'

The Times

'The writing is deft and smooth, the characters well-drawn and Fizz and Tam are a couple worth keeping an eye on' Donna Leon, *Sunday Times*

'Fizz and Buchanan are an extremely engaging couple . . . They are well drawn characters who are perfect foils for one another' *Shots*

'A good story, light-hearted, full of fascinating characters, and it makes me look forward to more of the exploits of Fizz and Buchanan' *Birmingham Post*

'A brilliant, sassy debut' *Crime Time*

Bitter End

Joyce Holms

headline

First published in 2001
by HEADLINE BOOK PUBLISHING

First published in paperback in 2002
by HEADLINE BOOK PUBLISHING

10 9 8 7 6 5 4 3 2 1

ISBN 0 7472 6344 2

Typeset by
Letterpart Limited, Reigate, Surrey

Printed and bound in Great Britain by
Clays Ltd, St Ives plc

HEADLINE BOOK PUBLISHING
A division of Hodder Headline
338 Euston Road
LONDON NW1 3BH

www.headline.co.uk
www.hodderheadline.com

To John.

Chapter One

Fizz had been keeping an eye on Buchanan for two days. He'd never been the most frolicsome of bosses but you could usually get a smile out of him now and then if you tried hard enough. Not recently, though.

It certainly wasn't like him to sit at his desk for minutes at a time, staring blankly into space, with an expression on his face like he could feel the entire population of Edinburgh walking over his grave. She was fairly certain it wasn't an affair of the heart, but something was definitely preying on his mind and he was refusing to admit it, either to Fizz – who had already tried several pseudo-casual probes – or to his secretary, the Wonderful Beatrice.

'So, you reckon it's not something to do with work, Beatrice? Buchanan hasn't made a bit of a hash of something, maybe, and is worried about getting found out?'

Beatrice's eyes glittered behind her specs: a lioness defending her cub. '*Mr* Buchanan doesn't make mistakes,' she said, barely parting her teeth sufficiently to let the words out. 'Not mistakes of *that* calibre, at any rate.'

Fizz was happy to agree with that estimate of her boss. She might prefer the simple things in life but she had no intention of working for one. She said, 'Well, but accidents happen, Beattie.'

'Not since I've worked here,' Beatrice stated, leaving Fizz to draw the obvious conclusion from that. 'I can't imagine Mr Buchanan having any professional worries, and I'm quite sure he wouldn't thank you for poking your nose into what is clearly none of your business, no matter how charitable your intentions.'

'How do you know it's none of my business?' Fizz retaliated. 'If the firm's about to go bust I want to be the first up at the Job Centre, don't you?'

'The firm's not going to go bust, Fizz, I can tell you that. Old established law practices like Buchanan and Stewart don't collapse overnight, and thank God for that because the Job Centre's not much good to a woman in her fifties.' She rapped the spacebar on her keyboard to clear her screensaver and started to hammer the keys like she was playing 'The Flight of the Bumblebee'. 'So clear off and give me peace.'

'I wonder if Dennis would crack under interrogation,' Fizz mused, looking out the window at a bunch of passing tourists on the open-topped City Tours bus. The tourists stared back at her with as much attention as they were allocating to the other sights of Edinburgh. One of them even raised his camera but lowered it again when he saw she was giving him the finger.

'Dennis?' Beatrice stopped typing and slipped her specs up on to her ferro-concrete perm. 'What makes you think Dennis would know any more than I do?'

'I'm not suggesting he *knows* more than you do, Beattie.' Fizz headed for the door, pausing to send her a sad smile. 'I'm just saying he might be more likely to *talk*.'

Beatrice didn't rise to that one, according to it only a hollow laugh, which could mean she knew no more than Fizz did after all. That left only Dennis, the junior partner, and Fizz didn't really want to visit him in his office. He was too likely to get between her and the door and start practising his pathetic seduction technique. One had to draw a pretty careful line with Dennis: somewhere between poking him in the eye and actually giving him an inch, and she didn't feel up to it at three-thirty on a Friday afternoon.

Instead she extracted the Mail In book from the front office and took it into the filing room to see if it might contain some hidden clue as to what had put a burr under Buchanan's saddle. Some of the letters that had been logged over the past few days were identifiable as referring to current, and equally dull cases; others were familiar to Fizz because she still did some filing, now and then, when Buchanan had no paralegal work for her to do. The half dozen remaining entries were easy enough to track down and all but one of them proved to be uniformly unproductive, no matter how you looked at them. The sixth, however, had possibilities.

It was an official letter from the Lothian and Borders police informing Buchanan that the inquiry into the death of Mrs Vanessa Grassick had now been completed and, the coroner's verdict being accidental death, the probate of her will could now go ahead.

The letter in itself was not all that unusual: people were for ever driving off the road or taking a header down tenement stairs and they all needed clearance before their wills could be processed. What was unusual was the name. It wasn't by any means a common name in this neck of the woods; in fact, Fizz could recall coming across it only once, and in that case it referred to Lawrence Grassick, probably the most respected and influential advocate in Edinburgh as well as being someone high up in the political scene. But had he been a client of Buchanan and Stewart, Fizz could hardly have avoided knowing about it. It was unlikely, in any case, that Lawrence Grassick would put any of his, or his wife's, legal affairs into the hands of a solicitor other than one of his own associates – not unless it was some sort of deal that he wanted to keep very hush-hush. One could imagine him turning, in such an instance, to Buchanan's father who had also been much respected in the city's legal fraternity and had only recently retired but, if he had, it had been kept very quiet indeed. There was nothing filed under Grassick in any of the cabinets.

How curious, Fizz thought, rapidly losing all interest in Buchanan's mental state and zeroing in on this new – and much more interesting – enigma. She returned the Mail In book to the front office before someone noticed it was missing and resumed a systematic search of every file that might reveal the intriguing contents of Mrs Vanessa Grassick's will. It didn't take long, however, to establish that it was either in Buchanan's safe or the devious woman had used her maiden name; either state of affairs more or less constituting a blank wall.

Fizz sat frowning at the problem for a while, refusing to be balked. There were still possibilities, of course. One could ask Dennis, but (a) chances were he wouldn't know, and (b) the usual reasons. One could bring up the matter casually with Buchanan next time he was in an expansive mood, but (a) he didn't like it when she snooped around, and (b) he could be quite cutting. Alan Stewart, the other partner, might be easier to schmooze into parting with some sort of clarification, but he was in court today and might not even be in the office on Monday. The Wonderful Beatrice, even if she knew the truth, wouldn't reveal it under torture and Margaret, lately promoted to office manager, had maintained immunity to Fizz's charms for over two years now and would immediately – and with the greatest pleasure – report any unauthorised curiosity to Buchanan.

That left Buchanan's father, known around the office as Big Daddy. It wouldn't be too difficult to fabricate an excuse to phone him at home. Fizz had been helping him, in the intervals between lectures, tutorials, studying and working part-time in his son's office, to research his memoirs. This was an ongoing project which served him as an excuse for sitting in his study half the day playing Mine-sweeper on his computer, but he was well used to her phoning him up with the odd query. Keeping an ear open for the sound of Buchanan's door opening, she snuck into Alan Stewart's empty office and dialled the number fast.

'Mr Buchanan? Hi. It's me. Fizz.'

'Hello there, Fizz! How are you? How's the studying

going?' He said the same thing every time she phoned him, invariably followed, as now, with, 'Good . . . good. Glad to hear it. And what can I do for you?'

'Just a tiny query about the Morris case. Do you need the entire transcript or will a summary be enough?'

'Eh . . . Morris . . . let's see. Oh, you'd better send me the whole thing I suppose. My memory isn't exactly infallible these days and that one was quite a few years back. I'd better have the whole transcript to hand. Don't want any mistakes creeping in.'

'Okay. I'll get it in the post tonight.'

'No rush, m'dear. It'll do when you have a minute. Anything else?'

'No, that's everything for now.'

'Fine. Tell Tam his mother's wondering if he's left the country, will you? Maybe he'll drop by over the weekend.'

'I'll do that. He's with a client right now but I'll see him before I leave the office – oh, there *is* one thing you could help me with. I want to get this filing finished before I leave and I have a document for someone called Grassick which doesn't appear to have a home. Any ideas?'

'Rudyard Grassick,' said Big Daddy immediately. 'It'll be filed under the firm's name. Rudyard Grassick, Commercial Artists.'

'Great! That saved me a bit of time. Thanks a lot, Mr Buchanan. Talk to you soon.'

The name Rudyard Grassick rang no bells. It turned out to be one of the many small firms that didn't bring in a lot of legal business. The few documents in the file were mainly to do with the setting up of the partnership, three years ago, and with the purchase of some office space in Nicholson Street. But Mrs Vanessa Grassick's will was there, all right, and it made interesting reading. Interesting, not only because it bequeathed virtually all her worldly goods, plus her share in the business to her business partner, Joseph Rudyard, but because it had been drawn up – replacing all previous wills – barely six weeks ago.

5

The earlier will, which was still on file, had left the bulk of her estate to her husband, none other than the celebrated Lawrence. It wasn't such a vast amount of money – a paltry twelve thousand pounds, which was peanuts compared to some bequests Fizz had dealt with recently, but Vanessa had made damn sure that her husband wasn't getting a penny. Which, Fizz couldn't help thinking, was agonisingly intriguing, especially when you considered the fact that the woman had died in the sort of accident that required a police inquiry.

And one had to ask oneself: could there be some association between this coincidence and the mysterious anxiety that had been irking Buchanan for the past two days?

Buchanan's client, at that moment, was one of those people who, having fully discussed every aspect of his legal problem, had to hang around for a further twenty minutes to be reassured – and re-reassured – that everything was going to be OK.

By the time Buchanan was able to ease him towards the door it was well after five. The office was deserted apart from Margaret and Beatrice who were, as usual, vying to be last to leave, as though that alone established one's precedence over the other. He let them tough it out and went back to his own office, loosening his tie as he went and thanking God for weekends. For the next two days he intended to put his worries to one side and enjoy himself: dinner and theatre with an old pal this evening, a cousin's stag night on Saturday and on Sunday, rain or shine, a round of golf with his usual coterie followed by a long lunch in the clubhouse. By Monday, with a bit of luck, maybe his problems wouldn't look so complicated.

He was clearing his desk when Fizz breezed in, looking as fit as a laxative advertisement and manifesting as much surplus energy as if it were nine o'clock on a Monday morning.

'Well, that's another week nearer retirement,' she remarked, dropping like a felled oak onto the spare chair, which groaned in protest.

Buchanan finished sliding papers into his briefcase, locked the safe and swept his pencils and pens into his desk drawer. There were times when Fizz dropped by for a chat merely to pass the time and there were times when an unexpected appearance meant she wanted something. This visitation showed indications of falling into the latter category. Two years into their relationship, Buchanan was learning to stay, just occasionally, one step ahead of Fizz and he could read the signs.

When she wanted something there was an air of vivacity about her. She invariably looked younger, which was ludicrous considering that, for all she was in her late twenties, she rarely appeared a day older than sixteen. She looked prettier: her eyes shone, her lips dimpled at the corners and even her outrageous golden hair which, to Buchanan, almost had a personality of its own, appeared to froth and curl and jiggle and sparkle more – if that were possible – than it normally did. Also, her expression was an exaggeration – just a faint, carefully judged exaggeration – of the cherubic innocence she radiated all the time. This time, she had managed to twist her chaos of curls into something resembling a coil, thus presenting an unnaturally tidy appearance which he knew from experience would last no time at all.

Now was the moment to make a fast exit: he understood that perfectly, but curiosity made him hesitate. 'I thought you'd gone home.'

'I had things to finish. Also your daddy gave me a message for you. He says your mummy misses her baby boy and do you remember their address?'

Buchanan smiled at her with saintly patience. He didn't need to ask if the phraseology was his father's or Fizz's: she never missed a chance to take a poke at his ego. He opened his bottom drawer and swivelled his chair so he could prop his feet on it. 'Message received. Any other little news items you want to share with me?'

Fizz allowed her gaze to rest on him just a fraction of a second longer than it needed to. She knew he was on to her and he watched her take a second to re-think her tactics. 'Actually . . . yes. I just wanted to hear your thoughts on the Lammerburn Estate sale. I suspect we may have some problems there sooner or later.'

Buchanan was immediately uneasy. Buchanan and Stewart rarely handled property deals of such magnitude and he wasn't all that confident that Dennis, who dealt with the conveyancing, was up to it. 'What sort of problems?'

'Their brochure has just come in from the printer's and it reads like the prospective buyer is being offered a private little kingdom. Dennis had no problem with the text when the vendors discussed it with him but there have been one or two subtle changes and now you'd think we were selling a piece of virgin territory. No mention of tenants in the estate cottages and no mention of the right of way that I seem to remember running through the estate from Colton Bridge to the sea.'

'You're familiar with the area?' Buchanan asked, forgetting to be suspicious of her intentions.

'Not recently, but I had friends in that part of Berwickshire when I was at school and we regularly walked that right of way. It's not on our map of the area but I'm almost certain it ran across Lammerburn land.' She scratched her forehead where a wispy blonde ringlet was tickling her. 'The advert went into the papers yesterday and if we get any early interest I'd like to have my facts right. You know the stink the Ramblers Association and the Rights of Way Society are liable to cause if there should be any infringements on access later on.'

Buchanan felt he could do without a run-in with the Ramblers, who had a lot of clout, but he was even more concerned with the danger of kickback from a buyer who ended up with considerably less privacy than he'd thought he was purchasing. 'What does the estate factor say? He ought to know the details.'

'I left a message on his voicemail this afternoon but he hasn't contacted me. I tried to find someone else to talk to but the only people I could raise were household staff who hadn't a clue about anything beyond the garden.' She gave her head an irritated shake and more ringlets made a break for freedom. 'I suspect even the owners won't be familiar enough with the land to be much of a help.'

'That's possible,' Buchanan admitted. 'It was bought about fifteen years ago by a family firm we've looked after for two generations. Menzies Ale. I gather it was used mostly for corporate entertaining.'

It was annoying to be unsure of the facts but, as his junior partner would certainly point out, it wasn't the end of the world. Dennis should have been the one to pursue a solution to this minor irritation but the firm's image was not a matter that weighed heavily with Dennis: he would be quite happy to leave mention of the estate's shortcomings to the purchaser's surveyor. Justifiable perhaps, but in Buchanan's view, shoddy practice. He hated the idea of Buchanan and Stewart appearing incompetent, especially in a deal worth a couple of million. Now he knew he wouldn't rest easy until he had ascertained what sort of dishonesty the Menzies family was trying to get away with.

The fastest way to clear up any doubt was simply to drive down to Berwickshire and see for himself. It might take an hour or so each way but, it suddenly occurred to him, there was an added advantage in making the trip: his route would lead through the village of Chirnside where Lawrence Grassick's wife had recently met her end. Maybe a close look at the scene of that tragic event would help him decide what to do about it.

He swung his feet to the floor and kicked the drawer shut. 'Leave it with me, Fizz,' he said, surprising her with his sudden briskness. 'I'll get the information for you by Monday.'

'How?' she wanted to know.

He hadn't expected to smuggle that one past her and he knew what was coming but he had to say, 'I'll take a quick run down there and check it out.'

'Right. I'll come with you.'

'No need . . .'

'The start of the right of way is awkward to spot. I can save you a bit of time . . .'

'I'm sure I'll manage just fine, Fizz.'

'Well, I could do with a day out of town anyway. I don't often get the chance.'

Buchanan tried not to grind his teeth. He knew quite well that she hated to be stuck in town at the weekend and *she* knew quite well that he was a sucker. 'Well . . . sure, if you really want to go . . .'

Fizz bounced to her feet, emancipating the few curls that remained under restraint. 'Roger. What time? Eleven o'clock, say?'

'Fine. I'll pick you up.' Buchanan had been thinking of early afternoon but it really made no difference to his plans. Except, he realised as the door shut behind her, that he'd now probably have to buy her lunch as well.

Chapter Two

Lammerburn Estate had grown considerably since Fizz had last seen it about ten years ago. It was just a pity, she thought, that it had not grown in a southerly direction because, if it had, it might have taken in the right of way she'd lied about. In actual fact, the lovely wooded path wound its way seaward, as it always had done, missing the estate boundary wall by a good half mile.

'It's all changed so much,' she defended herself. 'The estate's much bigger, for a start.'

'Not much,' Buchanan said heavily, beginning to exhibit faint signs of distrust. 'The Menzies family bought up a small estate along their boundary by the Whiteadder river a couple of years back but there have been no changes in this direction. It looks like you were mistaken about the location of the right of way.'

'Looks like it.' Fizz met his eyes with a look intended to transmit total purity of heart. 'But, like I said, it was at least ten years ago so I couldn't be sure. At least we've eliminated one problem.'

Buchanan deployed an eyebrow. He was evidently not convinced that she'd got him here purely on business grounds, but she felt she could bank on him being too diplomatic to say so until he had solid proof.

'Do you have a clearer picture of where the estate cottages are situated?' he asked politely.

'Oh, absolutely. You can't miss them. You go through the village and out the other side and they're about quarter of a mile further on.'

Fizz felt she was on firmer ground with the cottages. They formed an integral part of the high wall that surrounded the original part of the estate: a terrace of six or eight little gems, as she remembered, each with its tiny dormer window and its strip of garden, and built of rose-red sandstone like the wall and the estate house and, indeed, almost everything else in the vicinity. The probability was, of course, that they had been derelict and standing empty for years but she was quite surprised to discover that for once, Fate was on her side. They were still there, still beautiful and still occupied.

Buchanan pulled the car into a parking bay on the other side of the road and, for a moment, they sat admiring the neat front gardens, the glittering paintwork and the other signs of loving occupation. Two youngish-looking men had paused in their gardening to have a chat across their common hedge and both turned their heads incuriously as they heard the slam of the car doors.

'A great day for gardening,' Fizz greeted them, as she and Buchanan crossed the road.

'Aye, it is that,' said the closer of the two; a thin chap with the beginnings of a beer belly. He put up a hand to shade his eyes from the sun. 'Although the ground's still a bit soft for mowing the grass after all that rain through the week.'

His neighbour's darkling stare swept over them both, taking particular notice of Buchanan's tan leather jacket and Armani slacks. He didn't appear overly impressed by what he saw so Fizz gave him a hundred-watt smile and said, 'I hope we're not intruding, but we're from Buchanan and Stewart, the people who're handling the sale of the estate, and we were—'

'Aye, I thought that's who ye were, either that or some toffs come to look at it.'

Fizz added a pinch of wistfulness to her smile and tipped her head a little to one side. 'You don't seem too happy to see us.'

12

'Too damn right, missy. You'll not find many around here that'll be spreading the welcome mat for you.'

'Naw, naw Geordie, it's no' these folks' fault,' the thin guy muttered, frowning with embarrassment. 'It's that Niall Menzies you should be complainin' to, like, no' his lawyers.'

'Not at all,' Buchanan said quickly. 'If you have any worries about the sale, now's the time to let me hear them. Better that than raising objections once the deal has gone through.'

The two guys exchanged looks, then the thin guy said, 'Seven years we've been in this house and Geordie here's been twelve years in his. And you should talk to Mrs Pearson, second from the end. She was born in that cottage and her father came to it in nineteen forty-five, when he was thirty.'

'You mean, you've received notice to quit?' Fizz asked, not entirely surprised. In her experience, top dogs were almost invariably sons of bitches.

'Aye, a month ago.' Geordie had clearly expected them to be aware of that little detail. He waved his gardening shears in a sweep that encompassed the length of the terrace. 'Paid off and told to get out. The whole row. You saying you didn't know?'

Buchanan evidently judged it best to say nothing that could be quoted in evidence. He followed Geordie's gesture with his eyes. 'All of you? You're all estate workers then?'

'We were. Up till the end of last month.'

Buchanan very rarely looked angry. In fact, he very rarely looked anything. Fizz was fairly sure he had taken a post-graduate course in Hiding Emotions. Right now, however, he was looking suspiciously red across the forehead, which Fizz usually took as a warning to be elsewhere.

'So we're talking about . . . eight families, right?' he said quietly.

'Aye, but there's more than us involved,' Geordie growled. He had an unnerving habit of flashing his shears

13

about as he talked and now swung them round to point down the road. 'The whole village will know the difference. There's seven kids in these cottages. If they all have to move away – and they will – the school will have to close. In a wee village like Lammerburn even eight families can make a big difference – to the shop, for instance, and the local pub, and the church. We only get a minister once a month as it is. My dad owns his own house – all his money's tied up in it. You think he'll be able to sell it? No chance. Not in a ghost town.'

'And there's folk in these houses that's important to the village too,' put in his pal. 'See Olive Pearson, along there? She used to be a nursing sister and she would turn out at all hours for women in labour, like, or if there was an emergency. She was great with our Tamsin when we were waiting for the doctor to come from Chirnside.'

Fizz was horrified to hear that a landowner could get away with this kind of thing in the twenty-first century but she was somewhat gratified to realise that, had she not used the sale of the estate as a lure to get Buchanan down to this neck of the woods, the Menzies family could have had the whole business signed and sealed before anyone noticed. It was still quite possible that the deal could go through as planned but now at least both she and Buchanan would be pressing for some sort of rethink on the vendors' part.

Buchanan took his leave of the two guys, managing to do so without making any promises, yet leaving behind the implication that he was concerned and would be taking the matter further. Both Geordie and his thin friend smiled and waved to them as they drove away.

'This is a shocking state of affairs,' Fizz burst out, thoroughly incensed. 'You'll have to do something about it.'

'You don't have to nag me,' Buchanan retorted with what struck Fizz as unnecessary crispness. 'It's not my business to question my client's morals. All I can do is

14

advise him that he might be biting off more than he can chew. I'll have a quiet word with Menzies and find out what he thinks he's doing. Right now I want a second look at Lammerburn so that I know what the extent of the problem is going to be.'

'It's going to be vast,' Fizz told him, counting the houses between the terrace of cottages and the edge of the village. 'The population can't be more than a couple of hundred and there's no way people are going to find new jobs around here. You'd probably have to travel all the way to Berwick to find work, and travelling that distance in winter would be horrendous on these narrow roads. Three or four inches of snow and you'd never get up the hills.'

They drove slowly through Lammerburn, a higglety-pigglety collection of rose-red sandstone villas, a white painted hotel, a general store-cum-post-office, a garage, a sawmill and a small stretch of mowed grass with some swings and a see-saw in the middle. Pretty enough in the summertime, when there was good hillwalking and trout fishing all around, but too small to sustain any clubs or winter activities other than drinking and going to church. Fizz, having grown up in just such a remote spot, was anything but envious of the locals.

Small communities like that around her grandfather's farm in Am Bealach were still, even after all the legislation that had been passed to prevent it, at the mercy of large estate owners. Anyone with enough money to buy up huge tracts of land – and there were plenty of billionaires nowadays – could allow cottages to fall into disrepair and refuse to renew the tenancy of rented farms. Ever since the Highland Clearances in the nineteenth century, the people who belonged to the land had come a poor second to the wishes of those few fat cats who wanted to divide up the surface of the planet amongst themselves and make the rest of humanity stick to corridors. It was one of the few things that got Fizz really pissed off.

'You'd think the local people would have tried to fight back or something,' she said as they left the village behind and headed towards the junction with the main road in the valley below. 'There's been nothing about it in the newspapers, no demonstrations – nothing! If it were happening to me, I don't mind telling you, I'd make sure the bastards wouldn't try it again in a hurry!'

Buchanan made no reply but his sigh was a comment on the concept of the direct approach. Fizz knew it was a waste of time nagging him to get tough and could only hope that he would at least give the Menzies family the business end of a ball-point. She had known him perform miracles in the past but he moved in mysterious ways to do so.

She waited until they were almost at the main road before she said, 'I don't know about you but I could eat a small branch of McDonald's.'

Buchanan's answering grunt was not an unmitigated rebuttal so she murmured, 'I seem to remember rather a nice little pub in Chirnside, just the other side of those woods. Maybe we could get a pie and a pint.'

'Mmm-hmm,' said Buchanan non-committally, but he turned the car in that direction all the same and, a few minutes later, the chimneys of Chirnside came into view. But before they reached the village proper, at the end of a short spur road on their left, Fizz spotted the burned-out shell of what must once have been Vanessa Grassick's weekend retreat.

There wasn't much of it still standing. The lower half of one gable wall was still there, and you could just about make out the line of the other outside walls, but within that boundary there was nothing but a black pit. What remained of the garden was splattered with rubble and bits of charred wood and scraps of household rubbish, reminding Fizz of images of bomb damage she'd seen on TV. On the ornate wrought iron gate was a now obsolete sign that announced Brora Lodge.

Just as she was about to suggest they stop for a closer look she saw Buchanan lift his foot from the accelerator. He pulled on to the verge and sat staring past her at the ruin as though he knew that's why they were there. This left Fizz with a choice: either she could ask him why he was stopping, thus implying that she knew nothing about the incident, or she could just shut up and admit, by implication, that she had suckered him again. The trouble was, she was fairly sure he already had her sussed, so trying to lie her way out of it would only make matters worse. Ah, she thought, and not for the first time, what a tangled web we weave!

Buchanan had been quite clear in his mind, from the moment he saw that the suspect right of way was nowhere near Lammerburn Estate, that Fizz was pulling his strings. The fact that there did, after all, appear to be a problem pending with the cottages tended to alleviate his chagrin, but he had a strong suspicion that Fizz had been as surprised about that as had he himself. The question was: should he slap her down for it and spoil what was actually quite a pleasant afternoon drive or should he save face by pretending he had known what she was up to all along? The outcome would, of course, be the same whatever he did. Fizz would pretend contrition, admit that her nosiness and manipulative behaviour were totally unaccept- able, and continue to operate with a level of adroitness and chicanery that would shame a weasel.

He felt her stir uneasily beside him. Swivelling his eyes, he met her deadpan denim-blue gaze and returned it with equal blankness. After a moment she broke and said, 'Are we going for a closer look or what?'

'Certainly,' Buchanan said, hardly sounding smug at all, 'since that's what we're here for.'

She ducked that one by getting out of the car fast and walking ahead of him down the driveway while he was locking up. She had her hair loose today – it always ended up that way anyway, fighting off all attempts to restrain it with Houdini-like ease – and the breeze was making it struggle madly as though it resented being rooted in her scalp. Every time he saw her like this, stomping around in her Doc's with her hands in the pockets of her jeans, he was struck by the disparity between her child-like appearance and her quite terrifying assurance. The incongruity wasn't so clean-cut when he saw her in the office – maybe the darker clothes she wore for work made her look taller or more grown up – but, in jeans and the same baggy sweater she'd worn the first time she'd blasted into his hitherto placid existence, she could still pass for a school kid – and a decidedly cherubic one at that.

When he caught up with her she was staring down into the hole left by the explosion.

'Looks like they had a cellar down there,' she said, pointing at an area of plastered wall that showed signs of having once been shelved. 'I can't imagine what sort of blast it must have been to have caused such destruction.'

'Gas,' Buchanan told her, wondering where she'd scavenged her information and why that detail had escaped her. 'There's no gas mains in this area so, apparently, the Grassicks stored several gas canisters in the basement. They used gas for cooking and also for one of those fake log fires. One of the canisters must have been leaking for days. The house probably full of fumes when Mrs Grassick arrived and she struck a match or something. That's the trouble with North Sea gas: you can't smell it like you could the old stuff. Not so easily anyway.'

She bent and picked up a piece of paper but saw nothing of interest on it and threw it away. 'Okay, so the police are quite happy about the case – accidental death, as far as they're concerned – and you have the go-ahead to pay out the cash, so what is it that's worrying you about the case?'

Buchanan was astounded. Was she reading his mind? 'Who says I'm worried?'

She looked at him with strained patience. 'Buchanan,

you've been sitting around with your knuckles in your teeth for three days. There's something about this business that's got you running scared. Yes or no?'

Buchanan wasn't going to lie to her but that didn't mean he had to give her any information she didn't already possess. 'Who put you on to this, Fizz? Beatrice?'

Fizz hooted rudely. 'Beatrice? Buchanan, you've got to know that Beatrice is as tight as a Trappist monk on Good Friday. She lives but to do your bidding.' She kicked sullenly at a piece of debris and decided to come clean. 'I happened to see the letter from Lothian and Borders police . . . the one saying they weren't taking the matter any further. I was curious so I looked it up in the files.'

'You were curious.' Buchanan nodded comprehendingly. 'Well, well. You *curious*, Fizz? Whatever next?'

Fizz showed him her middle finger and stalked away to the edge of what had recently been a patio. Buchanan followed her for a better view of the three widely separated houses that shared the side road.

The remaining buildings were probably over a hundred years old, which was far from unusual in the Borders. With their solid construction and big gardens they would each have been valued at something around two hundred thousand pounds had they been in the Edinburgh area. Here, Buchanan suspected he'd be lucky to find a buyer at anything over fifty-five thousand. The basic design of the remaining three houses was identical – an indication of what Brora Lodge had probably looked like: sturdy, pantiled, with two dormer windows set into a steep roof, and a stone-built porch to keep out the winter winds. They were set haphazardly with reference to the street, which was probably a newer addition: two facing it, one sideways on, as Brora Lodge had stood.

The closest house had taken a fair bit of the blast. All the windows on its near side were boarded up and there seemed, from this distance, to be no sign of life around it at all.

'So, what's the big deal regarding Vanessa Grassick?' Fizz persisted, sticking forth her bottom lip. 'She's Lawrence Grassick's wife, isn't she? Why does that make you nervous?' She took note of Buchanan's exasperated expression and ploughed on. 'She was still married to him, I take it?'

'Yes, Fizz, she was his current wife,' Buchanan barked without looking at her.

'Wife.' She was silent for a couple of restful minutes, her absorbed stare drifting from her boots to Buchanan's face and back again. Then she nodded. 'Right. Lawrence Grassick's wife. Right. You don't want to make an arse of yourself on this one, do you? You don't want to pay out the filthy lucre and then have it turn out she was murdered after all. She left the lot to her business partner, right? Every last penny.'

'Virtually every last penny. Yes.'

'Uh-huh. But something is making you jumpy, isn't it? Come on, Buchanan. I've seen you like this before. Cough it up.'

There was no way she'd ever drop the matter now, Buchanan realised, and if he were to face the truth, he'd have to admit to himself that it would be a relief to share the problem with her. She had her faults but sometimes her devious mind saw solutions where his didn't.

'There are one or two anomalies that are making me . . . well, just a tad uneasy,' he admitted. 'For a start, there's the question of what Lawrence Grassick's wife was doing, turning up at their weekend place at two-twenty-five in the morning.'

'Is that when the explosion happened?' Fizz's stare was as intent and unblinking as that of a cat at a mouse hole. Buchanan could almost hear her brain whirring. 'Maybe she had been there for hours and the gas had just leaked out.'

Buchanan would have dearly loved to agree with her on that. 'That's what the police believe. However, one of the neighbours claimed he heard Vanessa's car draw up not more than a few minutes before the bang. Nobody is taking him seriously, since he was the only person to hear it and there was nothing to corroborate his statement – but it makes me uneasy just the same.'

Fizz turned to look down the hill at the nearest house, the one with the boarded-up windows. 'If it was the guy who lived there you'd think he'd be close enough to know what he was hearing.'

'He didn't live there,' Buchanan said, fighting an increasingly black depression. 'The chap who lived in that house wasn't at home at the time of the explosion. He was here . . . with Vanessa Grassick . . . and he was blown to bits.'

Fizz's eyes widened perceptibly at that and she cast a quick glance at the ground around her as though she dreaded to see pulverised body parts besprinkled through the gravel.

Buchanan summoned up a smile. 'Don't worry. The police have been over and over the ground with fine-toothed combs. You can be sure that all traces of Vanessa and her neighbour – one Jamie Ford – have long gone.'

The breeze swirled round the remains of the gable wall causing a tight whirlpool of dried leaves and rubbish at their feet and stirring up a smell of wet charcoal. In the distance a door banged, clearly audible in the silence, and, from the furthest visible house, a person in tan trousers emerged, followed by a brown and white spaniel.

Fizz turned her back on the figures and fixed her eyes on Buchanan's. 'What you're wondering is,' she stated, 'whether the police were maybe too scared of Lawrence Grassick's influence in high places to start de-skeletonising his cupboards.'

Buchanan himself would not have put the matter so strongly. He had more respect for Lothian and Borders police force than Fizz had, probably because he had got up its collective nose, and suffered the inevitable repercussions, less often than she had. 'I don't really have any firm suspicions at the moment. I just don't want to do anything too precipitous till I'm a little easier in my mind.'

'Yeah, yeah,' she said, as though it were merely a matter of semantics, and without turning round, stuck a thumb over her shoulder and added, 'There's one of the neighbours. Aren't you going to stop him and see what he has to say?'

Buchanan was by no means sure that he wanted to take that line of action – not yet, at any rate – but before he could reply it became obvious that the choice was not going to be his. The neighbour, who transpired to be a well-built, middle-aged woman, clearly had him in her sights and was moving fast to cut off his escape.

'Something I can help you with?' She bellowed the words as soon as she came within earshot, but the tone of her voice translated them into something more akin to, 'What the hell do you think you're doing in there?' She had a large florid face and her eyes, behind the thick lenses of her spectacles, looked like tadpoles in a jam jar. From the hip joints up she was a substantial cube in a fawn anorak, but below that line she was only a pair of skinny legs in black leggings. Buchanan couldn't help but be reminded of an animated Weetabix.

Fizz leapt into the fray as usual, smiling with all thirty-two teeth, and tripping forward to meet the Fury like a toddler approaching Santa's grotto.

'That's very kind of you,' she crooned. 'We're from Buchanan and Stewart, Mrs Grassick's solicitors. This is Tam Buchanan.'

'And your name is?' said the Fury, making it clear that she would have no hesitation in checking out their bona fides.

'Fitzpatrick. I'm Mr Buchanan's assistant.'

That was stretching the truth a bit but, as Fizz well knew, Buchanan wouldn't quibble in front of witnesses. He held out his hand. 'It's good to know that someone's keeping an eye on things.'

'Jean Pringle.' She shook it, but her big square face showed little sign of mollification. She had one of those voices you'd have difficulty in classing as male or female. 'You wouldn't believe the number of people we've seen prying around. Looking to see what they can pick up, I've not the slightest doubt. My husband had to stop someone carrying off one of the stone troughs last week. I told Mr Grassick about it when he was here but I see no sign of him doing anything to make the garden secure.'

'He's very lucky to have such thoughtful neighbours,' Fizz told her, laying it on thick. 'I'm sure this whole business must have been quite a strain on all of you.'

'Dreadful.' Mrs Pringle cast her eyes around to check on the dog, which was sniffing around a heap of rubble with an avid interest that, regardless of what he'd just told Fizz, made Buchanan's stomach churn. 'They've been coming and going for days – fire brigade, police, ambulances and goodness knows who – knocking on doors, taking statements, annoying people. You've never seen the like.'

'Ambulances?' Buchanan said, just checking. 'More than one?'

'Well, they took something away in an ambulance not long after they got here. Something in a body bag.' She shook her head in pretended distaste that didn't quite mask the enthusiasm in her voice. 'It was dark, of course, except for the flames, so we couldn't see properly till they got their floodlights going but I imagine it must have been what was left of Mrs Grassick or Jamie Ford. And then, later on, there was another ambulance to take Poppy, Jamie's wife, to hospital. Badly cut with broken glass she was, poor little thing, when the windows came in on her.'

'Is she still in hospital?' Buchanan asked, his mind exploring the possibility of having a word with her. If anyone could explain why her husband had been with Vanessa Grassick at two-twenty-five on a Saturday morning it would be she.

Mrs Pringle folded her arms under her substantial bust, hitching it up a little, and, for a long moment, appeared to be admiring the countryside. Buchanan was starting to wonder whether she had heard the question when he realised that she was deep in thought. Apparently she was in some doubt whether to confide in him or not. Finally, she drew an audible breath and said, 'That's a thing that's been worrying me.' She withdrew her gaze from the middle distance and looked firmly at Buchanan as though she expected him to argue with her about that. 'On Tuesday we went to visit Poppy in hospital. Elizabeth Armstrong and myself.' She indicated the Armstrong household with a nod: a modernised version of her own which had had its beautiful sandstone walls coated with an ugly pebble-dash. 'Such a sweet little thing she was, Poppy Ford. No bigger than you, dear. Quiet as a little mouse, but we all liked her. We went in Elizabeth's car and took some fruit and magazines with us but, when we got there, we were told that Poppy had been discharged two days before, on the Sunday.'

Fizz stuck her head forward like a pointer. 'She didn't come back here?'

'Nobody knows where she is,' Mrs Pringle growled deeply, hugging her bosom. 'It's so unlike her to just take off like that without even phoning to let us know she was all right. We notified the police on the way home, naturally, but we've heard nothing from them or from Poppy all week. I'd have thought she'd have been worried about Jet, but no. Not a word.'

'Jet being . . .?' Fizz inquired in a gentle voice, designed to avoid interfering too much with her discursive flow.

'Jet . . . her cat. He's dead, of course, but Poppy wouldn't know that, would she? So you'd have expected her to have phoned to ask Elizabeth or me, or even the police for that matter, to look out for him. But no. Nobody has heard a word from her since she left the hospital. It's uncanny.'

Buchanan felt Fizz's eyes on his face but didn't want to receive the message she was sending. He could see for himself that there was no way he could honourably turn his back on this investigation. He didn't need to be told he was in a cleft stick. He could feel it tightening inexorably around his throat.

Chapter Three

If Buchanan was overjoyed to discover that the 'nice little pub' of Fizz's recollection was, in fact, the Chirnside Hall Hotel, he managed to hide it well. He accepted without comment her plea that it must be under new management, but was probably swayed more by the thought of a decent lunch instead of a pie and a pint.

The service, as befitted a five star establishment, was suitably relaxed which gave Fizz time to dispose of a large gin and tonic before eating – thus getting the full benefit of the alcohol content. She was in a particularly good mood, not just because of the gin, but because the flimsy hint of mystery surrounding Vanessa Grassick's death was suddenly showing signs of becoming something she could get her teeth into. Meanwhile Buchanan, for much the same reason, was looking as grim as something chiselled out of Mount Rushmore.

'Oh, cheer up, for pity's sake,' Fizz told him with her usual compassion for a fellow traveller on Life's stony road. 'Even if Vanessa was murdered by her business partner – or any other beneficiary, for that matter – they can't defrock you for paying out her estate. You're covered by the police inquiry and the coroner's verdict. It's not up to you to query it.'

He stopped grinding his teeth to take a spoonful of chowder. 'I have to query it, Fizz, you know that. The least I ought to do, if only for my own peace of mind and the reputation of the firm, is to find out what the police think

about Mrs Ford's disappearance. But even that's not going
to please Lawrence Grassick, is it? It's obvious he doesn't
want any adverse publicity like a murder investigation and
– if that should happen – he won't easily forget that I was
the one to set it in motion just when the case had been
closed.'

It wasn't easy to deny this reading of the situation, Fizz
had to admit. There couldn't be a worse person to cross in
the entire Scottish legal system than the man who had
been dubbed Ghengis Grassick since his student days.
There were plenty of stories about his vituperative attacks
on junior counsel, and any witnesses bold enough to try
lying to him in court were liable to be on Prozac for the
rest of their lives. There were three ways to avoid dentures,
so the saying went: brush after meals, visit your dentist
regularly, and don't cross Ghengis Grassick.

It said much for the man's professional capability, however, that he was unarguably top dog in Scottish law, and
Fizz herself would have killed to get a job in his chambers
in any capacity whatsoever. There was no chance of that –
not unless she got first class honours in her finals plus all
manner of distinctions, a personal recommendation from
the prof, and character references from the Prime Minister,
the President of the Bank of England, and God. Yes, *and*
had a sex change operation into the bargain, since
Grassick was a known misogynist as well as a despot.

'Don't do it, Buchanan,' she said earnestly. 'It's not
worth it – really, *really* not worth it. The grief that man
could cause you for the rest of your working life doesn't
bear thinking about. Hell, if *he* doesn't care who gets his
wife's money, why should you? For God's sake, let's just
drop the whole thing and go home.'

Buchanan raised his eyes from his plate and blinked at
her for a minute as though he couldn't believe she would
willingly turn her back on an interesting inquiry at this
stage in the game. Fizz could barely believe it herself. The
only motive she could find for suggesting such a course

was to avoid witnessing a colleague – OK, a friend – commit professional suicide.

Buchanan finished his soup in a morbid silence before he folded his arms on the table and shook his head. 'It wouldn't work for me.'

Fizz started to argue but he wouldn't budge.

'I hear what you're saying, Fizz, and a lot of it's perfectly true, but you know what I'm like. I'm a lawyer because I like being a lawyer. Not because my dad was a lawyer. Not because I was forced into the business. But because I believe in truth. If I did what you want me to do, if I did what I know to be wrong to save my career, it would be on my conscience for the rest of my life.' He toyed with his cutlery and grinned a bit sheepishly. 'A long time ago I heard a psychiatrist say that most cases of mental illness had their roots in a guilty conscience. I've no idea whether there's a grain of truth in that but I reckon I'm one of those people who have a genetic weakness in that area and I believe in prevention rather than cure. I *need* my self-respect.'

It was so unlike Buchanan to bare his soul like this that Fizz was left unable to respond. She hadn't entirely realised just how seriously he was taking this thing but it was now beginning to worry her, too. After all, her own future, if her plans came to fruition, was likely to be tied up with Buchanan's. She had invested a lot of time, ever since she first enrolled for a law degree, in making sure she had a job with Buchanan and Stewart when she graduated. There was horrendous competition for traineeships in Edinburgh, and the Buchanan and Stewart partnership was one of the choice berths. As yet, nobody had promised her anything even semi-permanent, and the arrival last year of Dennis, the new junior partner, had brought the personnel up to fighting strength, but she still had hopes of carving herself a niche by the time she needed one. What a laugh it would be if the fortunes of Buchanan and Stewart were to take a dive in the meantime. Not.

Neither of them said much for the rest of their meal. Fizz's ebullient mood had now plummeted. It was standing out a mile that, in her own interests, she should be continuing to nag Buchanan to keep his doubts to himself, but it was equally clear to her that he wasn't exaggerating when he claimed he'd suffer for it if he did. She'd known about his love affair with the truth for a long time and, in spite of herself, she was finding it hard to leave that factor out of the equation.

Worrying about other people's peace of mind was not something Fizz did. She'd grown up the hard way, virtually on her own from the age of fourteen, and she'd had problems enough just keeping body and soul together without losing sleep over things that were not of immediate concern. When it came to a choice between her own needs and those of someone else, she could seldom afford the luxury of being generous. But there was something about Buchanan that made her feel sorry for him – not often and not a lot – just the sort of twinge of uneasiness you'd feel seeing a dog trying to cross a busy road. He simply didn't have the same sort of carapace over his emotions as Fizz had grown during the hard years. He believed in people, he trusted them, he strove for them, and half the time they just took what he had to give and scarpered. Too late to change him now: what he needed was a thoughtful friend to slap him about the ears from time to time.

'Well, what about a compromise?' she suggested after a while. 'We can do a little digging around . . . talk to a few people. Try to ascertain whether there's really any need to take the matter further. We . . . you could be worrying for nothing.'

'Yeah.' He tried for a grin but it didn't come off and he didn't persist in the effort to look hopeful. 'Well, no, actually. That idea doesn't grab me at all. For one thing, I'd hate Grassick to catch me being underhand about it. If I decide to make my own inquiry I'll tell him I'm going to do it. And for another thing, we already know there's more to this business than meets the eye. We already know I've cause to be concerned. Better to get it cleared up and have done with it. The chances are it won't turn out to be anything too embarrassing for Grassick. I hope not anyway.'

There didn't look to Fizz to be too many options. It wasn't the sort of thing Buchanan was likely to change his mind about after a good night's sleep, and there was as much chance of Grassick giving his blessing to a review of his wife's demise as of his donning a tutu and performing an *entrechat* in the forum of the High Court.

She excused herself to go to the loo and, on the way back, made a detour to speak to the two waiters who were hovering attentively by the doorway. It didn't take much to get them chatting about the burned-out house down the road, a news item which rated, locally, as something on a par with the shooting of JFK.

'It must have been some blaze,' Fizz suggested, wide-eyed with interest. 'Was anyone killed?'

'Aye. Two people blown to bits,' said the waiter who had attended her table, and added, as an aside to his partner, 'Lenny told me they were picking up pieces for two days.'

'Who's Lenny?' Fizz asked him, seeing that Lenny must have had a ringside seat.

'Lenny Napier. He's the postman. He hears all the news when he's delivering the mail. He says an old couple who lived across the road were near thrown out their bed by the bang. Two-thirty in the morning! They thought it was world war three starting. They're not over it yet, the pair of them.'

Fizz looked deeply sympathetic. 'Were there only two people living in the house?'

'No, no miss. Just the one of them belonged to the house,' the other guy put in, smiling at her. He was middle-aged and heavy with it but he still bore the signs of being a heart-throb in his youth. 'The woman was Vanessa

Grassick – her husband's a famous lawyer – you'll maybe have heard of him. They came in here for dinner all the time. But the man that was killed with Mrs Grassick wasn't her husband. He was one of the neighbours.'

Fizz, out of the corner of her eye, caught sight of Buchanan crossing the room towards them, and knew he meant to stop her from asking questions before he had okayed it with Grassick. Quickly, she raised her eyebrows at the two men. 'At two-thirty a.m.?'

Both of them chuckled, exchanging glances.

'Aye, miss, you may well ask,' the older one admitted, 'and I'll not deny there's been more than you putting two and two together, and maybe making five. But I'll not believe there was anything between them. Mrs Grassick was too much of a toff to take up with Jamie Ford, decent enough lad though he was.'

'You knew them both?' Fizz asked, but the other waiter was ready for a turn at putting in his ten pence worth and he didn't go along with his pal's opinion.

'She was much younger than her husband, you see. Thirty-three, it said in the paper, and he's grey-haired. Must be near enough fifty. Yon place wasn't a weekend cottage, if you ask me, it was a love nest.'

'Och no, Andrew,' his pal insisted, shaking an emphatic head. 'A terrible thing like yon happens and right away folk are seeing bogles, asking if it was really an accident, getting suspicious about damn all, making up things so it's more exciting. It's just foolishness, that's what it is, aye and speaking ill of the dead.'

Buchanan loomed up at Fizz's shoulder and cleared his throat to draw attention to the fact that he was waiting with his wallet in his hand. 'Sorry, Fizz, but we really have to rush,' he said pointedly and nodded to their waiter. 'That was a nice meal. Can I pay for it, please?'

Andrew, the younger guy, started apologising and dashing around with the check etc giving Fizz the chance to isolate his colleague. 'Why are people saying it wasn't an accident?'

He looked sideways at Buchanan and tried to wriggle
out of it by saying, 'Och, it's just gossip like I was
saying. Just some daft old folk making mountains out of
molehills. We don't get a lot of excitement round these
parts so we have to make the most of it, know what I
mean?'

'But who—?'

'Come on, Fizz, we really must go now.'

Buchanan had a firm hold of her elbow so she had to
leave gracefully, for the moment – but only for the
moment. The minute she could get shot of Buchanan she'd
be back.

In point of fact, as soon as he had made the decision to
follow his conscience, Buchanan felt instantly better. It
was as though a weight had been lifted from his shoulders.
To call it an onward-Christian-soldiers feeling might have
been putting it too strongly, but not much. Now that his
future was in the lap of the gods, all he had to worry about
was bearding Ghengis Grassick in his den and that
encounter, distasteful as it would certainly be, wasn't going
to deflect him from performing what he saw as his duty.
He knew himself to be non-confrontational to the last cell
in his body but he also knew he couldn't be bullied.

First thing Monday morning he phoned Grassick's
chambers for an appointment and was somewhat abashed
to be squeezed into the great man's lunch hour, a privilege
that reflected the esteem – largely earned by Buchanan
père – in which he held the firm. Buchanan's father and
Ghengis Grassick were not exactly buddies but they went
back a long way together and had always treated each
other with mutual respect. Since the old boy had retired,
however, Buchanan had known he was on probation.
Grassick had risen in the profession the hard way and
made no secret of his disdain for those 'daddy's boys' who
inherited a career.

All morning, as he got on with his other work, a part of

33

Buchanan's brain was rehearsing what he was going to say. Fizz wasn't much help, popping in and out with hawkish suggestions, and as he left the office for the appointment, she grinned at him fiendishly and whispered, '*Nos morituri te salutamus!*'

Buchanan gave her a gladiatorial salute but, if he were about to die, it wasn't bothering him unduly. In fact a sort of madness had taken hold of him, opening his eyes to the boredom of long hours spent behind a desk and to the repetitiousness of much of his workload. So, what if he did find himself no longer able to attract the class of business he'd been used to? It wouldn't be entirely catastrophic. He still had his health and strength, goddammit, and in the long run he might be infinitely happier working his way around the world, doing any job that came along, as Fizz had done for seven or eight years. She'd had some hair-raising experiences, if half of what she told him was true, but she'd *lived* more in those eight years than Buchanan had in thirty-two.

Grassick had his chambers in a newly refurbished building in Chambers Street, a stone's throw from the law courts but a good fifteen-minute walk from Buchanan's office. At that time of day, however, the traffic was such a bind that it was six and half a dozen whether he took the car or walked, so he chose the latter to get a bit of exercise.

It was the first time he'd been in Grassick's chambers since the firm had moved there a few months back, and he was struck by the stark modernity of the decor which contrasted sharply with the traditional wood panelling and heavy furnishings of his previous lair.

When Buchanan had passed through several pairs of secretarial hands he found Lawrence Grassick relaxing between sessions. His wig and gown were suspended from a hanger on the back of a cupboard door and his fly-away collar and white tie were undone. For all he had made time to see Buchanan, he didn't look all that welcoming, and by the time they'd got through all the formalities of commiseration at his recent bereavement he was already beginning to show signs of impatience.

'Something to do with the will was it, Tam? No problems, I hope?'

Buchanan took a slow breath and tried to break it to him gently. 'Not in the normal way, no. The bequests are perfectly straightforward. Apart from a small gift to a local charity your wife's entire estate goes to her business partner Joseph Rudyard.'

'Yes, yes. I'm aware of all that.' Grassick shifted the position of the papers on his desk and tapped them impatiently. 'So? "Not in the normal way"? What does that mean?'

'It means, I'm afraid, that I have reservations about the efficiency of the police inquiry into your wife's death. I'd like the opportunity, before winding up her estate, to satisfy myself that a proper—'

'What sort of nonsense is this?' Grassick interrupted, snapping down his eyebrows in a long bar above his nose. 'I've no complaints against the police. They conducted a very intensive investigation into the cause of the fire and concluded – well, you know all that yourself if you've seen a paper recently. The *Evening News* had a field day on the strength of it.'

'Yes, I've read the reports,' Buchanan said, 'and I'm quite sure that what you say is, on the whole, true. There are, however, one or two minor points I'd like to clarify, merely to put my own mind at rest before I wind up your late wife's estate.'

'And what minor points are we talking about?' Grassick's voice was still calm, dangerously so, but his thin, aesthetic face appeared to be not only reddening, but swelling.

Buchanan allowed a moment to pass before answering, in the hope that Grassick would get a grip on his temper, and then said quietly, 'There's no explanation in the police report as to why Mrs Grassick should have arrived at the house in the middle of the night. Nor have I seen an explanation as to how a close neighbour came to be involved. Also, there are . . .'

He broke off, involuntarily, without being aware that he had done so, silenced by the realisation that he was about to witness one of Grassick's famous rages. It didn't start with a bang: it built up silently but with an appalling sense of power, like a tidal wave, and then it broke about Buchanan's ears with such violence that he was momentarily stunned.

'You *what*, you damn fool interfering imbecile? You think you're going to start sticking your snout into my personal affairs, rooting about for some sort of scandal that you can use to make a name for yourself? Oh no you don't, my lad. You won't be using me to claw your way up the ladder. That's the way it's done these days, isn't it? Not by being good at your job – oh, no! – by becoming a household word! You think you're setting yourself up as Edinburgh's Miss Marple, don't you? Totally exceeding your remit, interfering with police business, getting your face in the papers, arsing about like an idiot in the middle of the Festival parade, for Christ's sake! Oh, yes! I heard about that disgraceful business and it didn't do you any credit, let me tell you . . .'

The last cut was a little too close for comfort, since the memory of that episode had barely faded into a mental bruise, but Buchanan was determined not to let it show. He kept his eyes steadfastly on the twisted and engorged face and stopped listening. Gradually, the pitch of Ghengis's delivery lessened and the torrent of words ebbed to a strong current. The personal abuse mutated into a more divergent diatribe but the delivery was just as deafening.

'I've had the police and the fire brigade and the bloody media damn near living in my pockets for days, pestering my staff both here and at home, tramping my garden into a quagmire, taking photographs, measuring, nitpicking and making bloody nuisances of themselves to prove what everybody knew in the first place: that Vanessa died as the result of an accident that could have happened to anyone. And now, not content to take their opinion as read, I'm supposed to put up with a damn daddy's boy who knows nothing about anything, swanning in where he's not wanted and raking out the whole business again.' His bullet-hard brown eyes bored into Buchanan's as though he believed he could face him down. 'Well, you can forget it, laddie. If you thought I'd give my blessing for that sort of exercise, you were wrong!'

Buchanan cleared his throat and sat up as though he were rousing himself from suspended animation. 'With respect, sir, I didn't come here to ask for your permission. I came, as a matter of courtesy, to inform you of my intentions. My inquiries – my *entirely proper* inquiries – should not take more than a day or two and I don't anticipate inconveniencing either you or your staff.'

He got to his feet and Grassick rose with him, leaning across the desk on his two clenched fists. 'You're a fool, boy!' he bawled in a voice no longer pitched to the back row of the gods but still painfully loud and shaking with uncontrollable fury. 'Carry on the way you're going and your reputation won't be worth a tinker's cuss. You'll end up the laughing-stock of Edinburgh. I just hope your father's proud of you!'

'Thank you, sir. I believe he is. However, I still have my work as a solicitor to accomplish and I intend to do so to the best of my ability.'

Buchanan no longer had to work at appearing calm. Much as he admired Grassick as a lawyer, he could only despise his use of personal abuse and intemperate shouting as a preferred means of expressing an opinion. OK, he'd just lost his young wife in a horrific accident so you had to cut him a little slack, but it wasn't easy to witness such a performance without losing a large slice of one's respect for the man.

'I'm truly sorry,' Buchanan said as he moved towards

the door, 'to have to add to your afflictions at this time, but I see it as my duty to make sure there are no serious repercussions at a later date.'

'Serious repercussions?' Grassick snarled. 'By Christ, you'll know what serious repercussions are all right, if I've anything to do with it. Don't think you'll be instructing *me* next time you need counsel, you damn cocksure young brat! Now get out of my sight!'

Buchanan inclined his head slightly. 'Thank you for seeing me, sir. Good morning.'

He'd meant to exit on that line but a sudden madness intervened. Maybe it was his disappointment at discovering his idol had feet of clay; maybe it was the realisation that he had already signed his own death warrant and could sink no deeper, but some demon goaded him into scanning Grassick's purple face and remarking, 'You know you're killing yourself, don't you?'

There were several more people in the outer office than there had been when he went in and he was aware of their awestruck stares as he passed through. No doubt Grassick's half of the conversation, and his own momentary insanity, had been clearly audible to the entire staff and would be common knowledge throughout Edinburgh's legal fraternity by this time tomorrow.

Fame at last.

Chapter Four

Fizz was seriously unsure whether to laugh or cry when the news reached her. The first time she heard it, which was from a messenger delivering a packet of deeds, she didn't believe it for an instant.

'Somebody's got it wrong,' she assured a gobsmacked Beatrice. 'The bit about Grassick yelling at Buchanan – *that* I can swallow. The bit about Buchanan letting him do it: okay – I could more easily imagine him getting up and walking out, but – sure, fine, I don't have a big problem with that either. But, trust me Beatrice, he would never tell Ghengis Grassick to watch his blood pressure. Absolutely no way. He's never *ever* rude. Not to anybody.'

'If he lost his temper he—'

Fizz raspberried that without reserve. 'You are being facetious, I take it? When did you last see Buchanan lose his temper? Have you any proof that he actually *has* a temper to lose?'

'No,' Beatrice muttered unhappily, folding the two wings of her cardigan protectively across her motherly bosom as she habitually did when she felt the foundations of her existence teetering. 'But, Lawrence Grassick! Surely you know what people say about him, Fizz. He can be quite offensive. I've heard him myself – in court – and he would goad anyone into retaliating.'

'Not Buchanan,' Fizz insisted, perfectly sure in her own mind. If she herself couldn't get a rise out of Buchanan – and God knew she'd been trying for two years – nobody could. Buchanan might be a stubborn bastard, he might abominate bullies with a deep and implacable loathing but he was polite to the last ditch and, what was even more to the point, he had never once displayed suicidal tendencies. The gossip was either a tissue of lies or exaggerated out of all recognition.

'*You* didn't see him when he came in this morning,' Beatrice said. 'The minute he walked through that door I said to myself, "You haven't slept much last night, my lad. I wonder what you've been up to." I suspected he must have got himself a new girlfriend and, to tell you the truth, I was glad to think it because I don't believe there's been anyone – not lasting, I mean – since Janine . . .' Fizz was damn sure there hadn't been: she'd made sure of that. She might not – at the moment – want Buchanan for herself, but she wasn't having him bonking anyone else. '. . . but now – *now*, Fizz – I realise what must have been giving him a sleepless night: not feeling piqued about the bawling out, of course, but regretting what he'd done. You don't insult Lawrence Grassick and get away with it. Poor boy, he must be wretched.'

Fizz gave up trying to convince her. Beatrice was entrenched in her own opinion and, besides, right now it was more important to find out if there really *was* a new girlfriend in the frame.

It was only later, when Buchanan himself actually confirmed the accuracy of the communiqué, that she was forced to accept it as fact but, even then, she was too stunned to react. Buchanan . . . belligerence . . . It was impossible even to craft a sentence containing both words. The world was coming to an end, she thought. There would be signs, portents, fiery comets and showers of frogs. Hamsters would prophesy. Virgins would bring forth armadillos.

She studied Buchanan's face as though seeing it for the first time. There was no outward sign of his having been inhabited by a malevolent entity from another planet and,

if there were a new flintiness in his eye, at least there was
no suggestion of the onset of insanity. He had slept very
little last night, that much was obvious from the grooves
under his eyes, but he showed no sign of regret and that
only made her more alarmed.

'I've never known you to lose your temper,' she said,
totally in denial. 'I know Grassick can be a bastard but I
can't believe you let him get to you.'

Buchanan rose from his chair as though it had ejected
him and started to walk up and down behind his desk with
his hands in his trouser pockets. Fizz loved it when he did
that because – forget all his other faults – he had the cutest
bum in Christendom.

'I didn't lose it, Fizz. I wasn't even angry at him. I was
just sorry to see him out of control like that.' He stopped
by the window and stared out at the traffic. 'You hear
stories about his temper but you imagine it differently –
clean, somehow, and purposeful and deliberate. Like a
scalpel. But it was disgusting, Fizz. He wasn't *using* his
temper: it was using *him*. Watching him . . . it was embarrassing more than anything else . . . and alarming. He
looked like he was about to burst a blood vessel.'

'Oh, pooh!' Fizz had no patience with such rubbish.
'Even if his temper *were* killing him, it wasn't up to you to
tell him so. You have to let people go to hell their own
way.'

'Yeah, well, this time I didn't. Maybe he'd rattled me
more than I realised but, even now, believe it or not, I
don't regret saying it. And, anyway,' he twisted his lips a
fraction in a sardonic smile, 'he was already as mad at me
as he could possibly get. You've said it yourself more than
once, I seem to remember: the best kind of security is to
have nothing to lose.'

Fizz did recollect spouting some such nonsense, probably when under the influence of a few G&Ts, and there
were times when she actually believed it, up to a point. But
she'd been referring to the wonderful sense of liberty she'd

experienced when she was wandering the world with nothing but what she stood up in, and she very much doubted if Buchanan, who was used to a cushy lifestyle, could achieve the same sort of nirvana.

There wasn't much hope of Grassick regretting his threats once he cooled down. Nor was he likely to forget Buchanan's parting shot, not when it was ricocheting around town like a flu germ.

'Does this mean you're going to drop the investigation after all?' she queried, but seeing Buchanan's upwardly mobile eyebrows she knew it had been a silly question. There was no stopping now. The only thing to do was to forge ahead and get some positive result to prove to Grassick that Buchanan had been right to be concerned. 'So, where do we start on this one?'

He turned to look at her. 'We start,' he said with solid emphasis, 'by making you understand – and *accept* – that, much as I'd appreciate any behind the scenes help you feel motivated to give me, you have to keep a very low profile on this one. Nobody's even going to nod to me in the street for a while in case Grassick gets to hear about it and the last thing we want is for you to nip your career in the bud by being actively involved.'

Fizz hadn't actually got around to considering that aspect of the affair and although she was sick as a parrot at the thought of staying out of things, she wasn't going to argue. 'You're damn tootin'. I'll make sure Ghengis couldn't distinguish me from the Invisible Man.'

She wasn't daft, she told herself. She'd worked hard at her course for more than two years and it hadn't been easy, either academically or financially, so she sure as hell wasn't going to put all that effort to the slightest risk. But – hell! – it would be tough cheddar if she couldn't find a way to grab herself a part of the action. Grassick had never seen her and was never likely to but, anyway, it would be no trouble to disguise her appearance enough to foil any verbal reports that might get back to him. She'd done it often enough before. No need to mention it to Buchanan right at this moment, though, since it would only cause an argument.

Buchanan returned to his chair and drew his scribbling pad towards him, flipping to a fresh page. 'I'll have to talk to Vanessa's business partner, Joseph Rudyard, I suppose. He's the one – the only one, as far as I can see, to profit much from Vanessa's death, so he ought to be our prime suspect. Then there's the neighbours, Mrs Pringle and her husband. Then the other woman who accompanied Mrs Pringle to the hospital. Elizabeth something.'

'Elizabeth Armstrong,' Fizz remembered. 'The local postman, Lenny Napier, appears to be the local Reuters, so we should talk to him. And the older waiter at Chirnside House said something about some daft old folk who were making sceptical noises. He mentioned no names but I reckon, if we could talk to him again, he'd finger them for a half pint.'

'Okay. Probably the Pringles.' Buchanan added those leads to his list and sat back, studying them. 'We'd better make a start right away. I don't want to give Lawrence Grassick any time to put pressure on Dad – or the police – or anybody else – to have this thing stopped.'

Fizz swung her chair round to prop her feet on the corner of his desk. 'Are you, by any chance, thinking what I'm thinking: that Grassick's got something to hide?'

'Everybody's got something to hide, Fizz, if you dig deep enough, but we're not likely to be doing that. However, if you're asking me if I suspect Grassick of blowing up his wife, the answer's no.'

'Why not?' Fizz persisted. 'They say most people are killed by members of their own family, don't they? Grassick could have killed her in a temper.'

Buchanan clasped his hands behind his neck and stretched his spine. 'Grassick gets rid of his aggression by shouting, not by lashing out.' He clenched his teeth to smother a yawn. 'And anyway, why murder his wife when he could divorce her? It wouldn't make sense.'

Fizz was much inclined to believe that reasons for doing so could exist, even if they were not immediately apparent. If Vanessa's death really did turn out to be non-accidental, Ghengis Grassick was top of her list of suspects, whatever Buchanan thought.

She watched Buchanan add a name to his schedule. 'Another lead?' she asked.

'Not really. It's just a chap I play golf with who's a Labour activist. I might have a word with him eventually if things swing that way. I know Grassick is chairman of one of the Labour wards in the city, sits on various commit- tees, has a lot to say at their conferences. I don't suppose that side of his life will impinge on anything we're likely to be interested in, but you never know. Anyone else you can think of?'

Fizz stared at her toecaps for a minute. 'The police?' she suggested, half in fun.

'I've already spoken to the police,' Buchanan surprised her by saying. 'I had a brief chat with a DCI Virgo, who was in charge of the investigation. A *very* brief chat. I don't see us receiving much help from that quarter.'

'I'm not surprised. They can't stand anyone else taking an interest, can they? What about asking your old chum DI Fleming to do a little spying for us? He owes us one for handing him Mr Big on a plate. We did all the work on that case and he got all the glory.'

Buchanan drooped his eyelids at her. 'I suspect the now *DCI* Fleming viewed Mr Big as fair exchange for his not arresting you after your *previous* felony,' he said. 'I reckon we still have some work to do to build up our credit with him. I may have to lean on him eventually, but I'll post- pone it as long as I can.' He raised his chin from his fist to give her a hard look. 'Also, one doesn't want to nag, but it would be nice if we could stay within the law this time.'

Fizz returned the hard look in spades. 'It really gets on my tits,' she snapped, 'the way you always make it out that

I antagonise the police deliberately. If I take the law into my own hands once in a while – and it *is* only once in a while – it's because there's no other way out. I'm not stupid, you know!'

Buchanan closed his eyes and pretended to be asleep. A minute later she realised he wasn't pretending.

Vanessa Grassick's commercial art business, Rudyard Grassick, occupied spacious but unpretentious premises above an Indian restaurant in Nicholson Street. It was entered via a gloomy staircase with old stone stairs that were worn concave in the middle from the passage of many feet, but inside it was filled with light from tall Georgian windows. The minimum amount of money had been spent on turning the interconnected rooms into a congenial workspace but the staff appeared cheerful enough at their drawing boards and someone had a tape playing somewhere that sounded like a classic Chris Barber.

The Rudyard half of the partnership turned out to be a woeful-looking guy in his mid- to late-thirties, so thin that his ribs showed through the tee-shirt he wore under an open shirt. His hair was coal black and cut in an expensive but unflatteringly geometric style that skimmed his eyebrows and framed his ears in a C-shaped curve. It was very eye-catching but, in Buchanan's opinion, it only accentuated the angularity of his face. In one ear he wore a small gold earring shaped like an anchor, and that didn't make him irresistible either. Nevertheless, he looked just as amenable to being interviewed as he had sounded earlier when Buchanan had phoned to suggest a meeting.

'Bit of a mess in here,' he apologised, in voice that was already grating on Buchanan's nerves, and led his visitor into a cramped office. 'Things have been getting a bit out of hand recently. Somehow or other we never seem to get time to spend on organisation.'

Buchanan picked his way through a minefield of bottles, rolls of paper, tins of paint and small glass dishes and lowered his two-hundred-pound trousers on to a less than reassuring bentwood chair. The walls of the room were lined with shelf units containing a similar assortment of materials as did the floor, and the whole room smelled strongly of an unfamiliar chemical spirit. The door, the free-standing cupboards, and every available patch of wall was plastered with posters, photographs and cuttings, presumably samples of the firm's output.

Rudyard sketched a dismal attempt at a smile as he followed Buchanan's gaze. 'You see, when we started the business we were in such a hurry to get it off the ground, to get the money coming in, that we decided to leave the non-urgent stuff till we broke even. But now that the work's beginning to come in more regularly we can't spare the time to start ripping out walls etc. We'll get round to it one of these days.'

Buchanan nodded pleasantly. 'I believe there are firms that specialise in doing that sort of job over a weekend, while the premises are empty. With the bequest you stand to receive from Mrs Grassick's will, you'll be able to afford to pay extra for speed.'

'I suppose so.' There was something trapped under Rudyard's thumb nail that appeared to interest him more than the money. He picked at it with the end of a paper clip as he snivelled, 'I don't know what my plans are for the future. I may move to new premises, I may give up the firm altogether. Things will be difficult without Vanessa.'

'Difficult? Businesswise, you mean?'

'Uh-huh. Vanessa was the creative half of the partnership.' He lifted one shoulder in a spiritless shrug. 'I'm a good draughtsman – tell me what you want and I'll deliver it – but it was Vanessa who got us the orders. She had the contacts and the drive and the reputation you need in this scene and, most of the time, she was the one who came up with the clever ideas. I just don't know how things will go from here on in.'

Buchanan discovered he didn't give a shit, one way or

the other. In fact, he was finding Joseph Rudyard one of the most unappealing jellyfish he'd had to deal with for some time. His voice had a lot to do with that. It was pitched rather higher than average and had a nasal whine that weighed quite heavily on Buchanan's spirits. As well as that, he had a habit of tucking in his chin, thus forcing himself to roll his eyes up, exposing a line of white below his irises and giving him an irritating hang-dog expression. One could commiserate with his loss of a dynamic partner but, for God's sake, wasn't twelve thousand pounds and the said partner's share in the business enough of a compensation?

'Were you close socially, you and Mrs Grassick?'

Rudyard returned to picking his nails. 'We'd go out for a drink sometimes after work,' he said listlessly. 'Friday nights usually, but that was more of a business thing. I've been over to her house once or twice. She and her husband always had a mass of people round for drinks on Christmas Eve, that was something they laid on for friends they didn't meet up with regularly, business contacts, those sorts of people. When you come right down to it, we didn't really have a lot in common. But,' he added as an obvious afterthought, 'I'll miss her, of course. She was great to work with.'

Somehow Buchanan couldn't imagine Vanessa, or indeed anybody else, saying the same about Rudyard. That voice entered the ear like a dental drill: listening to it for eight hours a day would do anybody's head in.

'How about her weekend place down in Chirnside? Ever been down there?'

Rudyard smiled a humourless smile that barely creased his cheeks. 'No. They didn't have guests there, not unless Lawrence took some friends down for a couple of days' fishing. I don't think it was Vanessa's scene, to tell you the truth. She was more of a townie but she tagged along with Lawrence for the sake of a quiet life, I think. He can be quite . . . er . . .'

'Dictatorial?' Buchanan supplied.

'I was going to say self-centred but, yes, from the hints Vanessa dropped, he liked to get his own way. I suspect he dominated her a lot of the time.'

'Was she the sort of woman who hated being dominated?'

'Don't they all?' He looked, for a second, as if he'd be interested to hear Buchanan's opinion on that, but then continued, 'I don't suppose she enjoyed it but she just let it wash straight over her head – as far as I could tell, anyway.'

Buchanan would have been surprised if that had not been the case. It would have taken a strong woman to stand up to Grassick's temper, and two browbeaters of his class in the same household would never have lasted the ten years those two had clocked up. He said, 'Yes, quite. Yet, by all accounts, they jogged along together pretty well.'

'Yeah.' Rudyard's initial gratification at having his opinions solicited appeared to be ebbing. Evidently it wasn't as much fun as he had expected it to be, and he was now slipping deeper into what Buchanan suspected was his normal state of profound depression. 'But it wasn't what I'd call a marriage. They lived together and they socialised together but there didn't appear to be much else to it, as far as I could see. They both had their own careers and it looked to me like they didn't see all that much of each other – especially since Lawrence started to get so involved in politics.'

'Takes all kinds,' Buchanan murmured. It was almost reassuring to hear that the Grassicks' marriage was grounded more in convenience than in passion. In spite of everything, he didn't really want to find that Grassick had arranged his wife's death and he couldn't help feeling that where there was no passion there was less reason for one of those involved to boil over. In his experience, a husband/ wife killing was usually a *crime passionnel*.

'Did it ever occur to you . . . Sorry, it's none of my

business . . .' Buchanan began but, receiving an encouraging lift of the brows from Rudyard, he continued, 'Did Mrs Grassick inform you of her intention to leave her entire estate to you?'

'No. Never hinted at anything like that. I don't even know why she'd think of such a thing. Except, maybe . . .' His nose wrinkled, widening his nostrils unattractively. 'She might have meant it to go towards building up the business but, if so, she never spoke to me about it. I suppose she would have explained her thinking to me if she hadn't died so suddenly.'

His lugubrious eyes hung on Buchanan's as though he expected sympathy for being so thoughtlessly treated. He should have been dancing on his tippy-toes with delight at his financial windfall like any other not-too-distressed beneficiary but, if that was what he felt like inside, he was hiding it well. It was always possible, Buchanan thought, that he was misjudging the guy for no good reason and Rudyard simply deemed it indecent to betray any jubilation at a blessing obtained in such tragic circumstances. Possible, but highly unlikely.

'Just one more thing you might be able to tell me,' he said, watching Rudyard's face. 'How did Mrs Grassick appear psychologically these last few weeks?'

'Psychologically?' That brought his head up. For a moment Buchanan thought he detected a flicker of humour in the mournful eyes. 'You think she might have committed suicide? Is that what you meant earlier when you said there were matters you wanted to clarify?'

'No.' Buchanan had never thought that likely, but one could never tell. 'I don't imagine many people would choose that way of putting an end to their life. I was simply curious to know if she seemed happier or sadder than usual.' What he'd really wanted to know was whether she looked as if there was a new interest in her life – like a love affair with a neighbour, for instance – but that wasn't the sort of thing he could ask Rudyard straight out so he covered up by adding, 'Worried about anything maybe? Something that might have distracted her thoughts when she was turning on the gas supply?'

'Naw,' Rudyard said, without bothering to think about it. 'She was real mad about some guy clearing people off an estate somewhere near their cottage but she wasn't the sort to let it get to her like that. Vanessa was a nice quiet lady on the surface but, when you got to know her, she was cold steel underneath.'

It was always nice, Buchanan thought, when you got the answer to a question you'd never have thought of asking.

Chapter Five

'I'm beginning to form a really interesting picture of this Grassick woman,' Fizz told Buchanan as they headed back to Chirnside that evening.

It was lashing with rain but she was feeling quite pressured by the need to push ahead and get out of Grassick's hair as soon as humanly possible. Buchanan had muttered a bit as she'd expected, but he could hardly deny the need for alacrity. And, quite coincidentally, since they had set forth directly from the office, 'pushing ahead' also meant that he would have to buy her dinner.

He lifted his eyebrows and said, 'Yes? How do you see her?'

'Well, she was nobody's whipping boy, I reckon,' Fizz submitted, feeling quite confident that she knew what she was talking about. 'Vanessa took what she wanted from that marriage, a position in society, a luxury lifestyle, possibly even very good company – when Grassick wasn't in Ghengis mode. She may have loved him dearly – in fact, I'm sure she must have done – but when he *was* in Ghengis mode I can see her just leaving him to it and getting on with her own life.'

'How do you come to that conclusion?' Buchanan spared her a quick glance and then concentrated on the rush-hour traffic. There had been a time when he'd have greeted Fizz's prognostications with imperfectly concealed amusement but he'd grown up a lot since then.

Likewise, Fizz was man enough to admit in the privacy

of her own thoughts, there had been a time when she couldn't have traced back the line of her own reasoning. Now she had grown used to explaining herself to Buchanan and was able to say, 'Nobody with any savvy whatsoever could have put up with Lawrence Grassick's temper for – how long were they married?'

'Ten years.'

'Right. However, we know Vanessa *wasn't* simple because she was making a success of her business in a competitive field, and we know she was capable of putting her needs across because she was the one who went out and got the orders. I can't see anybody fighting Grassick with his own weapon – women can't shout that loud for a start – so the only way she could have lasted *this* long was by teaching him that he wouldn't get away with bullying her.'

'Rudyard said she went along with his preferences just for the sake of a quiet life.'

'That's by the way. You swear to that at the altar.' Fizz wriggled into a more comfortable position and tucked her feet under her, being careful to remove her Doc's first since Buchanan was still pernickety about his new Saab. 'I'm talking about pushing her too far. She wouldn't take that for long. According to your chum Sunshine Rudyard, Vanessa wasn't the kind to let anybody walk all over her, so she must have had some way of keeping Ghengis Grassick in check. Maybe he was crazy about her and was scared she'd ditch him. Maybe she had some other big stick to hit him with.'

'Hm-mm,' Buchanan said as he overtook a car-transporter lorry in a shower of spray. The weather being what it was, he had taken the main A1 instead of the tourist route, and at this time of day it was like Le Mans. 'Makes me wonder just how mad she was about the sale of Lammerburn Estate. Rudyard said she wasn't pleased about it but I should have asked him if she'd been annoying the Menzies family. There's potentially a lot of money tied up in the sale of Lammerburn Estate so, if Vanessa Grassick looked like being a serious threat to the sale, it means we really have to add Menzies to our list of people to talk to.'

'Well, you were going to talk to him anyway, weren't you?'

'Maybe,' Buchanan admitted. 'If the letter I got Dennis to write him this morning doesn't have the desired effect.'

'You wrote to him already? What did you tell Dennis to say?'

'I don't tell Dennis what to say,' he had to point out, in the nitpicking way that got straight up Fizz's nostrils. 'We had a chat about it and Dennis considered it should be enough, in the first instance, to suggest to Menzies that he might want to think about the effect his plans would have on the village. We'll see what he has to say to that and take it from there.'

It was quite obvious to Fizz that Menzies had already considered the effect his plans would have on the village and didn't give a monkey's chunky, but she was ready to concede that Buchanan had more experience in diplomacy than she had.

'What sort of people are the Menzies family?' she asked, absently opening the glove compartment and helping herself to a stick of the chewing gum Buchanan habitually kept in there to guard against thirst on a long journey. 'Have you dealt with them before?'

'Not personally. They were Dad's clients till Dennis took over the conveyancing, but I understand they're quite well respected.' He accepted the offer of some gum without comment. 'Old money. They were big landowners in Aberdeenshire at one time but death duties hit them hard and they ended up, back in the fifties, opening their Victorian pile to the public. They started brewing their own ale, more or less as an added attraction to the house, but the business took off and it eventually restored their fortunes. Dennis has been dealing with Niall Menzies, son of the current head of the family. Apparently, the old man is in his late eighties now and doesn't have much to do with business.'

'What age is the son?'

Buchanan smiled, not looking at her. 'Dennis has him down as about fifty-five. Too old for you to try turning his head, I'm afraid, Fizz.'

Fizz didn't lower herself to answer that one, considering it a childish jibe and almost wholly unmerited, since the thought had no more than crossed her mind. Besides, the older they were, the easier they fell for her 'motherless child' approach.

'Where are we eating?' she said, noting that the turnoff for Chirnside was approaching. 'I rather liked that place we went to on Saturday.'

Buchanan put on a reasonable face which usually meant he was going to try to talk her out of it. 'Or,' he murmured, 'we could grab a bar meal at the Waterloo in Chirnside. That would save a bit of time and maybe let us get home at a respectable hour.'

'You have something you want to do this evening?'

'Nothing special, but I—'

'Neither have I,' Fizz told him sweetly. 'What time is it now? Nearly seven. Not a good time to be dropping in on people, I'd have thought. They'll all be eating, won't they? Of course, we could kill an hour or so in the pub before we go, have a few drinks. I'm easy. Thy will be done.'

Buchanan, no doubt considering how much she could drink in an hour, said that he quite fancied the Chirnside Hall after all and presently pulled in to the car park with a tolerably good grace.

In point of fact, Buchanan didn't really mind buying Fizz a decent meal. She was, after all, giving up her evening for him – even if her motivation for doing so was nosiness rather than solidarity – and besides, he was never totally convinced that she ate properly.

He was pretty sure she didn't have a lot of money. She'd been living for two years now on her student grant, plus what she earned from holiday jobs and such part-time work as Buchanan could find for her to do without appearing too charitable. She had a thing about accepting charity in any form other than food and drink – and those she cadged shamelessly from anyone at all. No doubt that little habit was one she'd picked up during the lean years – even leaner than at the present time – when she had lived virtually from hand to mouth. Or maybe she believed that she gave fair exchange for the food by being engaging company which, indeed, she was, when she wanted to be. Other times she'd drive you to drink. Most times, actually.

When they were seated, he said to her, 'Bear in mind, Fizz, that Lawrence Grassick is a regular customer in this place. He would be absolutely livid to think we'd been gossiping about him with the staff so, this time, can we just enjoy our meal and leave?'

'Absolutely, Kemo Sabe.' She twinkled at him flirtatiously, but with an air of facetiousness that precluded his taking her seriously, and returned to her perusal of the menu.

He said, 'No, look at me, Fizz. I really mean it.'

'Like I said – absolutely. I wonder if I should have the monkfish. What are you having?'

Buchanan gave up and applied his attention to choosing his dinner but he was not too engrossed to miss the fact that her smile to the approaching waiter not only acknowledged the fact that she remembered him but was also a blatant invitation to him to chat: an invitation which he was not slow to accept.

'Good evening, miss. Good evening, sir. Very nice to see you back again.'

'Couldn't resist it,' she assured him with a girlish giggle. 'It's so nice and cosy in here on a rainy evening – and such an exciting part of the country. Any more exploding houses recently?'

'No, I'm afraid not, miss,' said the waiter, grinning. 'But there have been—'

'I think . . .' Buchanan said, and then added innocently, 'Oh sorry. I interrupted you.'

'Not at all, sir. My apologies, sir. Are you ready to order?'

Buchanan admitted that, in fact, he was, and did so.

As soon as the waiter had swanned out of earshot he turned on Fizz with a glare. 'What did I just say?' he demanded angrily. 'Did I just ask you not to start on about the explosion or am I losing my mind?'

'You suggested it might not be a good idea to start cross-examining people in case Grassick got to hear of it,' she returned, with a childlike expression of wounded innocence, 'but you said nothing about allowing the staff to talk about the accident of their own free will.'

'That's semantics, Fizz. You know damn well what I meant!'

'Yes I do,' she agreed pacifically, buttering a bread roll. 'But the crux is: could I be quoted? There's no way the waiter could tell Grassick that I'd been asking questions, or even that I'd shown any undue interest. All I did – both just now and last Saturday – was make polite conversation, as any visitor would. What's wrong with that?'

Buchanan wasn't in a mood to argue with her but he made up his mind that he'd take damn good care she didn't get the chance to resume her polite conversation. He was already beginning to regret allowing her to help him deal with this business. She had always been difficult to keep on a leash and he knew beyond a shadow of a doubt that if she broke loose this time he'd end up, once again, in considerably deeper shit than he'd started out in.

At the end of the meal, while the waiter was helping Fizz with her coat, Buchanan heard him say, 'I hope we'll see you again soon, miss. We can't promise you another exploding house but I hear the last one might turn out not to be an accident.'

'Good heavens,' said Fizz, ignoring Buchanan's hand on her arm. 'An insurance fraud, do you mean?'

'Maybe. That's how the local gossip goes, anyway. There's an insurance investigator – Mr Cambridge – staying here at the hotel for a few days, so there could be some truth in the rumours.' He registered Buchanan's suggestion of impatience and backed off, trousering his tip. 'Thank you very much, sir. Goodnight, miss.'

Buchanan would have loved to stay and chat. The mention of an insurance investigator was a tempting bait but he was determined to play this case by the book and do nothing to give Lawrence Grassick cause for complaint. There was no need, in this instance, to gossip with the staff: he could phone this Mr Cambridge tomorrow and ask for a meeting. As Vanessa Grassick's legal representative, he had a right to know whether the insurance investigation was a routine one or not and, if Cambridge had serious doubts about the cause of the explosion, maybe he would be willing to swap findings.

Fizz was too furious for words and shook his hand from her arm as soon as they had passed out of the dining room. In the lobby she turned on him like a bonsai Ghengis Grassick, keeping her voice low only because there were people in the open-plan cocktail bar a few feet away.

'I don't believe you just did that,' she hissed, choking with frustration. 'You didn't even need to *question* the guy! All you had to do was stand there and let him run! We could have heard all the gossip from him instead of dragging it out of the neighbours like we were drawing teeth. Dammit! You just irritate the hell out of me, Buchanan, you know that? I can't count the times you've . . .'

Slowly it dawned on her what she – and Buchanan – had just heard through her whispered insults: the voice of the barman saying clearly, 'Mr Cambridge? A telephone call for you, sir.'

As they watched, a blond, good-looking chap rose from

a stool at the bar and walked to the end of the counter to take the phone from the barman.

Fizz looked up at Buchanan's face, her expression that of Stephenson glimpsing the potentiality of steam. 'Now *that*,' she murmured, 'was a gift from God, Buchanan. Don't tell me you're going to take a rain-check.'

Buchanan was far from it. There was a world of difference between gossiping with the staff and running into the insurance investigator in person. He took Fizz's arm and led her over to the two stools next to the one temporarily vacated by Mr Cambridge.

Fizz perked up instantly, probably at the prospect of her second gin and tonic of the evening, and let him see that his reluctance to converse with the waiter was a thing of the past. She removed her coat and fluffed up her already rumbustious ringlets.

'Okay, compadre, how do we play it? Are we innocent passers-by who're not particularly curious about the fire, or reporters from the *Berwick Herald*, or—'

'No lies, Fizz,' Buchanan said sternly, holding down her wrist so that she couldn't take her first sip of G&T till she listened. 'Not about our identity: not about anything. This chap could save us a lot of hassle. With a bit of luck he may be able to put my mind at rest and save me from having to alienate Grassick any more than I already have done.'

'Okay, okay. Have it your own way. I was only asking.'

She twirled sideways on her high stool and crossed her legs. She was wearing the usual navy blue dress and plain shoes she came to work in every day but suddenly she looked indefinably . . . classier. Or something. Buchanan couldn't quite put his finger on what the difference was . . . maybe she was holding herself straighter . . . maybe it was something in her expression . . . but she definitely looked different. From the corner of his eye he caught sight of Cambridge approaching and was immediately struck by how handsome he was.

He was about Buchanan's age or a year or two younger: lean and fit-looking with lazy, shadowed eyes and an easy-going expression. His clothes, slacks and a casual jacket with a black polo-necked sweater underneath, looked well cut and he wore them with a natural grace that turned heads as he returned to his place at the bar counter.

'Mr Cambridge?' Buchanan said right away before Fizz could do anything he hadn't anticipated.

The chap swivelled his eyes towards him over the rim of his pint. 'Hmm?'

'I'm sorry to intrude on you but I just heard your name mentioned and wondered if we might have a chat.' Buchanan slipped a business card out of his wallet. 'The name's Tam Buchanan and I'm executor of the estate of Mrs Vanessa Grassick. This is my colleague Miss Fitzpatrick.'

Cambridge set down his beer, whipped out a hankie and dabbed his lips. 'Glad to meet you. And you, Miss Fitzpatrick.' He shook hands with both of them, observing Fizz with unnecessary closeness as though he were memorising her. 'You know, obviously, that I work for Mrs Grassick's insurers.'

It was a polite way of saying, how in hell did you know my business, but Fizz saved Buchanan the trouble of explaining by giving a faint gurgle of laughter and saying, 'You're in Scotland, Mr Cambridge. Everybody knows everything about everybody, usually before it happens. We were having dinner just now and overheard a comment, that's all, and my boss here thought we should meet.'

It wasn't often that she referred to – or even *viewed* – Buchanan as her boss and it was peculiar that she should do so now, particularly as she had just been introduced as a colleague. It looked suspiciously like she was making it clear that their relationship was purely a business one. Abandoning the thought, Buchanan said, 'I hope your presence here doesn't mean that you have reservations about the cause of the accident?'

'I'm just doing a routine look-see,' Cambridge said, and

then flashed a wide, attractive and non-committal grin. 'But if I can earn myself a bonus by finding the company some loophole, well that's what this job is about. You know what insurance companies are like. They'll do anything to avoid paying out on a premium – and don't quote me on that, will you?'

Buchanan rather suspected that he was playing down his interest but, at the same time, he had hardly expected the chap to take him into his confidence on first acquaintance so he grinned back credulously and said, 'We're actually in much the same position ourselves: making a few low-key inquiries just to be on the safe side before paying out Mrs Grassick's estate.'

'Really?' He raised his brows, visibly more interested. 'Does that mean you know something I don't?'

Fizz laughed again. 'He's just a nasty suspicious character, that's all, and so nitpicking you wouldn't believe it. You know *who* Vanessa Grassick was, don't you?'

'I hadn't a clue till I got here this afternoon,' he said, nodding his smooth blond head. 'She was just a name on a piece of paper, to me, and to everyone else at head office. Now I hear that she was married to some sort of law lord.'

'Not exactly a law lord,' Fizz told him, 'but a very senior advocate and a guy with a lot of clout.'

Cambridge finished his beer. 'Yes? Well, I don't see it making a lot of difference to me – not unless it comes to a legal battle. I can't see that happening, not after a police inquiry, but I suppose I'd better make sure I get my facts right just in case.'

'Let me buy you another. Same again? Fizz?' Buchanan mimed the order to the bartender who was polishing glasses at the end of the counter. 'As you say, the police have already given their okay on the accident so there can't be much to uncover.'

He thought for a second or two that Cambridge wasn't going to come back on that one but, when the barman had delivered their drinks and gone back to his polishing, he sent Fizz a glimmer of his shiny grin and murmured, 'I suppose it would be the height of paranoia to wonder if Mr Grassick's exalted position in legal circles might have put some kind of pressure on the police? Not to falsify evidence, of course, but possibly to speed things up – maybe even to the point of carelessness.'

Fizz leaned across Buchanan to bring her head emphatically closer. 'Let me tell you something,' she said. 'I wouldn't be a bit surprised. We're talking about a seriously ferocious animal here. I can easily imagine Lawrence Grassick leaning on the inquiry team to do what was necessary as fast as possible and get the hell out of his hair. He'd put the frighteners on Hannibal Lecter, this guy.' She waved her glass at Buchanan. 'He went through the roof when Buchanan told him he wanted to check out things for himself. Didn't he, Buchanan? Go on, show him the teeth marks on your bum.'

Cambridge was hugely entertained by this sally. His grin was beginning to lose its appeal for Buchanan but not, he couldn't help noticing, for Fizz.

'So, it's possible we could find something the police have overlooked,' he said, looking down into his beer with an expression that morphed rapidly into one of sober consideration. Nobody said anything to that but after a moment he looked up at Buchanan and said, 'But it's not just that possibility that's niggling you, is it? There's something else. Something more specific.'

Buchanan shook his head. 'I'm not sure that it would be ethical for me to discuss my findings at this point . . .'

'Oh, come on, Buchanan,' Cambridge chided in an all-lads-together manner. 'If there's something going on here that should be looked into we'd do better sharing information, wouldn't you say?' He eyed both of them carefully and then, reading their silence correctly, added, 'Maybe I have information that might be of use to you.'

Fizz started to speak but Buchanan silenced her by nudging her with his knee and said, gently, 'I don't think that's likely, Mr Cambridge. Really I don't.'

Cambridge nodded briefly, as though that were that, but then leaned forward again and said, 'You know about the heater, then?'

'The heater?' Fizz breathed, her gin-scented breath tickling Buchanan's chin.

Cambridge put a hand in his hip pocket and produced a dark oblong of metal which he passed to Fizz. She turned it over and ran a finger across the raised print on its surface.

'Philips. Model number LX77731,' she said, and looked back at him questioningly.

'It was given to me by a Mr Pringle, one of Mrs Grassick's neighbours. It's part of an electric heater which, he claims, was scattered about the scene of the accident in a great many pieces – but not too many to make it unrecognisable as what it was. The police took away the rest of it but Mr Pringle insists that no such heater belonged in Brora Lodge.'

'How would he know?' Fizz asked, clearly not as riveted by the claim as Buchanan was.

The presence of an unaccountable electric heater in a house that had been demolished by a gas explosion was much more significant than the vague rumours that were all Buchanan had turned up so far. The news wasn't exactly what he had hoped for, but it certainly validated his decision to pick Cambridge's brain.

'Mr Pringle told me this afternoon,' Cambridge said, 'that the Grassicks had asked him if he would keep an eye on the house during the worst of the winter, when it was rarely used. He had a key to the back door and could let himself in to check for burst pipes et cetera and he was familiar with the furnishings.' He drooped a conspiratorial eyelid. 'I have a suspicion, from what he said, that he used the opportunity to have a good snoop around. He's that sort of guy. In his opinion, there was a more than adequate central heating system, besides which an old-fashioned heater of this model number would have stuck out a mile against the avant-garde furnishings they've chosen.'

'You're thinking it could have been part of some sort of explosive device?' Fizz asked, her eyes wide with a delight that Buchanan was unable to reciprocate.

Cambridge's eyes rested on her appreciatively. 'Dead right. Combined with the amount of gas the Grassicks must have had stored in the basement it could have made a very effective detonator.'

'But surely Mr Pringle must have mentioned his find to the police?' Buchanan suggested. 'So why didn't it prompt further inquiry?'

Cambridge shrugged. 'You tell me. All Mr Pringle was told was that the police had eliminated it as evidence, but if there was a rational explanation for the heater's appearance in the debris they're keeping it to themselves – which, in itself, is intriguing.'

Buchanan nodded his agreement, finally accepting the fact that he'd been right to be worried. There was still a possibility that the rumours were all false, of course, but either way it would take time to prove it and, in the meantime, he was going to be seeing a lot of this guy.

'Incidentally,' he said, with a certain amount of hesitation, 'the name's Tam.'

'Giles,' Cambridge smiled and turned an inquiring look on Fizz.

'Fizz,' she said, dimpling back at him in a way that made Buchanan even more depressed than he already was.

Chapter Six

It wasn't every day that Fizz ran across such supremely tasty men. At least ninety per cent of her fellow students were ten years her junior and living in penury, and such free time as she could spare from her studies was spent earning a crust. You could scarcely count either Buchanan or Dennis, the junior partner, who, on the surface, were both quite dishy, since Dennis was a complete piss artist and Buchanan was . . . well, Buchanan was Buchanan. No half measures for Buchanan. Start anything with him and you were liable to find yourself being dragged up the aisle in a dress like an explosion in a meringue factory.

Giles, now, he was just Fizz's type: not so tall he'd make her look like a pigmy, clever-looking but not starchy, and wickedly sexy. More importantly, he was probably not going to be around for more than a week or so, which meant that things were unlikely to get too complicated. Life was complicated enough right now and a meaningful relationship could – almost certainly *would* – cost her the grades she wanted in her LL B, but a transient interest as cute as Giles was irresistible. She finished her gin and tonic in a modestly explicit manner that encouraged Giles to suggest another round.

Buchanan looked at his watch and said, 'N—'

And simultaneously, Fizz said, 'Thanks, I'd love one.'

'But then we must be on our way,' Buchanan stated, in a voice that brooked no argument. 'We were planning to talk to the Grassicks' neighbours this evening, but it's almost too late already to be knocking on anybody's door.'

'Ah . . .' Giles rubbed a hand across his delightfully square jaw. 'Actually,' he said, 'it might be better if you left that for a day or two. I'm afraid I've spiked your guns a bit by quizzing them this afternoon. I imagine you wouldn't really want to be wading in again this evening. Sorry about that. If I'd known you were planning . . .'

'Not your fault,' Fizz said quickly. 'It just proves what you were saying: that we have to coordinate our efforts. You spoke to the other neighbours, the Armstrongs, did you?'

'Just Mrs Armstrong. Usually she and her husband are out at work all day but, luckily, she had a lousy cold and had taken the day off. However, neither of them had spoken to the Grassicks other than to pass the time of day and they were the type to keep themselves to themselves – unlike the Pringles who, I suspect, keep a pair of binoculars on the living room windowsill. The other house was empty. I'm told the owner was the man who died with Mrs Grassick in the explosion.'

Fizz let Buchanan reply to that because, sure as shootin', if she gave away any of their information she'd be doing the wrong thing.

He said, 'I'm surprised you didn't hear the Pringles' story about that. We met up with Mrs Pringle last weekend and she told us that Ford's wife was taken to hospital suffering from cuts from flying glass. However, when Mrs Pringle and Mrs Armstrong went to visit her a couple of days later, she had discharged herself and disappeared into the blue. No-one has seen her since.'

'Now, that's interesting,' Giles said, locking on to the information with an enthusiasm that Fizz entirely approved of. None of Buchanan's 'don't get fixated on one unsubstantiated clue' for *him*: he was in there like a terrier. 'Mrs Pringle wasn't at home when I called round and possibly Mr Pringle didn't think it relevant. But I must say, this opens up possibilities, doesn't it? The woman whose husband was with Vanessa Grassick in the middle of the night disappears immediately after his – and her – violent death. Does that strike you as suspicious, or is it just me?'

'Just what *I* thought,' Fizz put in, but Buchanan had to whip out his wet blanket.

'Presumably, the police had plenty of time to question Poppy Ford in hospital,' he said, swirling the ice in his double tonic water and looking as if, had he been wearing a judicial gown, he would have clasped its revers. 'If they allowed her to disappear – if, indeed she *has* disappeared, and not simply gone to stay with a friend – they must have been pretty well convinced she had nothing to do with the explosion.'

'You think so?' Giles said doubtfully, and then smiled. 'I know how cynical this sounds but, when you've been in the insurance business as long as I have, you don't trust anybody, not even the police. I've met more than a few bent coppers in my time and I've also known information damaging to a public figure to be suppressed. From what I hear of Lawrence Grassick he'd be very averse to having this story – if it's true – hit the tabloids. "Wife of Premier Scottish Advocate in Fatal Explosion with Lover." Whether it turned out that the perpetrator was the lover's wife or whether it was a suicide pact that went wrong, it's still something he'd want hushed up.'

'It's not likely that it was suicide, surely?' Fizz asked.

'If I thought there was no chance of it being suicide I wouldn't be here,' Giles said, lifting his brows in a you'd-better-believe-it way. 'Mrs Grassick doesn't get a penny unless she died as the result of an accident, or murder, or from natural causes.'

Fizz was astounded. 'You've got to be joking! Nobody could be so tired of living that they'd choose to blast themselves into garden fertiliser.'

'No, probably not, but I have to be sure that Mrs Grassick wasn't trying to gas herself and simply made a mistake. She may even have been dead before the explosion, had you thought of that? What better way to cover up a suicide than to blow up the body? At the moment, I admit, things are not pointing that way but there's a lot of money involved so I have to be sure.' He looked thoughtfully at his pint. 'However, even if it turns out to have been an accident, pure and simple, it's received very little media coverage, don't you think? Just one small paragraph in the *Scotsman*, which was far from specific, and a few brief reports in the evening papers. It's clear to me that Grassick wanted it all hushed up and – tell me if I'm wrong – Lawrence Grassick isn't short of clout, right?'

'He isn't,' Buchanan admitted. 'In fact I'm sure he'll be on first name terms with the Chief Constable, the Procurator Fiscal and half the Scottish executive. He's been a strong Labour activist all his adult life so, no doubt, even the Prime Minister owes him a few favours. But honestly, Giles, I can't believe that even he would have the influence to cover up a murder, or even a botched suicide. The occasional parking ticket, even a drunk driving rap, but not anything serious.'

Giles pursed his lips, something he could do without lessening his perfection. 'Well, you're probably able to judge the set-up here better than I am, but I reckon I'll make finding Poppy Ford one of my priorities all the same. If anyone is able to tell us what was going on between her husband and Vanessa Grassick, she's my number one hope. Which hospital was she taken to?'

'Mrs Pringle didn't say,' said Buchanan, clearly annoyed with himself for not quizzing the woman properly while he had the opportunity. 'It could have been any one of three or four, I imagine.'

'No matter. I can pop in and see the Pringles again tomorrow morning. You don't have any leads on where Mrs Ford might have headed when she checked out?'

'No,' Fizz admitted, planning to rectify that as soon as

possible. 'We haven't really started our investigation yet. Buchanan wouldn't raise a finger till he'd told Grassick what he planned to do. Like you, we have to be careful not to give him legitimate cause for a complaint against us.'

Giles broke into a grin. 'So, that's how you got your bum bitten?' he asked Buchanan, who looked unamused. 'I can imagine it wasn't a pleasant interview, especially as his goodwill would, I guess, be important to your career.'

This remark seemed to cheer Buchanan up, for some reason that wasn't apparent to Fizz till he said, 'You know, Giles, it's just possible that we could work together very effectively. If you would be willing to deal with the sensitive parts of the investigation – the chatting to neighbours, the poking around the site – in short, the parts that might get back to Grassick, I could reciprocate by talking to contacts in the Lothian and Borders police, and by following up any leads that extend beyond Grassick's immediate sphere.'

'Suits me,' Giles said, toasting the arrangement with his last inch of beer.

It suited Fizz too, she decided. She didn't want to be seen around too much with Buchanan in case it got back to Grassick, but she had no objections to being seen around with Giles. None whatsoever.

The Wonderful Beatrice, the following morning, was in one of her moods. Buchanan spotted it right away when, instead of greeting him with her usual bright smile and comment about the weather or whatever, she blinked stupidly at him and muttered the briefest of greetings.

Margaret, too, seemed even more irritating than was her supercilious wont and, to crown it all, it later became obvious that Dennis was determined to be as obtuse as he could possibly be without provoking a slap round the head. If Fizz had been present instead of attending a lecture, no doubt she would have hit on the reason for this mass provocation right away and taken steps to clarify matters, but Buchanan took half the morning to work it out.

He was washing his hands when he happened to catch an unexpected glimpse of his face in the mirror and was suddenly struck by the thought that perhaps it was his own ill humour that was making everyone appear so bloody annoying. Up to that point he had barely registered the fact that everything looked black this morning. Mornings were never his favourite time of day, with the prospect of eight hours behind a desk to look forward to, but he would normally have accepted the inevitable by the time the Wonderful Beatrice had fed him his first coffee, some ten minutes after he came in. Today was infinitely worse.

Fizz had once told him never to give in to depression because, if you did, it could become chronic. He had no idea whether there was any truth in this or whether it was just another of Fizz's dubious aphorisms, but he felt it was excuse enough to shelve the remainder of his morning's workload and toddle down to police headquarters. He knew a few people there who might give him the lowdown on the Grassick case and, hell, at least it would give him something to keep his mind occupied.

Ian Fleming was the obvious person to hit on. He and Buchanan – or more accurately, he and Fizz – had had their differences in the past but relations just at present ought to be at an all time high. It was only a few months since Buchanan and Fizz had handed him the head of the long-sought Mr Big on a plate: a service which had earned him promotion and a move to headquarters. That should have wiped out Buchanan's overdraft on his generosity, but whether Ian would be willing to get even remotely involved with what he considered a seriously disreputable alliance, was anybody's guess.

He seemed, to Buchanan, to be not displeased to see him and even met him at the elevator to conduct him along the corridor to his office.

'You're looking fit, Tam. No residual effects of that crack on the head, I hope?'

'No, I'm fine. And you? Enjoying your new job?'

Fleming chatted amiably for the length of time it took to get settled and organise coffee, and then said, 'But I take it this isn't a social visit, so what can I do for you, Tam?'

'I'm hoping for some inside information,' Buchanan told him frankly. 'Don't worry, it's nothing too privileged, just a small matter that has got my antennae twitching.'

'Yeah? Nice to know there's life in the old dog yet.'

Buchanan acted amused to keep him sweet. 'I'm executor for Vanessa Grassick's will,' he said and checked out Fleming's face to see that he was aware of the case.

Fleming nodded comprehendingly. 'Ghengis Grassick's wife. Nasty way to go, but at least it was quick.'

'Right. How familiar are you with the facts?'

'Not wonderfully – not my sphere of activity these days – but I have the general picture. A gas leak, wasn't it? Killed her fancy man as well.'

Buchanan uncrossed his legs. 'Ah, he *was* her lover, was he?'

'Oh, don't take that as gospel, Tam, for God's sake,' said Fleming, waving a disclaimer with nicotine-stained fingers. 'There may be nothing to prove that one way or another, but what were they up to in the middle of the night, the pair of them, if it wasn't a wee bit of hochmagandy?'

'Very likely,' Buchanan had to agree. It would have been nice if Ian had been able to confirm it though. He had a feeling that he wasn't going to learn much that he didn't know, this morning, but he pressed on. 'I know you had no direct input to the investigation, Ian, but I've spoken to the guy in charge . . .'

'Bob Virgo, yes. Dour big bugger. You won't get much help from him.'

The words were spoken lightly enough but Buchanan sensed a real animosity behind them and that gave him hope. Competition ran high in the Lothian and Borders police force and, if there was any suspicion that Virgo had skimped the inquiry, a little personal animosity might make Fleming all the more willing to uncover it.

'Since you're familiar with the case,' he said carefully, 'I'd be interested to hear your general impression of the speed at which it was carried out.'

Fleming looked vaguely at a loss. 'Speed? Slow, do you mean?'

'No, fast. Apparently the fire brigade and the police team were in and out in a couple of days. Isn't that unusually efficient?'

Fleming glanced indifferently out of his window as something screeched out of the car park with siren blaring. 'Not necessarily. Depends how cut-and-dried things were.' His eyes snapped round to focus on Buchanan's. 'Just tell me you're not implying that Ghengis Grassick tried to have the thing hushed up.'

'The thought had crossed my mind,' Buchanan admitted, making Fleming throw himself backwards in his seat with horror and exasperation.

'Jesus Christ, Tam! You shouldn't be allowed out without your mother! This is Fizz's idea, isn't it? You were never this psychotic before she came on the scene.'

'No, it's nothing to do with Fizz,' Buchanan sighed, no more certain of his sanity than Fleming was. 'I just feel I'm not fulfilling my executory duties properly if I pay out before I know the truth of how and why Mrs Grassick died.'

'You *do* know the truth. The police report lets you off the hook.'

'Legally, Ian, but not morally.'

Fleming put his elbows on his desk and clasped his head in his hands. Buchanan could hear him laughing deep in his throat. 'You're too sodding good for this world, y'know that? Fizz told me once that you'd be snatched up to the bright skies in a chariot at an early age, and it looks like this is it, chummie. Start making allegations against Ghengis Grassick and you won't last long.' When he lifted his head he'd stopped being amused. 'And all for nothing, Tam. You'll never prove that Grassick brought pressure to bear – financial or otherwise – and why would he bother anyway? There was nothing to find out. The explosion was an accident and all the peripheral scandal – if there is any – is nobody's business.'

'I hope you're right. However, Vanessa Grassick's insurance company have an investigator snooping around so, obviously, they're still not entirely satisfied. That means nothing of course, because, if the payoff is as much as I suspect it is, they'd do that anyway. As to peripheral scandal, I just hope that's all it turns out to be. If the truth turns out to be something I can live with, nobody will be happier than me.'

Humour him, appeared to be the thought uppermost in Fleming's mind as he took this in. He wasn't the most imaginative of chaps but he had to know that nobody stuck his nose into a wasps' nest merely to pass the time. He toyed with a handy pencil, considering the matter for a minute and, hopefully, weighing the advantages to himself if his colleague were proved guilty of accepting what must have been a substantial bribe.

'Okay,' he said finally. 'If it's that important to you, Tam, go ahead, but for Christ's sake keep your head down and don't drag me into it. I'm prejudiced against living in a cardboard box.'

'All I need is a little information,' Buchanan assured him. 'You know I wouldn't ask you to do anything that could be traced back to you, but I would be enormously grateful if you would just glance over the report of the investigation and tell me if it looked thorough.'

Fleming laid a hand flat on top of the pencil and started rolling it thoughtfully backwards and forwards. 'Anything in particular you have in mind?'

'A couple of things.'

Fleming stopped rolling the pencil. 'Uh-huh?'

'A neighbour, a Mr Pringle, found the remains of an electric heater scattered about the site. I'd like to know if this was eliminated as the cause of the explosion. Mrs Grassick's house had perfectly adequate central heating and the heater was an old, unattractive model. Was the heater established as belonging to her or her husband?'

'Okay. And the other thing?' Ian narrowed his eyes, looking intrigued but promising nothing.

'Poppy Ford. The wife of the alleged lover. She was taken to hospital immediately following the accident, suffering from glass cuts she received when her windows blew in. However, she appears to have stayed there less than a couple of days before discharging herself and disappearing. She hasn't returned to her home and no-one appears to have heard from her, but I believe a couple of her neighbours notified her disappearance to the local police.'

'Nothing sinister in that, Tam. Not necessarily.' Fleming went back to fiddling with the pencil. 'She probably just went back home to her parents. Anything else?'

'No, but if there's any forwarding address for her I'd like to have it. It would be a great help to me if I could talk to her.'

'I'll see what I can do, but remember, you didn't get it from me.'

Buchanan stood up and reached a hand across the desk, his spirits much lightened. 'That's one I owe you, Ian.'

'Not at all.' Fleming levered himself out of his chair so slowly that Buchanan was able to check the progress of his balding pate. 'And how's Fizz doing? She was looking like she'd been hit by a truck last time I saw her. Did it heal up okay?'

The memory, catching Buchanan unawares, hit him with such a wave of rage that, for a split second, he could think of nothing else. It was twenty years since he'd punched anyone, and he would condemn violence in any form, but the thought of the bastard who had scarred Fizz's baby face could still reduce him to the level of a savage. He managed to fake a smile and say all the right things until the elevator doors closed behind him, but all the way back to the office his teeth were grinding like the mills of God.

Chapter Seven

'What's got into Him today?' whispered the Wonderful Beatrice as Fizz was hanging up her jacket.

Fizz didn't need to ask which 'him' was being referred to: Beatrice always gave Buchanan an audible capital. 'Why?' she said. 'What's he been up to?'

'He came in this morning with a face like the Wolfman of Cracow, then stalked out again without saying where he was going, then came back in without so much as a glance at any of us. He's been in a very weird state.'

'California?' Fizz was tempted to say, but Beatrice had no sense of humour so she didn't. She gave her conscience a quick scan and, finding it relatively clear, decided that it would be safe enough to drop into Buchanan's office and take a look at him for herself.

He greeted her entrance with the blank expression he used on clients who were annoying the hell out of him. 'Is it important, Fizz? I've got a lot to catch up with.'

'No, not really,' Fizz said airily, dropping into the seat beside his desk. 'Just wondered if you had anything to report since last night. No serious setbacks, I hope?'

Buchanan threw down his pen in an aggravated manner and leaned back in his chair. 'What makes you say that?'

'Don't know. I just thought you didn't appear to be the droll, effervescent old Buchanan we've all come to love and trust,' said Fizz, sowing a little cheer and reaping a scowl.

'I spent half my morning talking to Ian Fleming,' he said, 'getting a promise out of him to check over the

Grassick report. And now I've just had Dennis in to tell me he's had short shrift from the Menzies estate.'

Fizz felt her own spirits sink at that news. 'Menzies is determined on the evictions?'

'Unconditionally. I've seen the letter and, I can tell you, he didn't leave any room for argument. In fact, he seemed to think we hadn't grasped the fact that he'd get more money for the place with the cottages empty.'

'Bastard.' Fizz was boiling with rage but felt, since Buchanan was feeling just as bad, that she should try to say something positive. The best she could manage was, 'Well, as my dear old granny used to say, the secret of success is the way you handle failure.'

'Yeah?' said Buchanan, not noticeably revitalised. 'Was that your original granny or Auntie Duff?'

'Auntie Duff. Before she married Grampa she held the Chair of Practical Philosophy at Am Bealach University.'

Buchanan allowed his eyes to crinkle just enough to convey polite acknowledgement of a pleasantry without slighting the intelligence of Auntie Duff who, he knew perfectly well, would have been risking a mental hernia if she'd tried to quote any such title, never mind earn it.

'Well, I'll be seeing Niall Menzies later today, in any case, to get his slant on Vanessa Grassick. No doubt the subject of the estate sale will crop up.'

'Oh, really?' Fizz said, letting him see that she was irritated. 'This evening?'

He had to be aware that she had made an arrangement with Giles to visit the hospital in the early evening, but he might also have considered the possibility that she would have liked to see what kind of a swine Niall Menzies was.

'Something wrong with that?' he said, twisting his brows. 'You can come if you want to.'

'I told Giles I'd go to the hospital with him to see what we could find out about where Poppy Ford might have gone. He's picking me up at the office. Didn't you hear us arranging it last night?'

'Uh . . . Oh, yes . . . Well I don't want to cancel. Does it matter so much?'

Fizz looked him in the eye. 'You did that deliberately so I wouldn't be able to come,' she seethed. 'You thought I might go for that bastard's jugular and lose you the sale. That's right, isn't it, Buchanan? Don't think I'm taken in by your conniving, 'cause I'm way ahead of you.'

'Not at all,' Buchanan said, obviously not giving a hoot whether she believed him or not. The trouble was, if he came right out and denied it like that he was unquestionably innocent. It was only when he didn't give you a direct answer to a question that you had to watch him.

Shite. She had been really looking forward to spending the evening with Giles but she might never get another opportunity to slide a verbal stiletto between the psychological ribs of a sub-human life form like Niall Menzies. Which to choose: personal gratification or the chance to strike a blow for democracy? Two considerations jostled their way to the fore: (a) Buchanan would buy her a meal, and (b) they still could meet up with Giles later to swap results.

'Right,' she told the barely interested Buchanan. 'I'll come with you. I can call Giles on his mobile and tell him to go ahead without me. What time are you seeing Menzies?'

'Seven. We'll do the same as yesterday: leave straight from the office and grab a bar meal in Lammerburn.'

A bar meal. Fizz debated with herself whether it was worthwhile trying to up the offer, which would mean suffering a ten minute lecture on the bankruptcy laws, but decided against it. A bar meal would be quicker and the sooner they got finished, the sooner they'd meet up with Giles.

It was only after his black mood had miraculously disappeared that Buchanan admitted to himself that it might have been induced, in part, by an emotion very similar to possessiveness. There was no denying it: he found Giles's entrée into the Fizz/Buchanan partnership something of an intrusion.

The atmosphere had changed subtly, last night, when Giles had joined them. The mellow, shoes-off, uncomplicated tenor of his relationship with Fizz had become a whole new board game, one where he knew neither the rules nor the part he was supposed to be playing. Fizz had metamorphosed from the familiar pal he saw every day into something verging on the exotic, something that attracted the eye and held the attention. She had certainly held Giles's attention and Buchanan had felt excluded. Excluded. Yes, that was the crux of the matter and he wasn't proud of it.

It was quite pathetic, really, to be acting like a schoolboy at the age of thirty-two, especially over Fizz with whom he had never been (and, pray God, never *would* be) romantically involved. Attractive she might be, when she chose, but she was also the sort of loose cannon an ambitious young solicitor could do without. One simply had to keep reminding oneself of that fact every time another Giles came on the scene.

He was determined that Fizz would have no chance to do her loose cannon act tonight. Neither she nor he himself had any right to browbeat Niall Menzies, no matter what course he chose to take with his financial affairs. He told Fizz so in no uncertain terms, not once but several times, on the way to Lammerburn and he felt, as they passed through the arched stone gateway to the estate, that she was for once resolved to keep her dogmatic opinions to herself.

Lammerburn House turned out to be one of those ersatz Scottish baronial halls built of dark stone and embellished with turrets, crow-stepped gables, and a porte-cochere. It reminded Buchanan of Stronach Lodge in Am Bealach, although lacking the Lodge's magnificent backdrop of old Scots pines and the peaks of the Ardoch Ridge. This house was a *Monarch-of-the-Glen* parody of the real thing but, in Buchanan's view, not an offensive one. Two deerhounds, a spaniel, a black labrador, and a golden retriever were milling around on the turning circle at the end of the drive, completing the picture of a country gentleman's retreat.

'Cor!' Fizz commented as she got out of the car. 'I didn't know there was a Disney World in these parts. All it needs is a couple of stuffed stags and a few – *Gerroff!*'

The pack of dogs reached her, overflowing with affability, excitement and saliva, but at her imperious command they transferred their attentions to Buchanan, who hadn't the heart to rebuff them. The deerhounds were the worst: they smelled the worst, they dribbled the worst and when they rose on their hind legs to lick his face it felt like they were damn near as tall as he was. Fortunately, Fizz being too amused to be of any assistance, he was soon rescued by a piercing whistle and the arrival of a small, portly man in a cardigan and cord trousers.

'Ben! Caesar! Here, you scallywags! Here!'

The dogs dashed up to him, then back to the visitors, then back to their master again, ricocheting in ever shorter trips till the distance between host and guests dwindled to a couple of yards.

'Sorry about that . . . they don't see a lot of strangers these days. Down, Goldie, there's a good girl.' He held out a plump, slightly damp hand. 'Niall Menzies.'

'Tam Buchanan, and this is my colleague Miss Fitzpatrick.'

'Delighted, delighted, delighted.' He had a round rosy face with a complexion like a girl's and no trace of facial hair, and his eyes were honest and open behind rimless glasses. 'Do come inside and have a sherry with Mummy, she's looking forward tremendously to meeting you.'

'Your mother?' Buchanan was surprised into saying. He had been given to understand that the family were no longer in residence and that Niall was only there for a few days to decide which furniture was to be kept and which sent to auction.

'Yes, I brought Mummy down with me, just till the weekend.' He led the way to the porte-cochere, the golden retriever trotting on ahead, flying her plumed tail like a banner, while the rest of the pack pranced along behind. 'My father is more or less housebound now – he has a nurse and other people to look after him, of course, but Mummy likes to keep an eye on things so she doesn't get out much. She needed a break, poor darling, and she wanted to be here to supervise the disposal of the furnishings. She's eighty-one now but still a wonderfully dynamic woman. Dear me, yes! Just wait till you meet her!'

Buchanan couldn't have said precisely what he expected to see – a cross between the Queen Mother and Margaret Thatcher, possibly – but he was certainly taken aback by the tiny creature they found ensconced in the drawing room. She was wedged into a wing chair with a selection of cushions that left so little of her showing that, had Buchanan not known what he was looking for, he could easily have missed seeing her altogether. Her face was the same shade of ecru as the lace antimacassar behind her head but her bold brown eyes and eagle's beak of a nose defined her at a glance.

'Those damn dogs of yours, Niall!' she bawled in a voice like a Brillo pad. 'If you can't teach them manners they should be put down. Get rid of them, for God's sake, before we start having buyers looking round the place.'

'I will, Mummy. Good idea.' Niall ushered his guests forward. 'This is Mr Buchanan and Miss Fitzpatrick.'

A hand like a hen's foot emerged from between the cushions and gripped Buchanan's like a vice. 'Has a look of his father, this one, but he'll never be the charmer his father was. And what's he bringing this wee girl with him for?'

Buchanan was nonplussed by these muttered remarks and was about to stammer some reply when she continued, in a clearer tone, 'How d'you do? You must be Thomas, the younger son.'

'I am indeed,' Buchanan said, recovering himself. 'I wasn't aware you knew our family so well. You've met my father?'

'Yes, of course I met him, silly boy. He took care of all our legal matters for years and I met him several times when my husband was doing business with him. A most urbane and delightful man. I used to think he was the double of Gregory Peck. How is he?'

Buchanan told her his father was fine and enjoying his retirement but, as he spoke, her deep set eyes swung back to Fizz and she started mumbling, 'Pretty little thing. Why doesn't she cut that mop of hair? Can't be more than sixteen though, so she's not his girlfriend. The clothes they wear these days . . .'

'Sherry anyone?' Niall cried, interrupting her thoughts, but with no sign that he saw anything abnormal in her propensity for speaking them aloud. 'Miss Fitzpatrick? Dry or medium?'

'Medium, please.' Fizz's face was alive with amusement and she avoided catching Buchanan's eye as though she didn't dare.

'Tam?'

'Not for me, thanks. I'm driving.'

'Driving, indeed. That wouldn't have stopped his father from taking a drink,' thought Mrs Menzies, and then barked, 'You had an older brother – Stephen. You see? There's nothing wrong with my memory! He was the good-looking one but he didn't have his daddy's eyes. Not like you, you lucky young rascal. My God, they broke a few hearts, those eyes did, back in the old days! I'll bet he never told you about that, did he? Eyelashes like a camel, my sister used to say, and the shapeliest little—'

'Stephen's living in England now,' Buchanan inserted, seeing the way things were going. 'He has twin boys.'

'Ha. I knew he wouldn't go into the family business. Told your father so twenty years ago, damn near.' She smiled at some pleasant memory and then snapped, 'Niall tells me you also act for that Grassick woman who was blown up. Bungling idiot! Couldn't even commit suicide without taking half the neighbourhood with her!'

'Now, Mummy, you know that's naughty. Never speak ill of the dead.'

'Oh, shut up, Niall. I don't need you to tell me what I can say and what I can't say. I speak as I find.'

Buchanan felt Fizz's head turn slightly towards him. She was bursting to enter the conversation but she was fighting the temptation and wanted him to note the fact. He leaned a little closer to the miniature creature beside him.

'You think it was a botched suicide, then?' he murmured. 'Rather than a straightforward accident?'

Mrs Menzies lifted the lids of her raptor eyes. 'If it was an accident, it was a fortunate one: that's what I said when I heard about it. It must have been a blessed relief.'

Niall put a generous glass of sherry in her claw and shook his head at her with gentle reproof. 'Please don't start all that again, darling. We hardly knew them, after all.'

'Oh, of course we knew them. For goodness' sake, your father and I knew Lawrence's family before you were born. I remember Lawrence as a boy, yes, and a damned bad-tempered, spoiled little swine he was too.' She swallowed a large gulp of sherry and thought, 'Must be worth a pretty penny now, though, swine or not. Turned out to have more brains than both our brats put together.' Then she hauled herself up in her nest of cushions and said, 'The day we went down to the church to see them married, I said to Hugh, "God help the girl," I said, "I hope she's either deaf or as spineless as a dishrag or she'll have had enough of him within the year." That's what I said. I never thought it would last ten years, I don't mind telling you, and I certainly never thought he'd drive her to suicide.'

'Was she spineless enough to take her own life, do you think?' Fizz asked, reaching the end of her patience.

The brown button eyes swung round on her like a

searchlight in a prison camp. 'You think it's spineless to take one's own life?'

Fizz pressed her lips together and made a pretence of questioning her professed judgement. 'Yes.'

Mrs Menzies nodded and uttered a laugh that was, surprisingly, easier on the ear than her pot-scourer voice. 'Well, well, you may be right – ninety-nine times out of a hundred, maybe. Hope springs eternal. Who can tell what miracle the morrow may bring, yes? But some people can't wait till tomorrow, you know.'

'Vanessa Grassick? Was she one of those?'

Niall topped up his mother's empty glass and Fizz's, clearly uncomfortable with the way the conversation was going. 'None of us knew Vanessa all that well, did we, Mummy? We didn't live here, most of the time, and we didn't socialise much with Lawrence after his marriage, so the only times we met the Grassicks were at other people's dinner parties where the conversation was really very superficial.'

During this speech Mrs Menzies was thinking her own thoughts but, with her son's voice overlaid, they were not quite loud enough for Buchanan to decipher. He risked a glance at Fizz and saw that she was enchanted with the old lady, not surprisingly, since she embraced the unusual in all its forms. She obviously had another question on the end of her tongue but before she could pose it Mrs Menzies announced, 'She wasn't as spineless as I used to think her, that's certain. She was a lot of disagreeable things but no-one could call her spineless. I disliked Vanessa Grassick from the day I met her.'

'Not from the day you met her, Mummy. You used to say—'

'I *used* to say,' his mummy rasped, impaling him with a look, 'that she was like that misshapen little rat of a Jack Russell you used to have. A two-faced bitch.'

'Coco was a sweet little—'

'Sweet as sugar! I agree with you, Niall, for once. She

was so sweet it's a wonder she didn't rot your teeth – right up to the day she ate the cat.'

'She didn't actually *eat* the cat,' Niall said, fiddling with his glasses and looking earnestly from Buchanan to Fizz and back again. 'It wasn't Coco's fau—'

'Only because I caught her at it.' Mrs Menzies twitched her head and stared angrily out of the window. 'Misshapen little mongrel,' she thought. 'Lived with Nippy for two years . . . butter wouldn't melt in her mouth . . . first chance she got, she had Nippy by the throat . . . by God, I really enjoyed shooting that brute.' She held her glass out to her son to be refilled. '*That's* the sort of person Vanessa Grassick was: smiling in your face and stabbing you in the back.'

Niall had given up trying to argue with her but he rolled his eyes and shook his head as he went round with the sherry decanter, as though to say, take that with a pinch of salt, won't you?

'Vanessa was a business woman,' he said gently. 'You don't make a success of a business unless you have a streak of toughness in your nature, do you? She and Joe Rudyard have made Rudyard Grassick into one of the foremost graphic design studios in the city. Quite an achievement in just – what? – a couple of years.'

'You're acquainted with Mr Rudyard?' Fizz asked, glancing up at him as he poured her drink.

He filled her glass like a practised hostess, cupping a hand beneath it in case he spilled a drop on her clothes. 'Not really, no. I've met him . . . I think at one of the Grassicks' Christmas drinks evenings, but I probably exchanged only a few words with him.'

'Living skeleton,' murmured his mother. 'Wouldn't trust either one of them as far as I could spit.'

Fizz was right in there like a flash. 'Why didn't you like them, Mrs Menzies?'

Mrs Menzies blinked at her haughtily for a moment, clearly wondering if Fizz were reading her mind. 'Rudyard?

I just don't like the look of that chap. Too narrow between
the eyes: that's always a sign of a mean nature. And always
moaning about everything. Never happier than when he has
something to moan about. But *her* . . . the Grassick
woman . . . *that* one's a trouble maker. She took to do with
this ridiculous protest—'

'Mummy—'

'Oh, hold your tongue, Niall! If you must disagree with
every word I say you can take yourself off and do something with these damn dogs of yours. They're crapping all
over the drive.'

Niall flushed a little but made neither reply nor move to
leave.

'What was I saying? Yes, Vanessa Grassick. The cheek
of the woman! Writing insolent letters to Niall here – well,
to my husband actually but Niall has to deal with them –
trying to tell us what to do with our own property.
Nothing to do with her, but would she take no for an
answer? Not a bit of it! Has to get everybody all wound up
– the people in the cottages, the locals in the village, letters
to the Ramblers, representations to the local council and
goodness knows who else! Threatened to stage a demon-
stration at our gates so that every prospective buyer would
know they'd be in for a fight! You ask me what Vanessa
Grassick was like? *That's* what she was like! A two-faced
bitch!'

Buchanan cleared his throat. 'She was no doubt concerned about the serious effect it would have on the
economics of the village – and, inevitably, on the value of
her own property – if you were to clear the cottages.
Losing eight families would be bound to cause a certain
amount of—'

'Oh, don't you start, for heaven's sake!' squawked Mrs
Menzies, flinging up her arms and whipping her head from
side to side. 'I won't hear another word about it! I've told
that woman and I've told your partner, Mr Whittaker, and
I'm telling you – I won't be dictated to about this.

Nobody's going to buy the place with eight occupied cottages tagged on to it, and that's the end of it. Enough. Finished.'

'I'm sure the effect on the local people won't be so very bad,' Niall said with his placid smile and, his mother and Fizz having drained their glasses, went round again with the sherry bottle. 'It's been my experience that very little in this life turns out to be either as bad or as good as you expect it to be.'

'What's he on about now?' his mother muttered into her sherry glass. 'When did *he* become a philosopher, for pity's sake?'

Annoyed though she was, she didn't appear to be at all agitated; her head, however, had developed a slight but disconcerting wobble. Buchanan was uncertain whether this was a symptom of tiredness or intoxication, but he took it as a hint that it was time to be going. Arguing with Mrs Menzies was, in any case, unlikely to be either a practical or a profitable exercise and if Niall was going to change his mind about clearing the cottages it would not be in her presence.

They took their leave as expeditiously as politeness allowed, while Niall pressed them to stay and his mother thought, 'Eyes like his father, though. And the same strong mouth. Hope he gets himself a better wife than that Dorothy what's-her-name his father settled for. Could have had his pick, in those days, silly bugger . . . Better have a pee now before I'm caught short again.'

As they reached the doorway she raised a hand to detain them.

'Tam, my dear boy, I want you to have a little memento of Lammerburn House. Your firm bought it for us and your firm is selling it for us; it's proper that you should have something to remember it by. Niall, that bundle we sorted out for Oxfam this morning . . . there was a stag's head in it.'

Niall's glasses slipped down his nose and he pushed them up again with one forefinger. 'The . . . um . . . the

stag's head, Mummy? Were we going to throw that out?
You know how much store Daddy set by that. It was the
only one he ever shot. Perhaps one of the musical boxes
might be a better choice.'

'*Mus*ical boxes?' cried his mother in the sort of tone
Lady Bracknell might have used when she said 'A *hand*-
bag?' 'What would a virile young man like Tam want with
a musical box? For God's sake, Niall, wake up! Put the
stag's head in the car for him and take care you don't
scratch anything as you do it.'

Buchanan was hot with embarrassment and made a
resolute stand against accepting the gift but he could make
no dent in her determination nor could he dissuade Niall
from carrying out her orders. There was absolutely no
place in his flat, or even in the office, where the enormous
object would look anything other than totally outrageous,
but he was stuck with it whether he wanted it or not, and
could only try to look genuine while he expressed his
thanks.

The dogs met them in the porte-cochere but were less
mettlesome this time and gave most of their attention to
Niall as, between the three of them, they manipulated the
magnificent twelve-pointer into the back seat. It hooked
on to everything en route and Buchanan was sweating with
concern for the fabric of his brand new Saab but, with one
at each of the rear doors and one leaning back over the
driver's seat, they eventually wedged it into place. Probably
for ever.

Niall patted the deerhounds' heads in a distracted manner and then thrust his hands in the sagging pockets of his
cardigan.

'Mummy likes to get her own way, you see. She hates
being old and impotent and she fights it any way she
can.' He smiled almost pleadingly at Buchanan, his blue
eyes huge behind his glasses. 'But you mustn't take what
she says too seriously, you know. She's apt to make
mountains out of molehills these days. You know how

old people can get when they don't have anything else to worry about. There was never any bad blood between us and the Grassicks. None at all. They were perfectly nice people.'

'Of course,' Buchanan said, affably. 'I can imagine how irritating it must have been to have almost an insurrection on her doorstep. Is the organised opposition still causing you trouble?'

'No . . . not since . . .' Niall stooped to stroke the dogs. 'It seems to have fallen away at the moment. At least, I haven't heard anything for a week or so.'

Fizz was replacing the elastic grip that was supposed to be keeping her hair under some sort of control. 'And you are still determined to empty the cottages before the sale?'

'It should have been done by now,' Niall said, almost pettishly. 'I gave them an extra month to get fixed up elsewhere. Nobody can say I haven't bent over backwards for them, as I told your Mr Whittaker, but they are pushing me to the limit. I may have to ask you to get a court order to evict them in the end.'

'I know you must be aware of the devastation that would cause, not just to the families in the cottages but to the entire village area, so I won't go into that again,' Buchanan said quickly, before Fizz could make matters worse. 'However, it seems likely that there could be serious hassle later, if not for you then for the next owner. You might be wiser to consider postponing the evictions and letting the next owner decide whether he wants the residents to stay or go.'

'Yes, but you see, it's a matter of price,' Niall explained as though to a simpleton. 'Mummy is quite insistent that we'll get a much higher price if the cottages are vacant, and your Mr Whittaker didn't disagree. I'm sorry about the tenants but I'm sure they'll find other places to rent, and anyway, I couldn't change Mummy's mind if I tried.'

Buchanan wasn't sure that anyone other than, possibly, a brain surgeon could change Mrs Menzies' mind. He glanced at Fizz to see if she had any ideas on how to handle this impasse but, for once, she was silent. Like himself, she was doubtless far from ready to admit defeat on this one, but it sure as hell was going to take some thinking about.

Chapter Eight

Giles was still having dinner when they arrived at the hotel, which didn't surprise Fizz in the slightest. She'd half expected him to be running even later since, when she had phoned him earlier, he had been en route to Glasgow on the trail of some lead or other which he'd deemed more important than visiting the hospital. Because he was driving at the time, and because the reception on his mobile phone was terrible, he hadn't gone into details but Fizz had gathered his purpose was more a matter of elimination than something crucial. She also had a private little suspicion that maybe he wanted to postpone going to the hospital till she was free to accompany him, and she wasn't going to complain about that.

She was halfway through her first G&T when he appeared from the dining room, looking perfectly scrumptious, and started to apologise for keeping them waiting. Buchanan brushed all that aside and bought him a brandy.

'So how was your day, Giles?' he asked, sipping his own double tonic water. 'Fizz tells me you shot off to Glasgow on a hot trail?'

'On a cold trail, as it turned out, but it took me all day to be sure of that.' Giles ran a hand through his hair, looking tired and discouraged. 'I went back to Chirnside this morning, as planned, to ask Mr and Mrs Pringle which hospital Poppy Ford had been taken to, only to find their house locked up and deserted. Their neighbour, Mrs Armstrong, was able to tell me that the Pringles have gone

93

to visit their daughter in Glasgow, which is something they do at fairly regular intervals.' He swirled the brandy in his balloon glass. 'I don't know why that struck me as unlikely. Maybe because, when I was in the house yesterday, I didn't notice any sign that they were getting ready to go away. Mr Pringle had just started a massive jigsaw puzzle and he said his wife had gone out to get tickets for a concert in Berwick.'

'Definitely peculiar,' Fizz said, starting to tingle with anticipation, and Giles gave her a quick smile.

'Exactly what I thought. Fortunately, Mrs Armstrong had the daughter's address – she'd held it for years in case of emergencies – and I talked her into giving it to me.'

'That was a bit of luck,' Buchanan said. 'So you tracked them down?'

'Nope. Cold trail.' Giles shook his head wearily. 'The daughter's there, but no sign of Mum and Dad.'

Fizz looked at Buchanan to see if that news made any sense to him but apparently he was as bewildered as she was.

'What did the daughter say?' he asked Giles. 'Was she worried when you told her that her parents had disappeared?'

'According to the daughter, they *are* staying with her,' Giles said, 'but they'd "just gone out for a walk". She was very jumpy. She wouldn't let me in the house and as soon as I'd gone she was on the telephone to someone – I could hear her through the door and she sounded nervous. I hung around till six-thirty, but the Pringles didn't come back, so either it was a long walk or they're avoiding me. Take your pick.'

Neither of those possibilities struck Fizz as at all likely but she could think of no other rationale. The Pringles had certainly not been out for a walk for seven hours, not if Mrs Pringle was as unfit as she looked, but they could conceivably have decided to go somewhere or do something on the spur of the moment, while they were out. Yes, but if that were the case, why was their daughter so jumpy? Was it her parents she'd been phoning so hurriedly or, if not, who was it?

'What could they be scared of?' Buchanan pondered aloud. 'You think Pringle may be regretting giving you that piece of electric heater?'

'I've been wondering about that.' Giles sipped his brandy for a moment as the bartender paused to clear the adjacent table and then, when he had moved on, said, 'It also makes me wonder whether someone has hidden them away in case they say too much.'

'Like who? Lawrence Grassick?' Fizz suggested, dropping her voice.

'He'd be the most likely person,' Giles nodded. 'What do you think, Tam?'

Buchanan spread a baffled hand. 'To be honest, I don't know what to think. I get the picture that somebody in this game is not just playing for matches, but . . . Grassick?' He pondered that possibility for a minute, sipping his tonic water, and then shrugged. 'Then again . . . when I think about it, it could be the sort of thing he might do . . . treat them to a holiday somewhere to get them out of my way.'

'Or bump them off?' Fizz suggested darkly.

'No. Not that,' said Buchanan. 'They must still be alive.'

Giles looked at him closely. 'What makes you say that, Tam?'

'If the parents were dead, why involve the daughter? She obviously knows what's going on and is lending her support. That makes it look, to me, as though the Pringles were acting independently when they took off.'

'I'm with you on that,' Giles said. 'Although, what I could have said to panic them into such an extreme reaction, I cannot imagine.'

'They knew something they were afraid to let out,' Fizz stated confidently.

The way she looked at it, it was perfectly obvious. The Pringles clearly made a hobby of knowing their neighbours' business – doubtless they were the 'daft old folk' the waiter had been referring to – and in all probability they were the only two people who knew the whole story. They'd know if Jamie Ford and Vanessa Grassick were having an affair. In fact, they'd had plenty of opportunity to snoop around inside Brora Lodge, so it would be surprising if they didn't know more about the Grassicks' personal life than even Grassick suspected. No doubt they'd have been willing enough to share with the insurance investigator the one or two indisputable pieces of evidence in their possession, but they were too much in awe of Lawrence Grassick to get dragged into the mire of a scandal. Especially if they knew things they'd no business to know.

Giles and Buchanan were too deep in thought to acknowledge this incisive piece of insight. They were both staring into space with a concentration Fizz was unable to match. She wasn't good at focusing her thoughts, especially in a public place with music playing and people milling about. She gave up trying to think after a minute or two and sat watching the people at the bar.

There was one guy there she'd seen before somewhere: a heavy-shouldered guy with a square head that was covered in a pelt of greying hair. He looked, she thought, like an ex-soldier – more like an ex-centurion, for some strange reason, maybe because of his beat-up face and his hugely jutting jaw. He had probably been in the bar the evening before, or maybe around the village the last time she and Buchanan had passed through. He didn't strike her as being the Chirnside Hall's average type of patron, more like one of the locals who'd just dropped in for a pint – though why he'd be paying cocktail bar prices instead of patronising the Waterloo was anybody's guess.

'We've missed out on the Pringles,' Giles said, reclaiming her attention. 'Trying to locate them would be like looking for a needle in a haystack. The way I see it, either they've vamoosed of their own free will or somebody leaned on them to go and, if the latter is the case, the first person I want to talk to is Lawrence Grassick.'

'No, Giles,' Fizz was forced to say. 'You don't want to talk to Lawrence Grassick. You really don't. I can tell you now that you'll get no help from him – back me up here, Buchanan – and, even if he *were* the person who chased off the Pringles, he's much too smart to let anything slip. Believe me, you'll learn more by keeping a low profile.'

'Fizz is right,' Buchanan agreed, as Giles waved to the waiter for refills. 'If Grassick finds out that you're digging into the matter deeper than he considers necessary he'll crib like hell. He has the okay from the police now, which would normally have closed the matter, and I dare say he'd use that justification to have your head office take you off the job. I'd keep out of his hair as long as there's a different line of inquiry open to us.'

Giles flashed his white teeth in a quizzical grin. 'We're not exactly snowed under with leads, Tam. In fact, if we're unable to trace the whereabouts of Poppy Ford we might as well throw in the towel and pay up.'

'Mm-mm. I've asked a friend in Lothian and Borders police to take a look at the police report for me. We might get something out of that. Also, we've just heard that Vanessa Grassick was possibly about to cross swords with a local landowner called Menzies. The Menzies family own an estate locally which they are currently trying to sell . . .'

Seeing that she was unlikely to hear anything she didn't know already, Fizz took the opportunity to pay a visit to the ladies. It turned out to be one of the 'powder room' variety, with boxes of tissues and scented soap and little gold chairs to sit on as you used them. It reminded her suddenly of similar rooms in several countries where she used to wash her smalls, surreptitiously drying them under the hot-air hand-dryer.

On her way back to the table she noticed the ex-centurion type at the bar and decided to have a word with him. She was curious to know where she'd seen him before and surmised that, if he were indeed a local, he might be worth chatting to for a minute. OK, the Pringles had disappeared but they had done plenty of gossiping before they went and they might have been saying a whole lot more than they'd told Giles. Probably the whole village knew what they'd seen – or imagined.

She squeezed herself into the small space beside the centurion and gave a virtuoso performance of someone trying to catch the barman's eye, simultaneously taking very good care that he didn't actually notice her.

'Is it always as busy as this?' she asked her target, with just a touch of pseudo-impatience.

The centurion pretended he was deaf.

'I said,' Fizz repeated, poking him in the side and making him jump, 'is it always so busy?'

'Uh . . .' He looked at her as though she were accusing him of being responsible for the crush. 'Uh . . . I don't know. I've never been in here before.'

'Really? I thought I'd seen you here. Maybe it was in the village. Are you a local?'

'No.' He shook his head in case she wasn't familiar with the word and then repeated it just to make absolutely sure she got the message. 'No.'

'Right.' Fizz nodded complete understanding. 'So, you're on holiday?'

He looked distinctly uncomfortable and Fizz could see his tongue moving in his cheek as though he were checking the accessibility of a suicide pill. 'On holiday. Yes. Just a few days.'

'Doing a bit of fishing?'

'Yes.'

'Any luck?'

'Uh . . . No, not yet.'

It was like drawing teeth. The poor bugger was either painfully bashful or thicker than yesterday's lentil soup and it was unlikely that he was the repository of the least scrap of information that would be of interest to anybody.

Abandoning hope, she bought a packet of crisps and returned to her table.

Both Giles and Buchanan regarded her with curiosity.

'A friend of yours?' Buchanan murmured, his expression asking the same question but with a good deal more criticism.

'Nope. I just remembered seeing him somewhere recently and couldn't remember where it was.' Fizz noticed with gratification that someone had bought her another G&T during her absence and made appropriate noises. She opened her bag of crisps and offered to share them but got no takers.

'So where did you meet him before?' Giles asked, grinning at her as though he were strangely entertained by her gall.

'Probably just around the village,' she said, and laughed at the thought of the poor guy's embarrassment: he'd probably inferred that she was trying to pick him up. 'He's just here for a fishing holiday and I suspect his mummy told him to beware of strange women because he didn't want anything to do with me!'

She glanced over at the bar but the centurion had beaten an ignominious retreat.

'By the look of him,' Giles said, catching Buchanan's eye for confirmation, 'it would be a *very* strange woman who would try to pick him up. Do you do that sort of thing often? Chat up men in bars, I mean?'

Fizz pretended to consider that one for a moment: Buchanan didn't. He resisted the temptation to comment but he burst out laughing fit to split his drawers, more amused than she'd seen him for some time. She did her best to ignore him but it was difficult to appear demure in front of a witness who knew you'd speak to anybody, any time, and anywhere without even thinking about it.

Giles, however, gave every sign of being enchanted which was just fine by Fizz, as long as it didn't get out of hand. The kiss on the cheek he gave her, as they prepared to depart in their separate cars, was decorum itself, but the close hug that went with it held the promise of better things to come.

Buchanan was tired and disheartened when he got home some time after nine-thirty. Not even the sight of Selina waiting for him behind the fanlight worked its usual magic. He could see her through the stained glass, pacing up and down the ledge and mewing impatiently at the sound of his footstep on the stair, but he scarcely registered the warmth of her welcome as he opened the door.

Throwing his briefcase on the couch, he went into the kitchen and put the kettle on and then checked his phone messages, Selina retaining her perch on his shoulder throughout. There was the usual harangue from his mother about nothing in particular, more excuses from the decorator who was supposed to be redecorating his lounge, and a curt news flash from DCI Fleming to the effect that he had nothing to report. The police inquiry, he claimed, had turned up nothing at all to suggest any cause other than carelessness.

'Bugger,' Buchanan muttered, wondering which would be the next lead to be nipped in the bud. He sat down for a minute but Selina instantly stopped rubbing her cheek against his and gave him to understand that, although his company was a delight to her, a little nourishment would not go unappreciated. He couldn't think properly with four agitated paws marching all over him so he had to feed her and make himself a coffee before he could give Fleming's message his consideration.

It struck him as unusual for Fleming to be so brusque, even on an answering-machine. There had been something very official in his phraseology, almost as though he had been reading from a prepared statement . . . or perhaps he had been taking care not to say anything too specific in case the wrong person were to hear the tape. Curious, Buchanan re-ran the tape, listening more closely to the stilted delivery.

'Ian here. Just wanted to let you know I drew a blank. The other guys did a great job and everything's a hundred per cent okay. Nothing to worry about. Cheers.'

'Uh-huh?' Buchanan said aloud, staring sceptically at the answering-machine as though it were Fleming's lying face. 'That was no report, Ian. That was a brush-off.'

Why? That was the question. Had Ian really discovered that there was nothing odd about the police procedure, or had he found a stick to beat Inspector Virgo with and wanted to keep it to himself? Why had he chosen to leave the message here rather than contact Buchanan at his office as he normally did? Had he hoped to find Buchanan not at home so that he could avoid talking to him directly?

A third re-run of the message tape afforded the information that it had been received less than an hour ago and that – evidence the sound of a siren in the background – Fleming had been phoning from work. OK. If he was on late shift he'd still be there.

Buchanan found himself grinding his teeth again as he dialled Fleming's number. He wasn't angry, he told himself, just annoyed at Fleming for giving him the run-around.

'Fleming here.' His voice, on the telephone, sounded like an unusually articulate silver-backed gorilla, whereas he was actually barely five-seven and weedy with it.

'Buchanan.'

Fleming drew an audible breath. 'Hi, Tam. I left a message on—'

'Yes, I got it. I just haven't a clue what you intended it to mean.'

'Mean? Couldn't you hear it?'

'Sure I can hear it and, frankly, it sounded like a load of codswallop to me. What are you trying to tell me, Ian? To piss off?'

'Tam . . .' Fleming's voice dropped a bunch of decibels. 'Let's not do this, huh? Just take my advice and leave this thing alone.'

Buchanan couldn't believe he was hearing this. He said, 'You know that's not going to happen. Not unless you give me some very cogent reasons.'

'Tam, please . . .' Fleming started to say, and then seemed to realise he was wasting his breath. His voice sank to a murmur. 'Not on the phone, then. Meet me for a beer somewhere.'

'The Pear Tree. Now?'

'Give me half an hour.'

There was an immediate click, as if Fleming couldn't wait to hang up, and Buchanan was left staring at his receiver in amazement. All this cloak and dagger stuff was about as unlike the prosaic Fleming as he could imagine, and he was at a complete loss to anticipate what might be the reason for it.

Selina watched him changing into his sweater and jeans with a jaundiced eye and then left via the two inch gap below the window that was left open for her convenience. Her manner was clearly intended to let him see that, if he was going out, he needn't think she would be sitting at home waiting for him.

The Pear Tree was half empty, which was normal for a Thursday night, so Fleming was visible straightaway, even though he was sitting at a corner table with his back to the door. Buchanan paused at the bar to buy a couple of pints and carried them over.

'You're a good lad, Tam.' Fleming finished his first pint and drew the fresh one towards him affectionately. The fact that his decrepit Polo was parked outside was obviously not one that weighed heavily with him.

'Okay. Hit me with it,' Buchanan said impatiently. 'That message you left for me wouldn't have fooled a half-wit.'

Fleming's bonhomie vanished like the top half of his pint. 'Listen, Buchanan,' he said tersely, 'I was doing you a favour. You'd be well advised to keep your nose out of police business.'

'So there *is* something interesting going on.'

'There could be. I'm not sure yet but, if there is, it's something that's best dealt with inside the force.' Fleming flipped a quick glance at a noisy group around the bar counter and then frowned back at Buchanan. 'I shouldn't even be talking to you about it, and if I didn't trust you not to drop me in the shit wouldn't even be sitting here now.'

'It's Virgo, isn't it?' Buchanan insisted. 'He's on the take.'

Fleming rolled his eyes. 'Chrissake, Tam! You don't expect me to answer that, do you?'

'So, he *is*. I thought as much. The question is, why? What's he covering up?'

'Just hold on a minute,' Fleming growled, gripping his glass with both hands. 'I didn't say he *was* on the take. I don't have a single iota of evidence against the man, all I have is a gut feeling and that's nowhere near enough ammunition to start a war with, and – listen to me, Tam – a war is what I'd be starting if it gets out that I'm making unfounded accusations against Virgo.'

'Okay. I hear what you're saying,' Buchanan said. 'You know I'm not going to blab around and you know that, whatever else you say about her, Fizz knows when to keep her mouth shut. I trust her with a secret like I trust myself and I can promise you that nobody's going to know about your involvement but us. But you've got to give me a break. Something gave you that gut feeling, Ian, and I have to know what it was.'

Fleming couldn't think without doing something with his hands. He picked up his beer mat and started tapping it on the table, each corner in succession. 'It's not something you can describe,' he said, watching his fingers spinning the card. 'You develop a sort of sixth sense in this job – call it a bullshit detector. Well, the needle on mine was way over into the red when I was reading that report of Virgo's. On the surface it was perfectly straightforward but if you read between the lines . . . if you read it analytically . . . it started to look as though, maybe, he was a little too willing to take things at face value.'

'Meaning?' Buchanan prompted, wondering if he'd ever get down to the nitty gritty.

'Well . . .' Fleming took a long drink of beer and wiped his lips on the back of his hand, stretching Buchanan's patience to the limit. 'The heater you told me about . . . You are sure about that, are you, Tam? Because there's no mention of any heater – or anything that could be mistaken for a heater – in the report.'

'*Noth*ing? But Pringle, the neighbour, claimed he had seen several parts of an old heater scattered about the site. He had even picked up the maker's plate. I've seen it. All the other pieces were taken away by the police.' Buchanan shook his head in confusion. 'But surely that's all you need to prove that Virgo's on the take. That heater was – well, maybe not proof, but at least a strong indication that the explosion was not an accident. Someone who knew that Vanessa Grassick was on her way to meet her lover could have turned on the gas cylinders and arranged the heater to detonate the gas as soon as she switched on the electricity. If you want proof that Virgo suppressed valuable evidence, you've already got it.'

Fleming tapped his beer mat and smiled sadly. 'Proof? Virgo could have accounted for the presence of the heater and felt it unnecessary to mention it in the report. That's what he'll claim. Either that or he'll say there never was a heater and what proof do I have to the contrary? You've seen the maker's plate but that doesn't mean it was found at the site.'

'Pringle—' Buchanan started to say and then remembered that the Pringles were not available for comment. 'You've tried to contact the Pringles?'

'Uh-huh. And that's another thing that made me wonder. Their spur of the moment decision to go awol happened at a lucky time for Virgo, didn't it?'

'But you still don't feel you have enough to confront him with?'

'Not by a long chalk,' Fleming said, scowling at his piece of card. 'If I had any worries about the safety of Mr and Mrs Pringle I'd have to try and find them, but I can't do that without declaring my interest, and I doubt if there's any need to panic just yet.'

'You're not worried about them?' Buchanan asked, wondering how far Fleming's inquiries had gone in that direction.

'No. The neighbour didn't know where they'd gone, and I couldn't be too upfront in my questioning without admitting I was a copper, but I got her to admit that they were really looking forward to their trip.'

So presumably, after Giles's visit, somebody had warned Mrs Armstrong not to be so helpful to callers. Possibly Virgo. Possibly the Pringles themselves. Possibly Lawrence Grassick. Possibly Niall Menzies. But, just as possibly, somebody else.

Buchanan divulged Giles's 'daughter-in-Glasgow' version of the story, just to clarify the matter, and then said, 'What about Jamie Ford's wife? Did you find out where she went after leaving hospital?'

'Poppy Ford?' Fleming grinned with perverse satisfaction. 'Virtually no mention of Mrs Ford in the report, other than that she had suffered from shock and superficial cuts from flying glass. No mention of hospital. And no note anywhere of her forwarding address.'

As far as Buchanan was concerned, that settled the matter. Anyone who could have had inside information about the situation at Brora Lodge had been spirited away and whoever had been the instrument of their departure, it was a fair bet that Lawrence Grassick had funded it. That conclusion wasn't one that Buchanan faced up to gladly. There was little to relish in playing David to Lawrence Grassick's Goliath. He had admired the man for too long to feel anything but distaste for the impending necessity to expose him. However, it was comforting – if totally ignoble – to reflect that, if Grassick were found to be guilty of subverting the course of justice, he would hardly be in a position to condemn Buchanan's meddling.

Fleming finished his pint and pushed his chair back from the table. 'I don't give a toss what you find out from other sources, Tam, but as far as the Lothian and Borders police is concerned, I want you to leave it to me. You've got to see that the two of us, not to mention the insurance investigator, asking questions – no matter how discreetly – is just not on.'

'How much information are you prepared to share with me?' Buchanan returned. 'If you turn up anything positive I want to know about it. You have my word that it won't go any further, but if you keep me in the picture, I'm willing to do the same for you.'

Fleming nodded as though he hadn't expected a better deal, and stood up. 'Just as long as you don't take that little poison-ivy pal of yours into your confidence. I still get recurrent nightmares about her.'

'Fizz isn't nearly as bad as she used to be,' Buchanan said, and at that point in time he really believed she wasn't.

Chapter Nine

Giles picked up Fizz at the university after a late session with her tutor and drove her down the coast road to Berwick for dinner. The rain clouds that had been hanging around for most of the week had at last rolled away and the Kingdom of Fife, on the far side of the Forth, was clear enough to pick out individual houses.

'It's taken me all day,' he reported, with visible irritation, 'to discover which hospital Poppy Ford was taken to. I tried her neighbour Mrs Armstrong first, but she was either not at home or just not at home to *me*. Then I went into the pub – the Waterloo, is it? – and chatted to a few of the locals. One or two of them knew Jamie Ford by sight but nobody had met Poppy and they didn't even seem to be aware that she had been hospitalised. In the end I had to lie in wait for the postman – a chap called Lenny who, I understand, precludes the necessity for a local newspaper.'

'Yeah, they told me about him. Where did you locate him?'

'I simply waited at the pillar box,' Giles grinned, evidently pleased with his lateral thinking. 'I reckoned somebody would have to turn up for the next collection at four o'clock and the chances were it would be Lenny.'

'And, of course, it was,' Fizz supplied, massaging his ego with an appreciative smile.

'Indeed it was, and quite a repository of miscellaneous information he turned out to be. Not particularly relevant information but plenty of it and all readily available on request – or even minus a request.'

Fizz got the picture. 'But he was able to tell you where Poppy had been treated?'

'He was able to tell me where Mrs Pringle and Mrs Armstrong had gone to visit her, which probably amounts to the same thing. All his information was second-hand, unfortunately, most of it gleaned from Mrs Pringle herself, so he wasn't able to corroborate her version of events. But, yes, he did seem to be certain that Poppy was in the East Borders Infirmary, just outside Berwick. With a bit of luck, and a few of your irresistible smiles, we should be able to find somebody who remembers where she was headed when she left.'

'Ah,' said Fizz, pretending to look huffy. 'So that's why you wanted me with you: to make use of my sex appeal.'

'Only on the male staff,' he defended himself, laughing. 'I'll mount my own assault on the females.'

'Fancy your chances, do you?' Fizz couldn't help saying, even though she could hardly expect him not to be aware that he was gorgeous.

He looked at her steadily for a moment, the amusement fading from his eyes. 'I don't know. How would you rate them?'

There were two ways to answer that, Fizz decided: the first way would pander to his conceit and possibly give him ideas above his station; the second way would leave him wondering, which was always good practice. She said, 'To be honest, I'm not sure what nurses go for in a man. Possibly a tropical infection or an interesting skin disease.'

'And what about you?' he said lightly, riding the punch. 'Is there a man in your life?'

'No. If I'm not earning a crust, I'm studying, so I don't have time for a man.'

'Don't you get lonely sometimes?'

Fizz studied the scenery, wondering if he meant 'lonely' as in *lonely* or 'lonely' as in *horny*. The answer to the former possibility was, 'No, I don't have time to be lonely' and the answer to the latter was, 'It's none of your sodding business, right?' In fact, come to think of it, none of it was any of his business.

She said, 'No. I don't do lonely.'

'You don't do lonely?' he echoed. 'That must be nice for you. How do you manage it?'

'I suppose I'm just used to being on my own,' Fizz hazarded. It wasn't something she'd given a lot of thought to, introspection being another thing she didn't do. Her grandfather had brought her up to be independent, which was a smart thing to do seeing as he had been in his mid-fifties when her parents were killed. He had taken pains to instil in her the precept that you should never get used to a crutch that somebody could kick away. OK, he had probably been referring more to drugs than to relationships but the principle held good for both. She'd tried teaming up with a guy once or twice and it had invariably ended in trauma – for the guy in question, not for her – largely because she'd felt that the relationship cost more, in time, in commitment, and in self-sacrifice than she got out of it. Regular sex was great, but it wasn't worth the shackles. Maybe, one day far away in the future, she might be tempted to team up again but it wouldn't be while she had goals of her own she wanted to pursue.

'What about your parents?' Giles wanted to know.

'Dead,' said Fizz shortly and changed the subject before he got too nosy. 'What about you? Is there a Mrs Cambridge and half a dozen little Cambridges waiting for you back home?'

'God forbid!' he said, laughing, and added with admirable directness, 'No, there isn't even a girlfriend right now. I'm like Tam: untrammelled.'

Fizz was way ahead of him there. She had a notion that he was curious to know precisely what sort of relationship she shared with Buchanan so she wasn't surprised when he went on, almost without a pause, 'He *is* untrammelled, I take it? I only ask because it would be a very understanding girlfriend who would be happy to let him spend so many evenings with you. Does that mean there isn't one?'

'I think she has a puncture at the moment,' Fizz said, which distracted him enough to let her change the subject again. 'Have you spoken to him today? I meant to phone him at lunch time to see if he'd heard anything from his police contact, but I got sidelined.'

'No, I confess I expected to get all the latest news from you. I hadn't realised you wouldn't be in the office today, but I dare say Tam would have called me on my mobile if he had anything to report.'

'He would have,' Fizz felt confident enough to say. 'So that means DCI Fleming is dragging his heels, which surprises me not at all. God, it's like drawing teeth! We don't seem to be able to get a clear lead from anybody.'

'Plenty of *un*clear leads, though. If we could just sort out the wheat from the chaff.'

More like the chaff from the crap, Fizz thought, enjoying her view of his perfect profile. It was a long time since she'd felt like sketching anything – art college had virtually cured her of that – but give her a piece of charcoal right now and she could capture his face in thirty seconds.

He frowned a little, unaware of her scrutiny, and said, 'Tam was telling me last night about the estate that's for sale. What's it called? Lammerburn? Yes, well, the word is that Vanessa Grassick was poised to make a whole lot of trouble for the owners.'

'Where did you hear that?' Fizz asked, snapping, mentally, to attention. 'In the Waterloo?'

'Yes. The locals were up in arms about the terms of the sale – I expect you know all about that? – and Vanessa Grassick was getting them all geared up for a full-scale protest. She had good contacts in the media and, of course, in the legal profession and she had intended, as soon as the estate was put on the market, to have every man, woman and child in the area out there with banners, celebrities, pipe bands and virtually everything but a fly-past of the Red Arrows.'

'Wow! Really? That's incredible! I knew she'd complained to the owners but I didn't realise she meant business on that scale.'

Fizz felt the faint stirrings of an unworthy suspicion way in the back of her mind. Giles had taken his time about sharing this tasty morsel of information with her. Had he been tempted to keep it to himself?

'You think it's important?' he said, taking note of her enthusiasm.

'Well, yes. Don't you? I mean, the Menzies family would have been spitting tacks if they thought she might knobble their sale. There's a couple of million pounds or more tied up in that deal and that's a lot of money, even to the Menzies family.'

'An ancient half-crippled woman and her spineless son? You met them, I didn't, but the picture I got from Tam—'

'I wouldn't put anything past that old witch,' Fizz insisted. 'She's been used to getting her own way for far too long and the very idea of "ordinary" people telling her what she can do with her own property would have her biting the carpet. Maybe she can't get around much herself but that milksop son of hers would hammer tacks under his toenails if she told him to do it.'

'What about her husband? He's still alive, isn't he?' Giles seemed only now to be appreciating the possibilities inherent in his information. 'Where is he right now?'

'He's back home in their Edinburgh house,' Fizz said, 'but I reckon we can forget about him. My money's on Mrs Menzies. She's the spider in the centre of that web.'

'You really think she could make her son commit murder?' Giles stopped at traffic lights and took the opportunity to look at her seriously. 'Murder, Fizz. Think about it. Think about the amount of pressure you'd have to be under to actually take someone's life. Mrs Menzies would have to be a real Svengali to do that.'

'I wouldn't be surprised if she were,' Fizz returned, knowing perfectly well that she would have been. Giles was probably quite right. Even her goofy son wouldn't go that far just to keep his mother's spirits up. He wouldn't have the bottle for it. 'I don't say I could imagine Niall putting a bullet into someone – nothing violent like that – but laying a trap . . . that's something else. He's not the sort to appreciate the effects of his actions. Not really. Trying to make him understand the human tragedy the evictions would set in motion was like trying to read *The Times* in a wind tunnel. It wouldn't take much to talk him into arranging a gas explosion in Vanessa's house if he thought it would go off when the house was empty.'

Giles nodded, taking that on board. 'Right. In fact the whole business could have been intended from the start to be nothing more than a warning to Vanessa to pipe down. Niall Menzies – or whoever set up the explosion – may have been unaware that she was meeting Jamie Ford there that night.'

'Um . . . yeah,' Fizz said, but more out of politeness than because she actually agreed with that conclusion. If Giles's reading of the facts were true, Vanessa's visit to Brora Lodge would've had to be purely coincidental and coincidences, in Fizz's opinion, were roughly on a par with solar eclipses. They did occur, but not often enough to make them a factor in your day-to-day calculations. Nope. Somebody had to have known full well that Vanessa Grassick would be meeting Jamie Ford there that night and had arranged a welcome for both of them.

And who would be so intimately aware of Vanessa's plans? Probably not her husband. Not, at least, if the meeting was what it appeared to be: a romantic rendez-vous. Joseph Rudyard, her business partner? He was in a position to overhear her phone calls or maybe glimpse her diary, and he was also the one to benefit from her death.

It was annoying that Buchanan had refused to allow her to sit in on his chat with Rudyard. She'd let him get away with it at the time because he had scared the shit out of her by spelling out what harm it would do her career if Grassick took against her, but now she was sure that was a load of codswallop. Whatever Buchanan thought about it, she was damn well going to have a close look at Vanessa's main beneficiary at the first opportunity.

They stopped for a meal at a great little bistro on the outskirts of Berwick, the sort of place Fizz preferred but Buchanan avoided like the plague. The colours were bright and the music was loud and the waiters were cheerful. It was fairly new and the management had gone for character and atmosphere in a big way, covering the walls with *trompe l'oeil* scenes of Italian harbours, fishing nets, floats etc and making a speciality of sea food, which Fizz adored.

Actually, the tuna steak she chose was dry as a bone and she could hardly hear what Giles was saying because of the background music but, hey, she wasn't paying for it. When the check arrived she could tell that Giles wished he wasn't paying for it either. He made no comment, and neither did she, but she noticed that he didn't leave a tip.

'How do you want to play it at the hospital?' she asked him as they got back into the car. 'Do you admit to being an insurance investigator or does that make people clam up?'

'To tell you the truth, I've never been in precisely this sort of situation before,' Giles admitted. 'I'll probably try not to identify myself at all if I can get away with it, but if they ask me if I'm a relation of Poppy's I suppose I'd have no option but to say yes. It all depends on the receptionist, doesn't it? If we're up against a petty bureaucrat we won't get any information at all unless we claim to be family – and maybe not even then.' He examined Fizz's face. 'Does that constitute a big problem for you?'

Fizz had to smile. It was so liberating, after two years of Buchanan's conscience-searching, to be working with a man after her own heart. 'Whatever it takes,' she said.

Visiting time was half over by the time they found the hospital. It left them only three quarters of an hour to find someone who would take the time to answer their questions but at least the rush at the reception desk was over and the two receptionists, a man and a woman, were getting on with their paperwork. It was the woman, a blonde with fat, dimpled cheeks, who stood up and came forward to speak to them, so Fizz shut up and left Giles to charm the pants off her, which he proceeded to do.

'We're looking for a Mrs Poppy Ford,' he said, looking at her as though she was the most interesting woman he'd ever seen. 'She was admitted a week past on Saturday, some time in the early hours of the morning. I'm afraid I don't know which ward she's in.'

'Poppy Ford,' Dimples repeated in a soft Highland accent, and her eyes swept Fizz with a quick appraisal as though she was wondering if she and Giles were an item. 'I can look it up on the computer for you. Bear with me a minute.'

Giles went on staring at her as her fingers jittered across the keys, and the faint curve of her full lips showed that she knew he was doing it. When she looked back at him her eyes showed a trace of not unpleasurable embarrassment. 'Mrs Poppy Ford, Whiteadder Road, Chirnside?'

'That's her.' Giles nodded, flattering her with his eyes and patently amazed that any creature could be so clever and efficient as well as beautiful.

'I'm afraid Mrs Ford is no longer a patient here. In fact, her record shows that she was only kept in overnight for observation.'

'But . . . surely that can't be right? She hasn't returned home.' Giles pushed distractedly at his hair and looked at Dimples with troubled eyes. 'I've been in hospital myself since the accident – they took me to the burns unit in Edinburgh Infirmary – and I wondered why my sister – Poppy – hadn't contacted me. They said she hadn't been seriously hurt but when I went to her house today she

114

wasn't there and there were signs that she hadn't been there since I last saw her. What on earth has happened to her?'

'I'm terribly sorry but I can't help you.' She was visibly so torn with sympathy that she was having to resist clasping his head to her bosom. 'All I know is that she was discharged on the morning of Sunday the fifth. Is there a relation she might have gone to stay with?'

'No. There's just the two of us now,' Giles told her, going, in Fizz's opinion, a trifle over the score with the pathos. 'If she had wanted company she might have gone to stay with her friend here.' He indicated Fizz with a jerk of his head that relegated her to the ranks of the insignificant. 'But, obviously, she didn't do that either. God, this is so worrying.'

'I wish I could help,' claimed Dimples, laying a hand to her cheek and caressing him with a droop of her lashes, 'but I don't know who I . . .' She paused, her glance fluttering to the phone at her elbow. 'I suppose I could find out if any of the nurses in Accident and Emergency remember her.'

For a moment Fizz thought Giles was going to shed a tear. 'Could you . . . would you do that for me? You're so kind.'

'I can try.' She turned to the phone with an expression on her face like Mother Teresa ministering to the poor, and started punching buttons.

Fizz drifted a step or two away and dragged Giles after her. 'This is a dead end,' she muttered, keeping half an ear on the receptionist's end of the telephone conversation. 'If Poppy was in here only overnight it's very unlikely she'd have managed to be on chatting terms with any of the nurses. You know what night nurses are like. If you're not likely to pop your clogs during their shift they just give you a sleeping pill and get on with their knitting.' Fizz had never, touch wood, been in hospital overnight but she'd heard stories and that was enough for her. 'Let's get out of here. I've thought of a better way to find out about Poppy.'

Giles snapped his eyes away from Dimples to look at her but, before he could say anything, the receptionist reclaimed his attention by saying, 'Yes, that's her okay. You remember her . . .? Yes, well she hasn't returned home and her family's worried about her. I don't suppose you'd know . . . No, I didn't think you would. She didn't order a taxi to anywhere . . .? Oh? Did you see the driver? What kind of car? Maybe it'll mean something to somebody. Okay, thanks, Maggie. See you later.' She dropped the receiver and turned to Giles. 'She was definitely here only a matter of hours. One of the nurses saw her out to the car that picked her up. A black Ford Ka, driven by a man in his thirties. Does that help you at all?'

Giles pretended to be searching his brain for a moment but Fizz had lost her patience and wanted out. Also, she wanted the matter closed in case Dimples thought of some way to use it as a link between her and Giles.

'A Ford Ka!' she exclaimed with a grin that could have been seen from the Mir space station. 'George drives a Ford Ka! Why didn't we think of George?'

Giles smote his forehead and rolled his eyes in a parody of Sir Laurence Olivier. 'George! Obviously! Of course he would take care of her. Her boss,' he added to the enchanted Dimples. 'They're very close but, somehow, my mind was on other tracks. I can't thank you enough for your trouble. You've been so patient.'

'Not at all,' beamed Dimples, hanging on his lips. 'I'm delighted to have put your mind at rest.'

Fizz waited a second to see if she would ask if she could do anything else for him but she didn't. Personally, she would have awarded Giles's performance only a B-minus, but she was willing to admit that there were plenty of people less discriminating than she and Dimples was obviously one of them.

As they sped up the coast road to Edinburgh, Giles was not despondent. 'It wasn't entirely a waste of time,' he claimed. 'We know that someone picked Poppy up and we know he drove a black Ford Ka. That information could be useful if we run across someone connected with the case who drives that model. I'll check out the Menzies family, any of Lawrence Grassick's staff, Vanessa's business partner – what's his name – Rudyard. Do we know what make of car the Fords themselves owned?'

'Nope, but I dare say the Armstrongs could tell you.'

Fizz found it difficult to be as upbeat about their findings as Giles was. The news about the car and its driver might turn out to be evidential but it also eliminated both Niall Menzies and Lawrence Grassick, neither of whom could be mistaken for a man in his thirties. Either of them could, of course, have employed a menial to do the actual pick-up, but proving that would take a lot longer than having the nurse identify a photograph.

She forbore pointing out her reservations, however, because Giles was so chirpy it would have been heartless to slap him down. Only when they arrived at her flat did it emerge that his high spirits stemmed more from unfounded optimism than from job satisfaction.

'Don't I get a coffee?' he asked somewhat plaintively as Fizz made to leave the car. 'It's a long drive back to Chirnside.'

This, as far as Fizz was concerned, was definitely pushing his luck.

'Sorry,' she said very sweetly. 'I can't ask you up tonight. I have an aunt staying with me over the weekend.'

If he didn't believe her at least he didn't make it obvious. Instead, he slipped an arm round her shoulders and kissed her, taking his time with it. 'Maybe next time,' he said, making it a question.

'Maybe,' she said, looking willing, but thinking, *And maybe not.* Giles was a great meal ticket but he was a bit on the pushy side and Fizz didn't like to be pushed. Not yet, anyway.

He stayed in her mind for as long as it took her to walk

to the foot of her stairway and was then buried under the weight of her more pressing problems.

Time was passing at an awesome rate and this investigation, which had looked like taking two or three days, at most, had now developed into something that had no end in sight. That was bad news for Buchanan, who was keen to get out of Grassick's hair as soon as possible, and it was bad news for her because she was falling behind with her studies.

Luck had been firmly against them all the way and the time was approaching when they'd have to start making their own luck. Fortunately Fizz had ideas along those lines, none of which were likely to grab Buchanan but – hey! – that had never stopped her before. If she had left things to Buchanan in the past at least two guests of Her Majesty's Prisons would still be at large and Buchanan himself wouldn't have been too healthy either.

All week she had been aware of the fact that Poppy and Jamie Ford's house was lying there empty and accessible and filled with all manner of interesting leads: address books, recorded phone messages, photograph albums, and who could tell what else? The windows were merely boarded up and only the Armstrongs – who were too far away to hear anything – were in residence. The place was simply begging to be rifled.

Chapter Ten

Sometimes it seemed to Buchanan that Saturday mornings were the only thing that kept him going. After five days of dashing about in a sharp suit, dealing with angry, worried, or, frankly, criminal people, it was a delight to slob around unshaved, lazily reading the papers and overdosing on coffee.

Selina was also into Saturdays in a big way, probably because Buchanan was around to talk to her all morning and because the various other neighbours who spoiled her with tidbits were usually at home in the afternoon. She was snoozing across Buchanan's lap when the bell of the entryphone shocked her awake and her claws went straight through his tracksuit trousers: just one of her sweet little habits that was beginning to make his thighs look like those of a heroin addict.

By the time he had collected himself she was already balanced on the transom of the front door peering out through the stained glass to see who was coming. Buchanan suspected he already knew. Nobody but Fizz ever rang his bell on a Saturday morning.

He wasn't sure whether he wanted to see her or not. He had spent a bad night wondering if she was still with Giles and, if so, what the hell she was doing. What really annoyed him was that he was behaving irrationally, since it was patently none of his concern who Fizz spent her time with, and he had just succeeded in banishing such lacerating thoughts to the deep recesses of his consciousness.

Seeing Fizz this morning could bring about a swift return to the drawing board.

The bell rang again, twice, which meant she wasn't going to take a hint and go away. She knew he was in there.

Hastily grabbing a T-shirt from the selection of clothes and other rubbish around him, he wriggled into it as he joined Selina in the hallway.

'Yeah?'

'Smee.'

'I thought it would be.'

'So, you're not disappointed. Let me in, I'm desperate for the loo.'

Buchanan did as he was told, and stood aside as she flashed past him into the bathroom. Selina, her welcoming dive thwarted by this turn of speed, dropped on to Buchanan's shoulder instead as though that was what she had intended doing all along. He carried her into the kitchen and gave her a Kitty Kake to console her while he made some coffee.

When he returned to the lounge he could hear Fizz still running taps in the bathroom and he suspected she was doing her regular stocktaking of the johnnies in the medicine cabinet. Fortunately, he had remembered to remove one or two since the last time she was here, just to keep her guessing.

When she walked into the lounge he saw her eye fall on the piles of junk, all of which had surfaced, in the usual mysterious way, since Dolores, his cleaning lady, had done her bi-weekly mucking out yesterday. Pausing in the doorway, she put her hands on her hips and regarded him kindly.

'Ever wonder if there's something wrong with your Feng Shui, Buchanan?'

He swept the room with a glance, which was, if the truth were told, the first time he'd swept it with anything. Housekeeping was not his forte but it never had been and Fizz had hitherto resisted commenting on the fact.

'It's no worse than usual,' he said, sounding more plaintive than he had intended.

'Buchanan, it's like a Bombay public toilet in here. Don't you ever put anything away?'

'That's what I pay Dolores for,' he said, but obviously that didn't please her either so he waved a hand at the full mugs and added, 'You want some coffee?'

'You always did know how to get round me, you sexy beast. Where's the biscuits?'

'You don't have time for a biscuit.'

'I'll make time.'

Buchanan got the biscuit tin. 'So, to what do I owe this pleasure?'

Fizz took three biscuits and fell on to the couch. 'I just thought you'd like to know how Giles and I got on last night.'

'If you really want to share it with me,' Buchanan said, hiding the tightness in his chest behind a brave smile. 'But don't feel you have to go into the gory details.'

Fizz made a rude noise. 'That'll be the day!'

'Does that mean,' Buchanan had to insist, albeit lightly, 'that'll be the day when you *tell* me the gory details, or that'll be the day when there *are* any to tell?'

She shook her head, her mouth full of biscuit, and kept him waiting for an answer while she chewed and swallowed. Even then, all she said was, 'Giles and I are just ships that go bump in the night.'

And that, Buchanan thought, could have been either a Freudian slip or simply her way of dodging the implied question, and either way he didn't find it particularly amusing.

'The bad news,' Fizz pressed on, replenishing her stock of biscuits, 'is that nobody could tell us where Poppy had gone. Giles did a reasonable job on the receptionist, who bust a gut for him, but she wasn't able to find anyone who could give us a forwarding address.'

Buchanan had never been hugely hopeful about that

lead but he was in a mood to be disappointed. 'So gimme the good news.'

'Well, it's not earth-shattering,' Fizz admitted, fulfilling his expectations, 'but, who knows, it might turn out to be useful.'

'Uh-huh?'

'Somebody remembered Poppy being picked up by a guy in a Ford Ka. A guy in his thirties. Who might that have been?'

'That's it? That's the good news?' Buchanan said bleakly.

'That's the best I have for you today, muchacho.' She flapped an uncharitable hand at Selina who was regarding her chocolate biscuit with open but misguided optimism. 'It's not a lot but it's better than a poke with a sharp stick. No doubt you've been forging ahead with guns blazing. Yes?'

Buchanan, this morning, was not immune to her sarcasm. It seemed to him that his life was falling apart, that the stars were aligned against him, that his destiny was in the lap of the gods and they were about to stand up.

'I met Ian Fleming for a quick drink on Thursday night but he was no further forward. Obviously, he's getting no help whatsoever from the Hawick branch so he's planning to approach the matter from Lawrence Grassick's direction: starting, that is, from the assumption that Grassick is guilty of topping his wife.'

The tip of Fizz's tongue appeared, capturing a crumb from the corner of her lips.

'Starting where, exactly?'

'Starting with the usual lines of inquiry: establishing Grassick's whereabouts that weekend, tracing the origin of the heater, who sold it, who actually bought it. That sort of thing. He thinks he may be able to get some information out of a Mrs Hewlett who acts as housekeeper in Grassick's Edinburgh house.' Buchanan couldn't help showing his distaste at Fleming's methods. 'Apparently, Fleming has discovered that Mrs Hewlett's elderly mother was in trouble for shoplifting a few years back – that's the price you pay for having a name that sticks in a copper's mind – so he is banking on the fact that she didn't share that fact with her boss.'

Fizz grimaced back at him. 'Blackmail is a fact of life, Buchanan. It's merely a useful tool for simplifying the process of decision-making, that's all. As long as he gets something worthwhile out of it he's got my blessing.'

Buchanan knew better than to start another of their regular arguments about the end justifying the means. He said, 'In the meantime I'm going to widen our own field of inquiry. It's possible we've been concentrating on the wrong aspects of Lawrence Grassick's life.'

'What other aspects are there?' Fizz wondered.

'Well, his political life for a start. I don't know just how much power he wields in Holyrood, or in what fields, but I know somebody who can tell me. There could be a whole can of worms there waiting to be uncovered.'

Fizz didn't appear to be overly excited by that prospect. She patted a yawn. 'Okay. You do that. Me, I have a yen to make the acquaintance of Mr Menzies senior. If he's anything like his wife – and after fifty-odd years of marriage most couples have become a composite of the two original partners – he'd be just the boyo to put out a contract on Vanessa. Somebody ought to check him out. I can tell him I'm a social worker, or something.'

'Honesty's the best policy, Fizz—'

'Yes, but it isn't the *only* policy,' Fizz returned with strained patience. 'If you want to tag along I've no objection. It'll be a waste of time as far as the evictions are concerned but, if he's in his dotage, who knows what he might let slip? This afternoon suit you?'

Buchanan shrank back into his chair. 'This afternoon?'

'Only, I have to get my library books back before the library closes,' she said, bouncing to her feet. 'Never mind, I'll scoot up there now and come straight back. We can have a sandwich or something and go straight over to –

what's their address? Blackett Place, isn't it? I reckon we'll have milked him white in under an hour.'

'Actually,' Buchanan said firmly, 'I was planning a round of golf this afternoon.'

She paused with one arm in her jacket. 'I thought you were frantic to get this business tied up before Lawrence Grassick whipped a restraining order on you?'

There was no denying that, Buchanan had to admit, and no recourse other than to ditch his plans for the afternoon and go along with hers. He made the necessary phone call, half hoping that Mr Menzies would be unavailable, but even that was denied him. It was all for the best, he supposed, particularly since it was starting to rain again, but, still, he could have done without Fizz's tireless enthusiasm.

He made some cheese sandwiches and opened a can of tomato soup while she was gone, thereby exhausting both his store cupboard and his culinary expertise. Luckily, Fizz was more a gourmand than a gourmet and scoffed her share, plus half of his, without comment. Given her current carping mood he half expected her to ask what had become of his recently voiced intention of improving his diet, but she appeared to have reverted to her usual stance of non-intervention. She was less than complimentary about the stag's head in the back of the car but Buchanan could empathise with that since he, too, was being stabbed in the back of the neck by the antlers every time he braked.

The Menzies' pied-à-terre in Edinburgh was a three-storey Edwardian mansion in a conservation area a couple of miles from the city centre. It was set well back from the road behind a screen of cherry trees and sported an imposing entrance with a magnificent stained-glass door. Annoyingly, there was a car blocking the driveway so Buchanan had to find a parking space a good hundred yards down the road and walk back. As he waited for an answer to his ring, he checked out the rest of the street and estimated that a decent-sized bomb in this area would probably put Lloyds out of business.

The door was opened to them by a mature lady wearing a cheap plastic raincoat over a nurse's uniform.

'Mr Buchanan? Yes, do come in. Mr Menzies is expecting you.' She led them into a hallway and added, 'If you'll excuse me for a moment I'll just make sure Mr Menzies is ready to see you.'

Fizz watched her disappear through a doorway big enough for a horse and cart and muttered, 'It's like St Paul's Cathedral. How do people *live* in places like this?'

Buchanan moved away from her without answering and checked to see if a painting of a woman in a big hat was indeed by one of the Scottish colourists. It was. It was an original Fergusson and probably worth several thousand pounds. Not in a place of honour in the drawing room but tucked away in a gloomy corner, flanked by a faded strip of tapestry and a Turner print. As he was about to draw Fizz's attention to this indication of nonchalant affluence, the nurse's voice floated back to them.

'What's this, Mr Menzies?'

She was answered by an indistinct rumble, presumably from Mr Menzies.

'Aspirins? No, I don't think so, sir. An aspirin *bottle*, yes, but these are your sleeping tablets, aren't they? You've been saving them up again.'

'You know damn well that one tablet's no use to me when my arthritis is bad!' quoth her patient, in a voice made just audible by irritation.

'You can talk to Doctor Russell about that when he comes in tomorrow and he'll probably prescribe something different. Two of these would knock you out for twelve hours, you know, and we can't have that.'

Her patient's voice dropped to a rumble again but they could hear the nurse speaking briskly to him as she tidied him up. Presently, she returned to the hallway smiling cheerfully.

'I hope you don't mind if I leave you in charge for a couple of minutes, Mr Buchanan. I'm just popping down to the pillar box at the corner to post a letter that must catch the uplift at three-fifteen. I thought I could be there and back before you arrived but I think I can still make it.'

'No problem,' Buchanan said, and added as an after-thought, 'There's no probability of an emergency, I don't suppose?'

'No, no. Mr Menzies is in fine fettle apart from his arthritis,' she smiled, buttoning up her coat and flipping her hood up over her hair. 'You'll have no trouble, I promise you, and I'll be back before you know I'm gone.'

She pushed open the massive door, ushered them through, and left them to make their own introductions.

The Menzies patriarch was big enough to have made four of his wife and at least two of his son, but he shared Niall's placid blue eyes and his air of geniality. He was ensconced in a long-legged chair by a coal fire and had been playing Free Cell Patience on one of those tables on wheels that can be pulled across the knees. He, or the nurse, had pushed the table aside but as he went through all the formalities of asking after Buchanan senior etc, his eyes kept flicking across to the unfinished game as though part of his mind were still at work on it.

'Yes, yes, Niall told me on the phone that he and his mother had had a visit from you during the week. Quite cheered Muriel up, he says. She's been on and on about your father ever since, seemingly, and reminiscing about the old days when we were just starting up the business.' He shook his gaunt, balding head and smiled, one knobbly fist incessantly massaging the other. 'Those were the good years, Tam. The years of struggle and worry and small triumphs. Not the years when we had made our packet and could rest on our laurels. No. It's better to travel than to arrive, you know. I never believed that when I was a young man like you, but it's true.'

Buchanan could hear the slam of the front door as the nurse returned, followed by the rustle of a plastic coat being briskly shaken.

'Money doesn't make you happy, huh?' Fizz piped up from her perch on the window seat. 'But you have to admit it makes unhappiness a lot less uncomfortable.'

Menzies bent a look of avuncular affection on her urchin face. 'And what would a lassie like you know about unhappiness, eh? Nothing in your head but boyfriends, at your age, and you'll have plenty of those, I've not the slightest doubt.'

Buchanan's breath caught in his throat but, luckily, Fizz was disposed to make allowances for his advanced age. She said, 'I'm unhappy about the sale of Lammerburn Estate, to tell you the truth.'

'Aye, well I'm not too happy about it myself,' he said frankly, wincing a little as he heaved himself round to see her better. 'Of all our houses, Lammerburn was my favourite but I'm told we have to be near a hospital – now that we're old and decrepit! – in case my wife or I should need urgent attention and, unfortunately, my dear, when you get to my age, it's a lot easier just to go along with the experts.'

'There are hospitals quite close to Lammerburn,' Fizz insisted. 'And even here, you're not so near the Royal Infirmary as you used to be before it moved out to Little France. If it were me, and I didn't know how long I had left to me, I'd make darn sure I made the best of what I had. None of us is going to live for ever so, if you can't do anything about the length of your life, you can at least do something about the quality. What's the point of living another year or two if you're not living it to the full?'

His tender gaze lingered on her for a moment or two as though in wonder at such sagacity from one of (what he perceived to be) such tender years.

Buchanan cleared his throat and said, 'The only thing that worries me, Mr Menzies, is the effect of the sale on the local community. There are eight families in the cottages and if they have to move away, the impact on the village will be severe.'

127

'Oh, yes. Someone said something about people complaining.' Menzies dragged his eyes away from Fizz. 'Niall is supposed to be dealing with all that. Surely he can come to some arrangement?'

'He hasn't discussed it with you?' Buchanan asked, barely beating Fizz to the question.

'Not in great detail, no, but I know some woman was making trouble.' He straightened his big body and jutted his chin questioningly. 'Is there more?'

'I fear there is, sir,' Buchanan told him, and spent ten minutes putting him in the picture. Fizz, as usual, lost interest immediately and filled in the time by applying her mind to her host's game of Patience. Every time Buchanan glanced at her he could see her eyes flicking from card to card and from column to column, but he was aware that she had one ear on his presentation and he'd be getting marks out of ten for it on the drive home.

'Well, I don't have to tell you, I knew none of this,' Menzies said when he'd heard everything. 'Come to think of it, I don't think my wife intended me to hear about Mrs Grassick's complaint either, but Niall was never very good about keeping secrets and he let it slip. It wasn't my intention to pass the reins into his hands, I don't mind telling you, but Muriel insisted it would be better for him to take some responsibility now, while we're still here to keep an eye on him.' He stared into the fire for a moment, smoothing swollen knuckles with twisted fingers. In the silence, rain rattled like gravel against the windows. 'Neither Niall or his mother had close ties with Lammerburn. Niall was away at school half the time and Muriel liked to be close to her friends up north – when she *had* friends, that is. Most of them are pushing up the daisies by now, so she prefers Edinburgh to anywhere else. Not that it matters much *where* we live, these days. We're never out of the house.'

'You'd at least be out in the garden if you lived at Lammerburn,' Fizz nagged, so mercilessly that Buchanan squirmed in his chair: Menzies, however, showed every sign of wanting to adopt her.

'Well, well, there's a lot of truth in what you say, lassie. I'll need to think about that,' he said, probably not meaning a word of it but humouring her just the same. His abrupt change of subject confirmed that suspicion. 'You're a Patience fan, I see, like myself.'

Fizz's pixie smile acknowledged a fair cop. 'I used to be hooked on it when I travelled a lot. I spent hours – days, sometimes – waiting for transport so I always carried a pack of cards in my pocket to pass the time.'

'You're familiar with Free Cell?'

'Oh, yes. It's on my computer at work.'

She had the grace to shoot a guilty glance in her boss's direction but, in fact, she was giving away nothing he didn't know already.

Menzies nodded at the game in progress. 'This one's a dead duck, I suspect.'

'No.' Fizz smiled an apology. 'You could put the nine in a cell and move the jack on to the queen, which would let you bring down the run of hearts. Then you'd have a space for the nine and the eight, move the seven over, and you have a straight run home.'

Buchanan stood up and walked to the window as they bent over the table. The rain was lashing down now with such force that he could see it bouncing a foot off the tarmacked driveway. It eased his frustration at the loss of his round of golf but it was going to make their sprint back to the car a bit of a bind. He extricated Fizz from a discussion about the supernatural characteristics of Patience (what next?) and left Mr Menzies to digest the implications of selling his estate.

They let themselves out into the lancing rain and sprinted for the shelter of the Saab. Buchanan had his golf umbrella but sharing it with Fizz meant that he got soaked.

Chapter Eleven

Fizz had few friends with wheels. The chap downstairs had a bike which he let her borrow from time to time and also Buchanan was pretty good at giving her the occasional lift, as long as she was pursuing an objective that had his blessing. However, it was unlikely that he would give his blessing to her housebreaking mission, so it looked like Gurbachan would be drawing the short straw again.

The High Street was thronged by the time Fizz completed her Saturday chores and set forth to look for him. There was no sign of him at his dad's mini supermarket across the road from her flat but the old boy, Rajinder himself, was sitting behind the counter watching his dear wife stacking the shelves. Rajinder and Fizz had known each other since she had first come to school in Edinburgh at the age of fourteen. They were both strangers in a strange land at a time when the capital had probably been as much of a culture shock to a native of Am Bealach as to a young man from Kalat.

'Hi, folks,' Fizz said, taking a wire basket and starting to fill it with vegetables. She'd already been in for her necessary shopping in the morning but she had a hundred stairs to climb to her flat and, there being no way she could carry a load up there all at once, she never climbed them empty-handed if she could help it. 'Is your amazing son around?'

'He is – amazingly,' Rajinder snorted, his heavy Edinburgh accent indistinguishable from that of his customers.

'It's taken him since three o'clock this afternoon to deliver a couple of orders down at the Cowgate and that's him just back. Is that amazing enough for you, eh? Gurbachan! Here's your girlfriend looking for you.'

Gurbachan was now nineteen but he could still blush, and his beautiful café-au-lait face, as he emerged from the back shop, appeared to be lit by one of those bulbs you put in fake-fire radiators. It amused Fizz no end to see the prim mask he wore in front of his despotic parents. Away from their sphere of influence, which was extensive, he made up for their repression with a vocabulary of invective, blasphemy and abuse which rivalled Fizz's own.

'Wassup?' he said, being gruff and casual, which was currently regarded as cool by his coterie of buddies.

'Are you doing anything tonight, Gurbachan? I need a favour.'

'A lift?' He always liked to get straight to the nitty gritty and, anyway, lifts were invariably all that Fizz required of him.

'Your Aunt Janna is coming to dinner.' His mother's soft voice floated forth from behind the breakfast cereals. 'I want you to at least eat with us, Gurbachan.'

His back to his parents, Gurbachan mouthed something obscene.

'That's no problem,' Fizz said, dropping her voice a notch. 'Any time after half-nine would be fine. Unless you had other plans?'

'Nup. You want me to come round for you?'

'Would you? I'll watch for you at the window.'

'Where're we going?'

Fizz avoided looking at his parents but she spotted her minute hesitation and got the message.

'Not far,' she murmured. 'I'll buy the petrol. Thanks, Gurbachan.'

'No sweat.'

As she turned away from him to pass her basket of vegetables to Rajinder her eye was caught by a vaguely familiar profile across the street and just visible through the stacks of canned goods in the window. A second look confirmed that it was undoubtedly the centurion, who was engrossed in perusing a stand of postcards in a shop doorway.

There was not the slightest justification for the bolt of uneasiness that hit Fizz amidships. He was only doing what every other tourist would be doing at some point in their holiday: exploring the medieval Old Town, window shopping down the Royal Mile, and buying postcards. He wasn't to know that she lived just a few paces away, and the fact that he had already crossed her path two or three times in the recent past was far from sinister but, all the same, she was suspicious enough to say, 'See that guy across the road, looking at postcards? The guy with the tartan umbrella. Ever seen him before?'

Rajinder, Gurbachan and Yasmin crowded up at the window to look, which would have been unfortunate if the centurion had glanced in their direction.

'Yes,' Yasmin said right away. 'I sold him a Yorkie bar right after we opened the shop yesterday morning. Why?'

'I just wondered if he lived locally,' Fizz evaded, and they all drifted back to what they were doing.

Nothing odd in the guy buying a Yorkie bar, she thought, waiting for Rajinder to weigh out her potatoes. However, the Royal Mile section of the High Street didn't begin to wake up till at least nine-thirty or ten. Apart from the newsagents, Rajinder's shop was the only one open at eight-thirty. Hardly the hour for a tourist to be wandering the streets, especially if he were based an hour's drive away in Chirnside.

She was tempted to kill time in the supermarket and watch to see what he did but patience had never been her strong point so she chose the alternative of the direct approach. A few sociable words with him of the 'Hello-we-meet-again!' variety would soon tell her whether the encounter was of the third kind or not.

133

Unfortunately, Rajinder was now disposed to be chatty and it was a further two or three minutes before she fought clear, by which time there was no sign of the centurion in any direction. This struck Fizz as even more ominous than if he'd been visible, and she had a momentary impulse to phone Buchanan and apprise him of her suspicions. Only the thought of her nefarious plans for the latter part of the evening stayed her hand. She didn't want Buchanan doing his mother hen act and insisting on sleeping across her doorway armed with a howitzer, as he had been prone to do in the past. Time enough to tell him in the morning, when she would be in the office and would, hopefully, have something more positive to report.

She spent the ten minutes before nine-thirty behind her window, waiting for Gurbachan and sussing out the shop doorways and the dark entrances to the closes. It was still raining intermittently and there were fewer people about than usual so she was able to take time to study those that passed, but she could spot nothing out of the ordinary. Nor, at any point in the journey to Chirnside, could she detect any sign that they were being followed. The roads were not busy enough to provide cover for a vehicle on their tail and after Gurbachan branched off the main drag to take the longer – but, on a motorbike, infinitely more exciting – route over the hills, it was easy to be sure that they had the road more or less to themselves.

Gurbachan was not at all happy to discover, upon arrival, that he was expected to assist in a housebreaking.

'You don't know what my sodding father would do to me if he found out, Fizz! Jesus! He'd have the skin off my back!'

He had lately taken to embellishing his speech with as many swear words as he could fit in, no doubt as some sort of rebellion against his father's autocratic rule and pious rectitude.

'Who's going to tell him?'

'The police, if we're caught! No, Fizz, I'm not bloody doing it.'

'We're not going to be caught, dammit. Look around you, Gurbachan. That house is burned down, that house is empty at the moment, and that one faces in the wrong direction for anyone to spot us. Nobody's likely to come down the road at this hour – it's a dead end. If we take care to be real quiet getting the wood off one of those windows – the one at the back where we'll have the house between us and the Armstrongs' place – nobody's going to know a thing about it. We can put the wood back afterwards and leave no trace of our visit.'

'No,' he said, refusing to get off the bike. 'You don't know my dad, Fizz. It's not worth the risk.'

'Risk? You think I'd be taking chances if I thought there was that much of a risk? If Buchanan gets to hear about this he'll have me strung up at the hatch covers and given three dozen of the cat.'

'That's your worry.'

Fizz took off her helmet and hung it over the handlebars. 'OK. I'll do it myself if I have to, but the least you can do is help me get in.' She reached inside her jacket and brought out the claw hammer and tyre lever she'd borrowed from Mr Auld across the landing. 'It shouldn't take a minute, Gurbachan, and then you can take off somewhere and leave me to nose around for half an hour or so. I'll keep watch while you do it and let you know in good time if anything stirs.'

Gurbachan rolled his eyes and groaned as he strove with the devil but he succumbed at last and accepted the tools Fizz was thrusting at him.

'Just . . . keep your eyes open,' he warned pathetically and skulked into the shadows of Poppy Ford's garden.

Fizz left the bike behind the wall where Gurbachan had parked it and walked a few paces away to where she had a better view of the Armstrong house as well as a prospect of the road in both directions. Nothing stirred. In the distance, the sky above the village was fuzzy with the pale orange haze of streetlights on rain, but only the faint hum of an infrequent vehicle drifted this far. If a car were to come within a mile of where she stood she knew she'd hear it instantly and in plenty of time to warn Gurbachan.

Only one light showed behind the curtains of the Armstrong household but it was at an upstairs window, which was probably a bedroom. That meant they were turning in for the night and, the curtain being already closed, there would be little chance of either of them taking a last look out the window. Even if they did, they'd see nothing: Gurbachan, the motorbike and Fizz herself were all well hidden.

Her skin was buzzing all over with excitement, reminding her of other occasions when she had lurked around in the dark like this, usually for iniquitous reasons like (just the once) digging up a corpse or spying through someone's window. Darkness held no fears for her. Back home, she and her brother had spent many a night in bivvy bags under the stars and she'd always loved the magic of it. It was like being on another planet: one with unfamiliar creatures, strange sounds and smells, and where the sun was just another speck in the Milky Way.

She could detect a discreet tapping coming from the Fords' house as Gurbachan did his dirty work but it was certainly not loud enough to carry to suspicious ears. It was too cold and miserable for anyone to be about and the night sky was still heavy with clouds: just about as good a night for devilry as Fizz could have wished.

Not having a watch, she couldn't determine how long Gurbachan was gone but she was anticipating the imminent onset of gangrene in her toes before he materialised against the gleam of the wet road, panting as if he had just run a marathon and speaking in tongues unintelligible to a well brought up young lady.

'It's open. You're in. I'm off,' he said succinctly, handing the tools to Fizz and throwing himself on to his bike. He freewheeled as far as he could before starting the engine and, a minute later, he had faded from both sight and earshot.

The night closed over Fizz like a blanket.

She took a last careful look around and then wound her way through the dripping bushes to the entrance Gurbachan had left open for her. She didn't dare use her torch but as she got nearer it was easy to pick out the pale oblong of board below the gaping window. She sidled towards it, careful to keep covered from the direction of the Armstrongs' house. There turned out to be a window frame still *in situ* and it was ringed with vicious teeth of glass that would make entry dangerous – and a fast exit even more so. Gingerly, she inserted an arm, loosened the catch, and the frame swung outward.

A noise – something that sounded like metal scraping against stone – abruptly froze her against the wall, jerking both her breathing and her heart to a standstill for the long seconds it took to establish that she was not about to be jumped on. She stayed there, at a crouch, with her eyes at their fullest f-stop as long as she could afford to wait, and then, as certain as she could be that she was alone, she clambered up on to the window sill.

Seconds later, after traversing an unexpected sink, she found herself in a pine-floored kitchen/dining room that, after the pure night air, smelled faintly of cream cleanser and bleach. Her torch showed her a spotless working surface, a pine table and chairs, a kitchen clock (still going) and glass-fronted cabinets full of china and gadgets. If Poppy had known what was about to happen to her husband and herself, the night of the explosion, she could not have left her kitchen tidier. It was like a variation on the change-your-pants-in-case-you-get-hit-by-a-bus theme. Even the glass from the smashed windows had been removed, presumably by whoever had boarded them up.

The living room, which faced the kitchen across an L-shaped passageway, was at the front of the house so she had to draw the heavy velvet curtains before she dared use the torch. It wasn't a big room but it contained, as well as the usual lounge suite etc, a shelved alcove full of books, a bureau, and a modern storage unit, all of which could hold valuable clues.

Before starting a fingertip search she made a quick tour of the upstairs rooms: two bedrooms and a bathroom, all of which were unnaturally tidy, even to the point of fresh towels in the bathroom. It was uncanny. Even in the tidiest house you'd expect to see a pair of shoes peeking out from under the bed, a few newspapers lying around, maybe a coat or something draped over the banisters. But no. This place was so tidy it was scary.

The wind had picked up, confusing her with ambiguous noises that might be either branches tapping against each other or the village bobby hopping in at the kitchen window. She squandered a couple of minutes on checking from every outlook point, just making sure that nobody was creeping around out there, and then headed back downstairs to the ink black living room.

In her imagination, the room felt different. Warmer? Smaller? She couldn't pin down the basis for such a weird impression but her torch showed no visible changes from her previous image of the room so she dismissed it from her mind and got down to work.

Leaving the books till last, since they would take for ever to examine, she let down the lid of the bureau and ran her torch beam along the line of pigeon holes. Every one of them was empty. So, it quickly transpired, were the drawers underneath. Fizz didn't take time to ponder the strangeness of this; she turned immediately to the storage unit, whipping open drawers and cupboards with the speed of a career burglar. It took only a few seconds to establish that it didn't hold so much as a paper clip.

She stood in the middle of the room and thought about it. The place had been sanitised. Not emptied but sanitised. It looked like Poppy, or someone else, had come back and removed everything that might give a clue to her whereabouts. Not taking the trouble to sort out the telltale from the innocuous, but grabbing everything personal as though time was of the essence. She was already sure that, when she explored properly upstairs, she'd find the wardrobes, the airing cupboard, even the bathroom cabinets, as clean as a surgeon's glove.

Now that she thought about it, neither of the two beds upstairs had been slept in. Both were made up with crisp duvet covers, the pillows propped up to display their lacy trims, and yet the explosion had happened in the early hours of the morning when Poppy would, supposedly, have been asleep in bed. Shocked and cut by flying glass, Fizz could hardly see her nipping back home to plump up the cushions before being carted away to hospital.

She went over every room in the house, scrutinising every empty drawer, running her fingers over the bottom of the cupboards, hoping that, against all the odds and in spite of all the sanitising, some small clue to Poppy's whereabouts might have been overlooked. But whoever had done the job had done it properly. She didn't even find a trace of dust.

There was no food in the kitchen, not even ice cubes in the fridge. The glassware in the cupboards was so shiny it looked like even the fingerprints had been removed. There was nothing that could be construed as pertaining to a cat, neither dish nor bed nor toy, and the only sign of previous occupancy was a half empty container of washing-up liquid beside the sink.

That left the books. She was already running short of time and there were upwards of fifty paperbacks on the shelves, but she had found books to be enlightening in the past, and not just because of their literary content. Either Poppy or her husband had been a fan of science fiction: more than half the books were of that genre and the others were an assortment of romances, historical fiction and family sagas.

Each row was neatly lined up at the front of its shelf, leaving a four inch gap at the back, but there was nothing hidden in the gap. Every shelf was the same but the arrangement, Fizz guessed, was probably so that Poppy could push them back, dust the front of the shelf and then bring them forward again. She lifted each book in turn to check that there was nothing underneath and then dashed into the kitchen to check her time. She was already ten minutes over her time limit. She knew Gurbachan was out there, probably swearing like a sailor's parrot with Tourette's syndrome, but she couldn't leave without searching the books.

Working at the speed of light, she whipped the books off the shelves and checked them for inscriptions, giving them a good shake to dislodge anything stuck between the pages before replacing them as found. Shelf one revealed nothing. Shelf two revealed nothing. She was three quarters of the way through shelf three when she heard a noise behind her.

Sweat burst out all over her like a dose of chicken pox. She switched off her torch and listened, her mouth ajar and her eyes popping. A second later it came again – a kind of hiss that identified itself to her as escaping gas. The thought exploded in her head like Brora Lodge. *Gas!*

For a moment the terror filled her so completely that she couldn't move, couldn't think, couldn't access any of her senses. Then, in the instant her adrenalin kicked in, she heard it a third time.

'Sssssssssssss.'

Her legs thrashed, carrying her across the passageway into the kitchen at a speed that would have left a bat out of Hell standing. At one microsecond during her progress she saw the silhouette of a man at the window but she was nose to nose with him before the sight had travelled the length of her optic nerve to her brain.

'For fuck's sake,' he hissed, sounding suspiciously like the supposed gas leak. 'I've been a sodding hour out there. I'm going.'

Fizz could have felled him for scaring her like that. She looked longingly at the hammer in her hand, took three deep breaths, and confined her response to teaching him a few new phrases that virtually blew his hair back.

'Christ!' he muttered and fell back to lick his wounds, while Fizz considered her options. There were still books to look at, she reflected, but it was unlikely that they'd hold any more information than the others had and, besides, her nerve was completely blown. She didn't even want to go back into the living room but she couldn't risk leaving any signs of her presence.

'Two minutes,' she said. 'I have to tidy up and go to the loo.'

'A second longer and I'll be gone,' gritted Gurbachan, who had recovered his aplomb and, with it, the fear of his father's wrath.

Fizz gave him the finger and ran upstairs to take care of the most urgent of her tasks.

The expedition had not been the success she had hoped for, she thought as she sat there, but neither had it been a total waste of time. It proved there was a suspicious amount of organisation surrounding Poppy's disappearance. Either she had been ready for the explosion – a contingency which carried several intriguing possibilities – or she had covered her trail pretty damn quick.

The problem this presented was: how to pass this intelligence on to Buchanan without admitting to a degree of meddling beyond the call of duty?

Chapter Twelve

It had rained all day Sunday and, although Buchanan had persisted in playing eighteen holes in the afternoon, he felt somewhat defeated to see the brilliant sunshine that greeted him on Monday morning. It streamed in the living room window, etching bright oblongs on the carpet and on Selina who chose to sunbathe there, just where Buchanan would trip over her every time he came out of the kitchen.

On the way to work he noticed, for the first time, that crocuses were in full bloom everywhere and the green spikes of daffodils were already four inches high in the tubs and window boxes. Spring was bustin' out all over and here he was, or would be in a minute or two, stuck in a gloomy office till the sun went down.

In fact, the office wasn't at all gloomy. The high Georgian windows looked straight up George Street and got all the light that was going, but that didn't affect the principle. People like Fizz seemed to be able to get out and about at odd times throughout the day: commuting between home and office, library and college, and still managing to fit in the occasional sortie to see people who might help them with inquiries, all without doing any harm to her grades.

She never took public transport if she could avoid it: too miserly, probably. Her Doc Martens were her preferred mode of transport and she'd be marching into the office at any minute, rosy-cheeked and smelling of ozone and filling Buchanan with a pernicious envy.

He couldn't face getting behind his desk but stood at the window reading his mail between intervals of staring out at luckier people. He saw Fizz come striding down George Street at five-to-nine with her arms swinging and her hair jiggling, the Oxfam coat she'd been wearing for the past two winters flapping behind her like Superman's cape. A cross between a Munchkin and a Sherman tank. You had to smile.

He could hear the faint stir of her arrival in the front office, a burst of chattering, a shriek of laughter and, for some reason, the sound lightened his mood and let him get on with his work. Three minutes later she was bursting into his office, her entry concomitant with her knock.

'Buenos días, amigo,' she said, assaulting the spare chair with her behind. 'How's it going?'

Buchanan threw his pen on top of his papers and yawned. 'Can't get started this morning.'

'Late nights, huh?'

'I should be so lucky. What about you? What sort of a Sunday did you have?'

If she'd been seeing Giles, Buchanan didn't really want to know about it but he couldn't resist asking. He needn't have worried, she was as evasive as ever.

'Oh, just the usual quiet Sunday: church in the morning, bible class in the afternoon, evensong in the evening, a little ram-raiding, a few lagers with the boys, a bit of a punch-up outside the pub and a night in a police cell. Same old routine. Heard anything from Giles?'

'Not yet. I expect he'll touch base this morning if he has anything to report.'

She shoogled her chair round and swung her Doc's up on to the corner of his desk. 'Well, whether he has or not, I certainly have. I think I'm being followed.'

Buchanan felt squeamish with shock. Fizz's safety had always been of the utmost importance to him but, since the attack that had left a permanent scar across her eyebrow, remarks like this tended to push him one step closer to neurosis. He put his elbows on the table and held his head for a minute.

'I could be wrong,' she said cheerfully. 'It could be pure coincidence, but I saw that guy again – the one I spoke to in the Chirnside Hall Hotel the other night, remember?'

'The guy in the cocktail bar?'

'Uh-huh. I'd seen him before that night – that's why I spoke to him – but I'm damned if I can remember where. About Chirnside, I think.' She smiled at him in a half amused, half reassuring way, and re-crossed her ankles. 'Then, on Saturday, when I was in that convenience store across the road – y'know? – there he was again, in a shop doorway, looking at postcards. But, like I said, it could have been a coincidence.'

It wasn't a coincidence. She knew that and Buchanan knew that. She had told him so often that coincidences were figments of the imagination that he had come to believe her. Crossing the guy's path twice – that was a fluke: crossing it three times, especially in two widely spaced locations, definitely stretched credulity. Furthermore, his recollection of the chap in the cocktail bar classed him as just the sort of character he didn't want anywhere near Fizz. Even at the time, with Giles and himself virtually at her elbow, he had been uneasy to see her laughing up into his lived-in face so trustingly and the very idea of such a thug (he was sure the guy was a thug) finding out where she lived was doing his head in.

'You'd better move out right away,' he told her firmly. 'Is there anyone you can crash with for a few days?'

Fizz gave a little spurt of laughter. 'You don't have to throw a wobbly, Buchanan. At the very worst he's only following me. If he wanted to do me any harm he'd have done it before now. He's had ample opportunity.'

'So, why's he following you?'

'You tell *me*.'

'Not for his own ends,' Buchanan hazarded. He noticed his fingers drumming on the desk and gave them a pen to play with. 'More likely somebody's paying him to do it.'

'You think he's a private detective.'

'It's possible. I wouldn't be surprised.'

'Oh shit.' Fizz lost her *joie de vivre* in an instant, thudded her boots to the floor and stared at him in open consternation. 'I know what you're thinking. Friggin' Grassick, right?'

Buchanan ground his teeth. 'I hope not, Fizz. God, I hope not but it's the sort of thing he'd do, there's no doubt about it. He must have had me watched and I led his bloodhound to you. Why didn't I guess he'd do something like this?'

Fizz was on her feet, pacing about the room, punching things and chain-swearing. Buchanan knew how she felt. How often had he told himself that his association with Fizz was guaranteed to end in disaster for at least one of them, if not both. This was the nightmare scenario he'd been predicting for years but it was a surprise to discover that it was the snuffing of Fizz's bright future that he regretted rather than the dimming of his own.

'OK,' Fizz said, after a while. She tidied her hair, which had sprouted a thousand excited tendrils, and set her hands on her hips. 'If Grassick already knows about my involvement the damage is done. There's nothing we can do about that and, anyway, how much harm can he do me? I always know that I can rely on Buchanan and Stewart to employ me even if nobody else will. Right?'

'Right,' Buchanan felt safe enough in saying, since he could hardly let her starve. If the worst came to the worst Dennis would desert the sinking ship without a backward glance and would have to be replaced. Alan Stewart, who had been his father's partner for thirty-odd years, might even take early retirement rather than tarnish his professional reputation by association with one accursed. Buchanan and Stewart wouldn't exactly be the first choice of employer for well qualified legal practitioners, so the chances were that Fizz would be the best he could hope for.

'Right,' she agreed, looking grim and determined but also unaccountably smug. 'However, the fact that Grassick is paying a detective to trail us must mean that he's running scared. He has something to hide, Buchanan – got to have – otherwise why is he so worried about what we might uncover? It doesn't have to be his wife's murder but it's something really really serious, right?'

'I imagine so.' Buchanan could see where this was going but he let her run with it.

'So, that's our ace. Our only chance is to find out what it is that he wants to keep hidden and use it to blackmail him with.'

Buchanan found this proposal less than cheering since (a) it was only another name for what they'd been trying to do all along and (b) blackmail was simply not his bag. And, for that matter, (c) it would be a brave man who tried to blackmail Ghengis Grassick.

'Tell me about the guy who was following you,' he said to change the subject. 'You spoke to him. Did you discover anything about him?'

'All lies, I suspect,' she said, coming back to her chair, and thudding her feet back up on to his desk. 'He told me he was on a fishing holiday but that was about all. It was like squeezing blood out of a stone. I thought he was just a little short on social skills but, of course, he must have been horrified at my spotting him.'

'Did you tell him you'd seen him before?'

Fizz sniggered. 'I did. I bet he was thoroughly cheesed off about it. He pretended he didn't have a clue what I was talking about and, frankly, I didn't think any more about him. I'd sort of hoped he might be a local and could fill me in about the hearsay in Chirnside since the explosion, but he was a dead loss. Naturally.' She tucked a curl behind her ear. 'I'll tell you what, though: either he's a brilliant actor or he has the mental capacity of a mayfly. So, if Grassick is paying him any more than fifty pence an hour he's being ripped off.'

As far as Buchanan was concerned either possibility was equally likely. Grassick could afford the best and the best would certainly be capable of acting dumb to put Fizz off the scent – as she *had* been. The deciding factor would be whether they could now succeed in losing him.

For the past few minutes he had been slowly working his way towards a decision. Obviously, he couldn't let Fizz go home to her flat tonight. It might not give her a moment's uneasiness to know that she was being watched but Buchanan knew he, personally, wouldn't shut an eye. Even if she had someone she could crash with, and he wasn't at all sure she had, she wouldn't dream of going into hiding. However, if they were out late together, she might consider staying over at his place.

'Grassick is speaking at the Central Library tonight,' he said. 'I saw it advertised in the *Scotsman*. It's a political talk but I thought it could be quite informative to find out more about that side of his life.'

Fizz looked less than thrilled to bits at this prospect. 'Politics bores me to death and politicians are the pits.'

'It's only a one-hour talk. You might find it interesting.'

'No thanks,' she said politely. 'If I wanted to listen to an arsehole I'd fart.'

Buchanan winced, as she'd intended him to, but answered her with nothing more than a look because the telephone rang. It was Giles.

'Anything new?' Buchanan asked him quickly, before he found himself having to answer that question himself. He had made virtually no progress over the weekend, not on the Grassick case, and he wanted to postpone sharing the news about Fizz's stalker until she wasn't sitting there listening to him.

'Not a lot,' Giles admitted. 'I've been checking up on the Grassicks' gas supplies this morning. I started wondering how much gas it would take to cause the destruction of a house like Brora Lodge and it seemed to me that the devastation was a lot more widespread than you'd expect from the normal week-to-week supply. I haven't got around to establishing whether that's true or not just yet but I did locate the Grassicks' supplier in Chirnside. It turned out that they'd been getting through more than usual over the last few weeks.'

'You think Grassick could have been stockpiling it?' Buchanan suggested. 'When you said they'd ordered more than normal, d'you mean they'd bought more than would be accounted for by the bad weather we've been having?'

Giles drew a thoughtful breath. 'It's difficult to be sure because there's nobody around who can tell me how often they stayed at Brora Lodge over the last few weeks. The Armstrongs never seem to notice anything and, of course, the Pringles are not returning calls. However the Grassicks' order changed from eleven kilogram cylinders to fifteen kilogram cylinders last time round which may be circumstantial to you but, to me, seems pretty conclusive.'

Buchanan was inclined to agree. He glanced at Fizz's alert face and took a desperate step. 'I'm going to hear Grassick speak at the Assembly Rooms tonight,' he told Giles. 'It's some sort of debate, I think, but I've been wondering about the political side of his life for a few days. It seems a bit extreme, I know, but his wife could have been murdered as a warning to him, or to bring pressure to bear. I think it merits an hour's research, anyway.'

'So do I,' Giles responded right away. 'I'll come with you – if that's all right with you?'

'Absolutely. I'll wait for you in the foyer. Seven-forty-five.'

Buchanan was not surprised by Giles's interest, nor by the rapidity with which Fizz changed her mind and decided that she did want to listen to an arsehole after all.

Fizz was already regretting telling Buchanan about her stalker. OK, she'd had no choice but to mention her suspicions but maybe she could have played them down a bit and saved herself the irritation of his paranoia.

He was trying to play it cool, of course, but she wasn't deceived by his sudden wish to be in her company. In fact, she had him sussed from the instant he suggested – oh, so indifferently – that it was scarcely worth her while to go home after work when they could share a carry-out at his place and go straight to the Assembly Rooms from there. It wasn't that she had anything against this arrangement, since it involved free food, but she did wonder what his plans were for later in the evening when, presumably, the centurion would still be *in situ*. It would be interesting to find out.

Giles met them in the entrance lobby, scrummy as ever, and gave her a quick hug and a kiss on the cheek in greeting. 'Brilliant venue,' he commented, rolling his eyes at the plate-glass mirrors and chandeliers.

'Haven't you been here before?' Buchanan asked.

'Once. I saw Julian Clary here, during the Edinburgh Festival. It was many years ago when he was "The Joan Collins Fan Club".'

Buchanan smiled. 'There are several differently sized meeting rooms. I'm just counting on the political meeting being held in one big enough to let us lose ourselves in the crowd. I don't particularly want to catch Grassick's eye.'

'In that case,' Fizz said, seizing the moment, 'you and I shouldn't take the risk of sitting together. I'll sit with Giles and you can—'

'No,' Buchanan said blandly. 'I think it would be better if Giles and I were to sit together. Just a row or two away. If you wouldn't mind being on your own, Fizz, there are one or two points I'd like to bring up with Giles while I have the opportunity. It would save a lot of time later.'

Fizz minded like hell since sitting next to Giles was precisely what she was here for but she would look pretty naff if she insisted on it. She might not be gagging to leap into bed with the guy, but she liked to keep her options open. It was small comfort to note that Giles was a tiny bit miffed as well.

'I hope we'll have time for a drink or a coffee afterwards,' he said. 'I don't know why it is, but I find discussing my problems with both of you helps to straighten out my thoughts on this business. I must come to a decision soon on whether to authorise the payout or not. I've already swung it longer that I should have – but I can't see any way forward.'

'Tell me about it,' said Buchanan tersely. 'I planned to spend a couple of days on this inquiry and it has dragged on for over a week already. We'll get ourselves a quiet table somewhere after the meeting and do some brainstorming.'

That suited Fizz fine since it left her free to have an hour's doze while the debate went on, which she couldn't have done had Giles been with her. She had no interest in hearing what either of the factions had to say, her sole experience of politics being tainted by reluctant association with a friend's husband, back in Am Bealach. It was, nonetheless, interesting to see Ghengis Grassick in the flesh.

It came as something of a surprise to find that he was not the beetle-browed, blackavised ogre painted, subconsciously, by her imagination but actually quite handsome, in a horsey sort of way. His nose was too big and his cheekbones too pronounced but he had a fine head on a strong neck that would look good cast in bronze. He sat immobile and withdrawn while the chairman introduced the panel of four speakers, none of them professional politicians but leading figures in medicine, social services, law and the media.

The first subject to come under discussion was anti-abortion legislation and since Fizz already knew where she stood on that she stretched out her legs, crossed her ankles and her arms and composed herself for a period of rapid eye movement. Normally she was able to black out anywhere, any time, in seconds but the first speaker had a particularly raucous voice and, although she agreed with every word the woman said – about women having the right to choose etc – the irritation to her eardrums kept jerking her back to consciousness.

The second speaker took the medical viewpoint which swayed Fizz not at all and she was just drifting into nirvana when another voice took over – a deep and powerful voice that compelled her attention – and started to say things that made her open her eyes and sit up. It was Lawrence Grassick, of course, and he was saying things that Fizz had heard before but in a way that made her distinctly uncomfortable.

He spoke, not on the legal aspect of the subject, but on the moral perspective and the psychological effect of abortion on the mother. His manner was neither bombastic nor dogmatic – in fact he was much less passionate than the previous speaker – but he put his argument across in a quietly compelling manner that had Fizz considering – *really* considering, for the first time – the points he made.

You could see he really meant what he was saying but that he was bending over backwards to see the opposition's point of view. Abortion was perfectly acceptable, he argued, where the mother's mental or physical health would otherwise be endangered, but the murdering of a foetus should never be considered as a form of contraception like the morning after pill. He spoke sensibly and unemotionally about the risks to a mother's mental health inherent in her decision to kill her child – or to refuse it life – and held calmly to his point of view throughout the free-for-all that ensued.

Fizz was not only hugely impressed but so fired up that, had it not been necessary to maintain her incognito status, she'd have been on her feet putting in her ten pence worth. It was infinitely more enjoyable than the debating society at the uni, which she also quite enjoyed, and went straight down on her list as one of the best free entertainments the city had to offer.

She found Buchanan and Giles in the entrance lobby, talking to a suit with a moustache, but the group broke up just as she joined them.

'Who was that?' she asked Buchanan.

'Phil Reece-Williams. He's a member of the Labour faction in the council.' Buchanan touched her elbow and pointed her towards the door. 'I was picking his brains about what committees Grassick was on but he had nothing interesting to tell me. He doesn't know of any crucial decisions that Grassick might be able to sway – nothing, by implication, that might be worth blackmailing him for.'

'Back to the drawing board,' Giles said, taking her other arm and giving it a brief but promising squeeze. 'One step forward and another step back.'

They headed for the nearest watering place, a hotel lounge half a block away, and installed themselves in a corner with a pot of coffee and, because Fizz's Chinese carry-out had scarcely registered on her appetite, a selection of fancy muffins.

'You said earlier that you were hoping to waylay the postman,' Buchanan said to Giles. 'Did you have any luck?'

'Lenny. Yes, I spoke to him,' Giles nodded, 'but he was in a bit of a hurry and wasn't willing to give me a lot of time. Apparently Vanessa Grassick rarely spent time at Brora Lodge during the winter months and Lawrence only used it intermittently. If he had work that he needed peace to concentrate on he'd take it to the cottage, usually at weekends but occasionally midweek as well. He'd been using the cottage every weekend for at least a month, if Lenny's memory is correct but, of course, he has no idea what project Grassick might have been working on.'

'Probably not a political one,' Buchanan surmised, 'judging by what Reece-Williams just said. And, if it's a legal project, it's not one that's on his calendar, that much I do know.'

'So, where does that leave us?' Fizz snapped, still suffering the traces of belligerence she'd had to suppress at the debate. 'He could be writing a book, for God's sake, or studying Sanskrit. There's no way we're going to find out what he was up to.'

Buchanan stirred his coffee thoughtfully. 'Not unless Vanessa knew what he was doing and mentioned it to Rudyard. Maybe we should pay him another visit.'

'I'll do it,' Fizz said. 'I want to see that guy for myself.'

She had half hoped that Giles would offer to accompany her but he wasn't in favour of overkill. The look in Buchanan's eye, however, told her that it would be a long time before she went anywhere without him.

Chapter Thirteen

Buchanan was bored out of his skull by the time he got rid of Giles. The three of them had stayed sitting there at their table reviewing evidence, tossing around possibilities and cudgelling their brains until gone eleven. Quite unnecessary and, as it turned out, a complete waste of time.

Of course, wasting time was the whole point of the exercise, as far as Buchanan was concerned because the later they parted, the more convincingly he could persuade Fizz of the advisability of staying overnight at his place. He had anticipated that either Fizz or Giles would initiate the close of business, but it was clear from the outset that they viewed the discussion as merely an excuse to enjoy each other's company and, for all he knew, play footsie under the table.

'Well, I have to admit I enjoyed that more than I'd expected to,' Fizz announced when they got back to the car.

Buchanan, having decided to make no mention of her obvious approval of Giles, replied rather dryly, 'Yes. I noticed.'

She turned her head and regarded him at her leisure for several seconds. He immediately regretted his stupidity and braced himself for the put-down he deserved, but all she said was, 'No, I'm talking about the debate. Ghengis is a powerful speaker, isn't he? It makes it all the more surprising that he has such a short temper. I mean, you'd imagine he'd be able to put his point across convincingly, during a disagreement, without getting all frustrated and losing the place.'

'Lack of vocabulary is one reason for tantrums,' Buchanan agreed, dawdling his way along George Street on a route that could be construed as leading to both their places of residence, 'but it pre-supposes an audience of equal intelligence to the speaker. I imagine super-intelligent people like Grassick get easily frustrated by stupidity.'

Fizz looked out at the virtually empty street. 'You'd have been quicker going the other way and up the Mound,' she pointed out.

'That's true.' Buchanan tried to sound as if he hadn't thought of that but knew right away that she was on to him and decided to come clean. 'I was about to suggest that you crash at my place tonight. It's pretty late and . . . to be honest . . . I . . .'

'If I were stolen away for the white slave traffic you'd feel guilty for wishing it on me so often. Am I right?'

'Only partly,' he said virtuously. 'The main reason being that I have evil designs on you and plan to slip you a shot of my mother's elderflower wine and ruin your reputation.'

'Hm. Is that your final offer?'

'Glenmorangie?'

'You interest me strangely. Can I have the bed?'

'Gad, you drive a hard bargain, woman!'

'Okay. Keep your pest of a moggie away from me and you've got a deal.'

Relief made Buchanan generous. He encouraged her to indulge herself with a long bath while he made up a bed for himself on the couch and then shared a considerable amount of his malt whisky with her while she dried her hair. His feelings, as he watched her sitting on the floor in his bathrobe fluffing up her ringlets, he put down to the effects of alcohol and drowned them in another dram which was enough to give him a good night's sleep.

Fizz was already up and about when he awoke. He could smell the coffee she'd made and hear Selina complaining about being shut into her travelling basket for the night. When he staggered into the kitchen, there was Fizz at the table surrounded by the makings of a hearty breakfast and reading his paper. She eyed him critically.

'You should stay off the liquor, Buchanan. You don't have the constitution for it.'

Buchanan grunted and reached for the coffee pot. In another half-hour, after he'd showered and shaved and disposed of the rest of the coffee, he might feel like conversing, but seven-thirty in the morning was no time for social intercourse. Fortunately Fizz was more interested in the morning's news and he heard nothing further from her than a sound of munching coming from behind the *Scotsman*.

She left for the office before Buchanan because, she said, she wanted to walk. This was completely in character because it was a beautiful morning again and the office was only ten minutes away, but Buchanan wondered if she was also being diplomatic. If they arrived for work together just once every member of staff would be aware of it and the obvious conclusions would be drawn. It was a pity, because he was tempted to walk with her but, he reasoned, he needed the car at the office in case he had to go out during the day.

It didn't occur to him till he was locking the garage door that Fizz's follower could have been waiting for her to emerge. Obviously, if the guy had traced her through her association with Buchanan himself he would look here for her as soon as he lost her trail back at her flat.

Cursing his stupidity, he jumped in the car and pushed his luck all the way to the office in the hope of catching her up. However, he saw no trace of her until he got there and found her happily keeping Beatrice off her work with a report on last night's political debate. He gave them both an equivocal greeting, carefully avoiding any allusion to the fact that he'd already seen Fizz that morning, and got on with his morning's work.

Because Fizz now worked flexitime, fitting in her hours between her lectures and tutorials, he was never certain whether she was in the office or not. It would be just like her, he suspected, to scoot off for a meeting with Joseph Rudyard without warning him she was going and to claim, later, that he had okayed her going alone. This made him so uneasy that he was forced to visit her hideout in the filing room and .point out to her that he intended to accompany her. She raised no objection, merely commenting that she had expected nothing better of him, and duly presented herself at his desk at three in the afternoon, raring to go.

They found Rudyard in the same kind of mess Buchanan had noted on his last visit. The passageway to his office was lined with rolls of paper and the sunbeams that fanned in at his grimy window illuminated a fog of dust particles and an amazing assortment of spiders' webs. Rudyard dusted off chairs for his visitors and made apologetic noises which Fizz received with a bright smile.

'The maid's day off?' she inquired politely, almost causing Rudyard to twitch his lips.

'You're still sorting out the snags in Vanessa's will, then?' he whined, slouching listlessly behind his littered desk.

'I'm afraid so,' said Buchanan. 'Just one or two loose ends I'd like to see tied up before I finalise matters. I don't anticipate it taking me more than a few days.'

'No rush.' His eyes were compulsively drawn to Fizz's golden halo which was illuminated by the sunlight behind her and he seemed infinitely more interested in the sight than in anything Buchanan had to say. Fizz, meanwhile, returned his regard with a hundred-yard stare as though she were reading a billboard in the distance behind his head. Buchanan held his tongue, letting the silence lengthen until Rudyard noticed it, blinked, and said, 'What was it you wanted to ask me?'

'I just wondered,' Buchanan said, 'if you might remember Vanessa saying anything about what her husband was working on just before the accident. It's my understanding that Mr Grassick was in the habit of escaping to Brora Lodge when he had important work that he needed to concentrate on, and I've recently learned that he had spent the previous three weekends there. It would be an enormous help if we could discover what was taking him there.'

Rudyard couldn't be bothered thinking about it. He fingered his earring and sighed. 'You should ask Grassick.'

'But he might not tell us,' Fizz put in with a mischievous, nudge-nudge-wink-wink sort of look.

'Not if he was meeting a woman, no, I don't suppose he would. But I wouldn't be likely to know about that, would I? It's not something Vanessa would talk about to me.'

'And what about work?' Fizz persisted. 'Did Vanessa mention anything about Lawrence working at the cottage that weekend?'

'Um . . .' Rudyard passed a hand over his smooth hair and blinked at an unhelpful pot of poster colour on the window sill. 'She may have said he was going down to the cottage but I don't remember her mentioning why he was going.'

'When was this?' Fizz said. 'The week before she died or previous to that?'

'Ah . . . I think it must have been some time that week . . . maybe the Monday . . . or maybe even the end of the previous week. Actually, I think he spent both weekends at Brora Lodge.'

'Can't you be sure?' Fizz's voice was showing just a trace of impatience.

'Not a hundred per cent,' Rudyard apologised, his nasal whine becoming even more pronounced. 'But I'm fairly sure he was there that weekend.'

Buchanan nodded in an encouraging manner. 'That's very interesting, Mr Rudyard,' he said. He had already known that had to be the case but he forced himself to be interested in hearing his suspicions confirmed so that he wouldn't be lying. 'And, I take it, Mrs Grassick was not averse to spending her weekends on her own?'

'She never said so to me,' Rudyard had gone back to studying Fizz's hair and could spare Buchanan only a flick of his eyes. 'She liked being on her own in the house. Liked the silence. She said *that* often enough. 'That's why they had no family. All she needed was her business and her painting and her garden.'

'She painted?' Buchanan asked, wondering why this had never been mentioned before.

'Daubed, that's all.' His mournful eyes took on a sly look and there was a hint of spite in his tone of voice. 'Her draughtsmanship was reasonable but, she admitted it herself, she wasn't really the creative type. It was just a hobby with Vanessa. She did some watercolours of the hills around Chirnside but she didn't usually go down there at all in the winter. It was Lawrence's scene much more than it ever was hers. I guess she only went with him in summertime for the look of things. Very keen on the look of things, Lawrence was.'

Fizz appeared to resist a shudder. Her eyes fell away from Rudyard's face and returned to it, after a moment, only with obvious reluctance. 'So, her visit to the cottage the night she was killed . . . it must have struck you as peculiar.'

Rudyard merely looked put upon. Evidently the stress of searching his short-term memory was beginning to weigh on him.

Fizz stood up in a sudden movement that startled him, and began to walk around the walls looking at their covering of postcards, photographs and cuttings. 'Surely you must have thought about it, Mr Rudyard?' She spun round to fix him with a frown. 'Why was Vanessa at Brora Lodge that night? Did she accompany her husband? If so, where was Lawrence when the bomb went off?'

It should have been the funniest thing since Buster Keaton but, in an odd way, it didn't look at all melodramatic. She wasn't acting. She just wanted to know.

Rudyard watched her warily. 'I thought about it but . . . yes, I suppose it was a little unusual, but she didn't always tell me when she was going to be there over the weekend. Maybe she decided, on the spur of the moment, to go with Lawrence.'

'That seems the most likely explanation,' Buchanan said. It *was* the most likely explanation, but that was because it was the *only* one. The weather over that weekend had been atrocious: certainly not the weather to tempt Vanessa from the comfort of her luxurious Edinburgh home.

Rudyard was chewing at the corner of his bottom lip, so obviously gearing himself up to say something that even Fizz noticed and waited silently for him to get it out. Finally, he lifted his head and, wearing the expression of a whipped hound, he said, 'Actually, she had planned to be in Inverness most of the weekend. She told me she was driving up on Friday morning, seeing some customers in the after-noon, and staying Friday and Saturday night with friends.'

'What friends?' said Fizz. 'What customers?'

'She didn't say.'

'What customers do you *have* in Inverness?'

For a moment Buchanan thought this was one question too many for Rudyard. He pressed his lips together and tucked in the corners of his mouth in a sullen expression but finally he succumbed to Fizz's encouraging stare. Taking his time to it, he spun his chair around to face a pile of junk behind him and, after throwing a leather jacket and a roll of shiny paper to the floor, revealed a computer. It took him only a few seconds to access a half page of addresses which, with a languid wave, he invited Fizz to copy down.

Buchanan watched her scribbling a while and then said, 'I take it that Vanessa didn't inform you of her change of plans?'

Rudyard shook his head. 'I didn't know she'd come back early till Lawrence phoned to tell me about the explosion.'

'What did you think when you heard she'd turned up at the cottage in the early hours of Saturday morning?' Fizz said softly, over her shoulder.

He looked at her back with an expression that could only be described as a sneer. 'I thought what you're thinking,' he said unpleasantly. 'I thought she'd gone there in the middle of the night expecting to find him shacked up with another woman.'

'Did she ever hint to you that she suspected her husband was being unfaithful?' Buchanan asked.

'No, but if I'd been Vanessa, I'd sure as hell have been wondering what he got up to in Chirnside every weekend, wouldn't you?'

'And if she had caught him out,' Fizz prompted, still scribbling in her notebook, 'what would have been her response? Would she have divorced him? Or was she the type to forgive and forget?'

But Rudyard had exhausted his meagre store of benevolence and didn't care to exert his grey cells any further. All further questions were met with a shrug and an apathetic refusal to speculate so Buchanan gave up on him and kept any further questioning for another visit.

'You looked as if you were enjoying that little *tête-à-tête*,' he teased Fizz on the way downstairs and she answered by miming a retch.

'That guy is the pits,' she muttered, casting a wary glance up the stairwell to make sure he wasn't listening. 'He's what Doctor Spooner would have called a "shining wit". I know you said he was no ray of sunshine but – bloody hell! – how can his staff suffer him day in day out? He'd depress a laughing hyena.'

'Takes all kinds to make a world,' Buchanan couldn't resist saying, since that was the phrase she invariably quoted when introducing him to her bizarre friends. She was not amused.

'I'm going home,' she announced when they got back to the car. 'I don't give a hoot if Grassick is having me watched. I'm not likely to be doing anything that he doesn't already know about and, anyway, I've got work to do.'

'I don't think that's a good idea,' Buchanan started to say but she wasn't having any.

'No, I didn't expect you would, but you always were an old fusspot. I don't plan on going out tonight and, if it makes you any happier, you can see me safely to my door. Once I'm home there'll be two locked doors between me and the world and you won't catch me unlocking either of them.'

'One of the other neighbours could accidentally leave the staircase door open—'

'It swings shut and locks by itself, Buchanan. You know that perfectly well.'

No matter how assiduously he ground his teeth Buchanan could find no argument that would weigh with her. He had to conduct her down the dark entry that led to her flat and up the hundred stairs to her door, stand on the landing till he heard her bolt click and her safety chain rattle, and then sit for twenty minutes in his car with his eyes peeled to make sure no-one was hanging around outside. He would, he knew, suffer the lash of anxiety until he picked her up the following morning but there was nothing he could do about that. A stake-out was out of the question in the centre of town. He wouldn't be allowed to park his car in the Royal Mile all night and he could scarcely pace up and down for long without risking hypothermia.

He was almost back home when it suddenly occurred to him that there was, however, good old Ian Fleming. The local bobbies would be unwilling to give Fizz police protection but Ian could – and probably would – arrange to have someone keep an eye on her, if only for the opportunity to have her 'centurion' picked up and questioned. Accordingly, he got on the blower before he even took his coat off.

'Ian? Tam Buchanan here. Listen, I need you to do something for me.'

'Uh-huh? So what else is new?'

'Listen, Ian, Fizz is being followed. I need—'

'Who by?' Fleming interrupted in a changed tone.

'We don't know who the guy is – a private detective, most likely, and if so I reckon he must be working for Lawrence Grassick.' Buchanan took the time to draw a breath and remove Selina from his collar. 'Fizz spotted him a couple of times around Chirnside but she didn't suspect anything till she caught sight of him close to her flat yesterday.'

'She's sure it's not a coincidence?'

Buchanan hesitated. 'It could be, Ian, but you know Fizz. She's not the imaginative type. I don't think she's exaggerating.'

'It's not all that unusual for people who've been beaten up like Fizz was to start suspecting that everyone who looks at them—'

'No. It's not like that,' Buchanan said impatiently. 'Fizz is not in the least worried by this guy, it's me who's worried. After what happened to her—' Realising what he was saying, he broke off and forced a laugh. 'And don't start insinuating that it's me who's becoming neurotic!'

'Tam, you've never been anything else. What do you want me to do with the stalker? Run him in or have him followed to see if he leads us to Grassick?'

'Run him in,' Buchanan said, removing Selina from his collar again, and then thought about it. 'No, hang on a minute. It would be better to see who he reports to if we can. The chances are he'll report to Grassick, and it won't do us any good to learn that because Grassick might have a good excuse for wanting to know what we're up to. But, on the other hand, he may report to someone else, and that *would* be interesting.'

'Exactly my thinking. Okay. So what does he look like?'

Buchanan dredged his memory for details of the man he'd seen only once, and from the rear, and added them to Fizz's description to give a fairly comprehensive profile.

'Okay. Leave it with me. I'll give you a ring when I have anything to report. How's the inquiry going? Are you getting anywhere?'

Buchanan found he was unable to answer either yes or no with complete confidence. Sometimes he felt he was on the point of a breakthrough and at other times he felt totally disillusioned with the whole business. 'To be honest with you, Ian, my brain's like tapioca tonight. I need to sit down with a pencil and paper and try to make some sense out of a welter of unconnected facts.'

'Tell me about it,' Fleming said with a smile in his voice. 'I've got a raft of cases like that on my desk right now and not one of them moving forward. No wonder I'm losing my hair.'

Buchanan disengaged Selina from his collar and held her in one hand while he kicked off his shoes. 'Just one thing before you go, Ian. Have you any idea where Lawrence Grassick was on the night of the explosion?'

'I seem to remember he was at home in Edinburgh. Is there a problem?'

'Not really, but I believe it was his intention to go down to the cottage that weekend. At least, that's what his wife believed. He does have an alibi, I suppose?'

There was a silence at the other end of the line during which Buchanan could hear his clock ticking. He held Selina on his knee and scratched her cheek to keep her there.

'Now, that's something I didn't check,' Fleming said slowly. 'I'd imagine he must have had an alibi of some sort but I'll look into it and get back to you. Probably tomorrow.'

'Cheers, Ian.'

Buchanan put the phone back on its rest and sat drumming his fingers on it and wondering where the hell he was going, and what the hell he would find when he got there.

Chapter Fourteen

Fizz had no objection to being picked up and driven to work by Buchanan. The morning was sunny enough but there was a bitterly cold east wind whipping in across the North Sea and the walk across town would not have been an undiluted pleasure.

She waited at the window till she saw his Saab rounding the corner from North Bridge and then scooted downstairs before a traffic warden could get to him. As she emerged from the end of the close he was, for some strange reason, just getting back into the car. He could have been cleaning the windscreen or doing something esoteric with the engine for all Fizz knew or cared, but there was something about the speed of his movement and the way he seemed to be watching for her approach that was, ever so slightly, peculiar.

'What were you doing?' she asked as they pulled away.

'What? Last night?'

'No. Just now. What were you doing out of the car?'

She knew he'd give her an honest answer, and he knew it himself, but she could see him casting around desperately for a third option before conceding, 'I was having a word with that chap in the leather jacket who was standing in the gift shop doorway.'

'Uh-huh? What word were you having?'

She wouldn't have been a bit surprised to hear Buchanan admit that he had been accusing the chap of being her stalker but, close on the heels of that thought, she remembered that he had seen her stalker and must have known that the chap in the doorway – who she herself had already examined from her window – was nothing like him. Then she knew.

'He was one of your friendly local heavies, wasn't he? Dammit, Buchanan. You're having me bloody guarded!'

Buchanan drew a long breath, probably expecting it to be his last. 'He was a cop, Fizz, and he was only going to follow your stalker—'

'Oh great! Oh, bloody great!' Fizz yelled, waiting for a red light so she could kick him. 'Now I have a cop on my tail as well as a moronic thug and you don't even have the decency to tell me about it! You're not short of nerve, Buchanan, I'll tell you that! What makes you think you have the right to treat me like I'm sixpence short of a shilling—'

And so on until she had run out of invective and, about the same time, realised the impossibility of ever making him see what a prick he was. He knew damn well, in any case, that after all she had experienced in her eight years of travelling, after all the close shaves she had got herself out of, after all the physical attacks she had foiled, it got right up her nose to see how little he respected her capabilities. She was so angry and frustrated she was in half a mind to get out of the sodding car and walk.

It didn't help that he wouldn't even condescend to respond to her remarks. He just sat there with his austere profile turned to her and his eyes on the traffic ahead and let her run on till she felt like a harpy. It was like punching a sponge cake. And all the time, beneath all the fury and frustration, there was the searing suspicion that maybe a calm, reasoned discussion might achieve more in the long run. It wouldn't, however, relieve one's feelings.

They drove the rest of the way in silence. Fizz had wasted all the breath she intended to waste and Buchanan, probably very wisely, was keeping his head down. He had to park half a block away so Fizz left him to it, walked ahead into the office and avoided him for the next hour.

After whizzing through the most pressing of the assignments awaiting her attention she applied herself to the list of Rudyard Grassick's Inverness customers, phoning each of them in turn and finding two firms who'd had a visit from Vanessa the day before her death. Buchanan had, long ago, imbued her with a reluctance to do any sort of questioning by phone but Inverness was at least a hundred-and-fifty miles away so, in this instance, she didn't have much of an option. However, a rather attractive scheme was beginning to take shape at the back of her mind so she was careful to lay the foundations for a further approach to the relevant informants.

When she had worked her way through the list she marked it with her findings and dumped it, without comment, in Buchanan's In tray. Then she went into Alan Stewart's empty office and dialled Giles's number.

'Giles, it's Fizz.'

'Hello, sunshine. What's new?'

'Nothing terribly exciting, I fear, but I've located two firms in Inverness who had a visit from Vanessa Grassick the Friday before the explosion. She was supposed to be in Inverness all weekend but, for some unknown reason, she returned in time for the explosion. I've already made contact with the two businesses but you know how tough it is getting information out of people when you're not talking face to face.'

'You think it would be worthwhile for me to run up to Inverness?' Giles said, sounding quite willing.

'Actually, I'd rather like to go myself but I don't want to suggest to Buchanan that I should go on the train. He's in a funny mood today because I told him I thought someone was following me.'

'Yes, he told me about it,' Giles admitted. 'What would he say to my driving you?'

Fizz permitted herself a small congratulatory smile. 'I don't know that he'd like the idea if *I* were to put it to him, but you could suggest it and see what he says. If you give him a ring he'll tell you about the list of Vanessa's Inverness contacts, so you won't have to mention that you've spoken to me.'

She heard him chuckle. 'You slay me, Fizz. You'd think you were as innocent as a newborn babe but there's a devious brain under those curls, isn't there? How long will it take us to get to Inverness? Three to four hours, I reckon. Okay. We'd better get moving. I'll give Tam a bell straightaway.'

Fizz rang off and waited, and about five minutes passed before she heard Buchanan open his door and call for her.

She kept him waiting a moment or two before she stuck her head round his door, carefully applying an expression of fragile tolerance. He was back behind his desk with the telephone to his ear and her notes in his hand and he went on listening as he beckoned her in.

'Yes . . . yes, well here she is. I'll ask her.' He covered the mouthpiece with his hand and said, 'This is Giles on the line. He wants to drive up to Inverness this morning and question these two customers who, it appears, claim to have seen Vanessa the weekend she died. He thinks that, since you have already established contact, it would be better if you were to go with him.'

Fizz moved a shoulder. 'I don't mind.'

'You're sure you can afford the time?' he said, looking very pinch-nostrilled.

'Yes.'

'No lectures this afternoon? I don't want you to feel—'

'I don't feel pressured. When do we leave?'

She couldn't always tell what Buchanan was thinking but she was fairly sure he was ready to ignite. He spoke a few more words to Giles, his consonants snapping like knicker elastic, and then said, 'He's on his way. He'll pick you up by eleven.'

'Fine.'

She left him to it and didn't even say goodbye when she left. She was just in the mood for a nice long drive with a scrummy guy like Giles, a guy who, far from treating her like a backward infant, actually acknowledged that she had a brain of her own. If she had originally viewed Giles as little more than a rather titillating meal ticket, she was now beginning to appreciate him for the thoughtful and understanding person he was. You didn't expect to find a caring soul who looked like Leonardo di Caprio but Giles was proof that it could happen.

It was a delight to be with someone who chattered inconsequentially as he drove, making her laugh with examples of outrageous claims his company had received in the past and the ridiculous lies claimants had expected him to believe. He had never been this far north before and was stunned by the majesty of the landscape as they crossed the Highland line and saw the Cairngorm mountains away in the distance.

'I hope you didn't have anything pressing to get ahead with today?' Fizz asked him, while she disposed of a haddock fillet in Blair Atholl. There was little on the menu of the restaurant they'd picked other than the universal choice of fish fillet, chicken breast, salad, or scampi but she knew they'd be lucky to find any sort of eating place at this time of year, let alone a more imaginative one, anywhere in the wilderness that lay between Blair Atholl and their destination.

'Frankly, I don't really have anything pressing to do today or any day,' he said lightly. 'Not on Vanessa Grassick's case anyway. In fact, I suspect I've already wasted just about enough time on her claim as I can afford to.'

Fizz swallowed hastily. 'You're not going to pay up and shut up, surely?'

'What else can I do? There's not a single indication that Vanessa's death was anything other than an accident, is there? There are plenty of suspicious circumstances, I'll grant you that, but none of them point to Vanessa as the agent of her own demise.' He waved his fork helplessly. 'I can't withhold the claim indefinitely in the hope that some illuminating clue will fall into my lap. I've spent a week here already – much longer than I intended to – but, in terms of a black and white answer to the question of Vanessa's death, I'm not one step further forward. Nor, if I may be so rude, are you and Tam.'

Fizz could scarcely deny that. 'So does that mean you're going back to Manchester?' she asked in a matter-of-fact tone.

'I don't have much choice. They don't pay me to swan around in beautiful places with beautiful women, I'm very sorry to say.' He reached across the table to touch her hand. 'It's only a few hours away and I hope you'll say I can drive up now and then to see you. But, for the present, it's back to the grindstone for me – unless we turn up something really enlightening this afternoon.'

He poked unenthusiastically at his quarter chicken and ate a chip while Fizz strove to look as if she didn't give a hoot whether he stayed or went.

'I was back at the scene of the crime this morning when you phoned me,' he said. 'I thought I might get some more information out of Mrs Armstrong. Flogging a dead horse, I admit it, but that's the stage I'm at. However, the place was like a ghost town. Every house was locked and empty and not a sign of life to be seen – except a chap looking for a lost cat who came along just as I was leaving.'

Fizz looked at him with an open mouth, waiting to hear him say that he'd asked the guy if it was Poppy Ford's cat he was looking for. Then she realised she may have forgotten to mention the Fords' moggie.

'What is it?' Giles said. 'Spinach in my teeth?'

'Oh sh-sh-sh—' she started to say and changed it, more or less in time, to, 'sh-surely I told you about the cat?'

Mutely, Giles shook his head, but already his face was starting to say, 'I don't want to hear this.'

'Poppy had a cat. It disappeared at the time of the explosion and everybody – well, the Pringles at least –

172

thought it was dead. But I'm afraid it looks very much as though Poppy sent that guy to look for it.'

Giles leaned back in his chair and let his eyes droop shut. Fizz knew exactly how he felt. They'd just missed out on what might have been their best chance of finding someone who would lead them to Poppy and, because of one tiny, apparently unimportant detail, they'd blown it. She swallowed and said, 'It could have been another cat he was looking for.'

Giles opened his eyes and looked at her with no visible affection. 'It wasn't,' he said bitterly. 'It was Poppy's cat.'

'How do you know?'

'I know by the way he acted. I was just coming out of the Armstrong garden and I had my back to him, fastening the gate, when he appeared round the hedge calling, "Puss, puss, puss!" He must have taken me for Mr Armstrong and said, "Still no sign of Jet, then?" Then he saw he'd made a mistake and shut up.' Giles rubbed a hand down his face and stared out the window at the hills. 'I said, "Lost your cat?" and he said, "Yes," and hurried away. I thought he was perhaps a little simple – you know, the village oddball – but, of course, he must have been biting his tongue out. I need scarcely add that he was in his thirties – though if he was driving a Ford Ka, I didn't see it.'

Fizz passed her collection of swear words under mental review but found nothing, in five languages, to relieve her feelings. Giles was quite red in the face with suppressed anger and much of it appeared to be directed at her, which, she had to admit, was not unreasonable. She was so totally sicked-off she couldn't even finish her lunch, which was a first for her. The only hope she could find to cling to was that the cat-hunter would return to the scene of the accident, but how long would one have to wait for him to turn up?

Back in Giles's car the atmosphere was no longer festive. Both of them made sporadic attempts to be chatty but, between times, there were long periods of depressed silence which the sunshine and scenery were unable to penetrate.

They reached Inverness just on three o'clock, after getting hopelessly lost, and diplomatic relations were strained to snapping-point by the time they found their first Rudyard Grassick customer. This turned out to be a tiny hole-in-the-wall printing company just across the Ness river from the castle and they had already driven past its unobtrusive premises at least twice. It was apparently staffed entirely by educationally sub-normal sociopaths with Attention Deficit Disorder who could supply only one word answers and didn't know anything about anything. Yes, Mrs Grassick had been there on the relevant Friday afternoon. No, she hadn't said or done anything out of the ordinary. Yes, she had visited them before in person. No, it wasn't likely she'd be seeing further customers, it being nearly five when she was there. And yes, it was possible she had been in a hurry.

'Great,' was Giles's verdict on the interview. He was now beyond even pretending that Fizz's charming company made up for every reversal. 'That was just the type of discussion that makes an insurance investigator's job worthwhile. Can the next one be any worse, I wonder?'

Fizz was in no doubt that it could. It had been a rubber-hose-up-the-exhaust-pipe sort of day from the outset and the best you could hope for was to be still standing at the end of it.

Their second port of call was another small business: this one based in a corner shop in Church Street and running a variety of sight-seeing tours and guided walks. Fizz had a good look at their display of pamphlets as she and Giles waited to speak to the manager and found them all produced – very well produced – by Rudyard Grassick.

Presently a chunky guy in a sweater and kilt arrived and ushered them into an office behind the counter. It was as cramped as Rudyard's and not a lot tidier.

'Angus Cameron.' He shook hands with both of them

and moved boxes off chairs till they all had a place to sit down. 'Sorry I didn't have time to chat this morning, Miss Fitzpatrick, but almost all our tours set off at ten a.m. and you can imagine the pandemonium. You were asking about Mrs Grassick's visit?'

'Yes,' Fizz said. 'You probably know that she died early the following morning.'

Cameron nodded soberly. He had a nice open, intelligent face and Fizz was encouraged to hope that perhaps they might have a rational conversation, if nothing else.

He said, 'I was really sorry to hear about that. Mrs Grassick was such a charismatic woman, so full of enthusiasm. I always enjoyed her visits.'

'Did you see her regularly?' Giles asked.

'No, not at all regularly. Not any more than once a year. I don't think any of her Inverness customers merited frequent visits – not like the big concerns she dealt with in Glasgow and Edinburgh. It was more of a customer relations visit.'

'When she did come,' Fizz said thoughtfully, 'did she make arrangements with you in advance?'

'Usually. Sometimes I have to go out with a tour – like if we're short-staffed or somebody's off ill or suchlike. Mrs Grassick knew that, so she'd almost always phone up a couple of days in advance and say she was planning a visit.'

'Did she do that last time?'

'Yes. She phoned – I think it was Tuesday or Wednesday – and said she'd be here Friday and Saturday. We arranged her visit for Friday afternoon at five-fifteen because Saturday is a no-no for me all day, even at this time of year. Ski trips, winter wonderland tours, Munro-baggers. We're always kept going at weekends.'

Giles crossed his legs and pinched the crease in his trousers. He was still showing the signs of his earlier chagrin but it was clear that he, too, had hopes, albeit fragile hopes, of Cameron. He smiled as he said, 'It's certainly a wonderful part of the country but I reckon, if I were coming north just once a year, I'd prefer to leave it till the summertime.'

Cameron nodded. 'Yes, you're right. We didn't usually see Mrs Grassick this early in the year. Our brochures for the coming season are already in production by the end of February so there's no reason for her to brave the elements.'

'Did she comment on the earliness of her visit?' Giles asked.

'No.' Cameron propped his chin on a fist and smiled thoughtfully to himself. 'She didn't refer to it and, I have to say, it never struck me as odd till this minute. Actually, I had a lot on my mind that day – staff problems! – and she didn't stay all that long. It was just a flying visit.'

The shine was beginning, just a little, to wear off Fizz's optimism. Why was it that people never thought to take note of salient facts? Why did they so rarely ask the right questions or view anyone with suspicion? Why did they take in so little of their surroundings and never remember conversations accurately and in full?

And, for that matter, why was it so difficult to ask the bull's-eye question: the question that would release an unexpected bonanza of information? You could talk to somebody for hours, hovering around that critical query, always within a hair's breadth of hitting the bingo button, and go home, in the end, empty-handed. Always, always, always there was this gulf between the interviewer, who couldn't guess at the information the interviewee had in his possession, and the interviewee, who didn't realise that the insignificant fact that he considered not worth mentioning would form the missing link that led to the buried treasure.

With commendable doggedness Giles kept on pegging away, dwelling on Vanessa's evident state of mind, references to future plans, etc, the main thrust of his questions being to determine whether she might have displayed any signs of impending suicide. Cameron answered them all patiently and as helpfully as could be desired, but he had clearly very little knowledge that would be of the slightest use.

'I suppose I didn't really know her at all,' he said, with some degree of surprised enlightenment. 'You see a person year after year, you sit and chat to them, have a coffee, tell them about your family and your hobbies, and you think of them almost as a friend. But when I think about Vanessa Grassick I realise that it was probably me who did all the talking. I know her husband was a lawyer . . . I know she went to the opera every chance she got . . . but I can't think of another personal detail she ever told me.'

'You think she was deliberately secretive or just reserved?' Giles asked.

'No, she wasn't deliberately secretive, but you couldn't call her reserved either,' Cameron decided after a moment's thought. 'She'd say things like, "Well, I'm off to see if I can find myself a smart pair of flatties. These shoes are killing my ankles," but she didn't go on about her home life. It was as if it wasn't at the centre of her universe, that's all.'

Giles uncrossed his legs and got his feet under him, preparatory to standing up. As he did so, he sighed and said in a tone that indicated this was his final question, 'Mrs Grassick was, I understand, here in Inverness for a few days but, although she has several customers here, she apparently saw only yourself and one other. Did she mention any other customers she might be calling on?'

'No. I'm pretty sure she didn't.' Cameron pursed his lips and thought for a moment. 'No. She wasn't seeing anyone else after she left me. Straight home to put her feet up, she said.'

'Home?' Fizz said sharply. 'She told you she was going straight home?'

Cameron gave a sheepish smile. 'That's what she said but, of course, she didn't mean "home to Edinburgh". She always tied in her trips to Inverness with visits to friends out at Gollanfield. She meant "home" to their place.'

'Gollanfield?' Giles demanded, almost before the guy had finished speaking and before Fizz could process what he'd said. 'Where's Gollanfield?'

'Out towards Culloden,' Cameron said. 'Not far.'

'Do you know her friends' name?' Fizz got out, hope springing, if not eternally, at least for the time being.

'Sorry, no. I don't think she ever mentioned it. They own a farm, though, that's all I know.'

It's enough, Fizz wanted to say, but resisted the impulse. Cameron's information might not produce any break-through evidence but at least it opened a further line of inquiry and it renewed her faith in the possibility of asking the bingo question sooner or later.

Chapter Fifteen

Cantraymuir Farm (you couldn't miss it) was about a mile-and-a-half past Culloden. Fizz was loath to pass up a brief pilgrimage to the battlefield where Bonnie Prince Charlie – and Scotland – had been brought low by the armies of the Butcher Cumberland. She had visited it often enough before but she wanted Giles to experience the atmosphere of doom that still hung around the scene some two hundred and fifty years after the event. She was far from susceptible to the ambience of places like that but she got a sensation in the back of her neck, not unlike being poked by a stag's antler, every time she passed among the graves of the clans.

Giles manifested a convincing interest as she pointed out landmarks to him and filled in the gaps in his scanty knowledge of the battle but he didn't take his foot off the accelerator as they sped past. Fizz was, however, just as impatient as he to hunt down the farmers who were, quite possibly, the last people to see Vanessa alive, other than Jamie Ford, deceased. These were the people who would know when, and why, Vanessa had changed her mind about staying the night and had left – surely so precipitately – to hurry back to Brora Lodge.

The building that revealed itself to them as they rounded the last bend was no farmhouse but a hodge-podge of stone structures that were partly residential, partly storage for farm implements and partly falling down. The main bit of the building was what looked to

Fizz like a thirteenth-century keep with arrow slits, a studded door and a crenellated tower. Cobbled on to this was a long two-storey building of some later date, but still very old, and at the far side, a row of arched bays that might, at some time, have held carriages or carts but had since been glassed in to provide more modern living space.

Giles got out of the car and looked uncertainly at the studded door as if he felt the need of a sword hilt to drum on it and summon the nearest vassal. There was, however, an iron bell-pull close by and he used this instead. After a minute, Fizz heard a window open some distance above their heads and a youngish woman leaned out.

'Hello there,' she called, a sweep of dark brown hair slithering, Rapunzel-like, over one shoulder. 'Is it me you're looking for?'

'Yes,' called Fizz. She could have been addressing the au pair, she realised, or the mad woman in the attic for that matter, but they could discuss that later.

'Hang around, then. I'm on my way.' The window slammed shut and Giles raised his eyebrows in silent comment. 'Right,' Fizz agreed, looking about her at the lichened stone walls and windows of thick imperfect glass. 'This should be interesting.'

They could hear no sound of approaching feet beyond the door but a couple of minutes later it opened to reveal the dark young woman smiling out at them and panting slightly.

'Sorry about that. Do come in.' She looked at them closely. 'I don't know you, do I?'

Fizz stepped into a stone-flagged hallway lit only by electric light and a single ray of sunshine that emerged from a window that was out of sight around the bend of a spiral staircase on their left. The walls of the square area were lined with weapons: long-barrelled pistols, dirks, broadswords and targes, a crossbow and a dusty, dark-red banner that was more holes than fabric. Everything smelled of dust and rising damp and, for some reason,

Fizz was uncomfortably conscious of the weight of masonry above her, supported, one imagined, only by the barrelled ceiling and the exceedingly rotten-looking stone. Giles, meanwhile, was explaining their purpose there with his inimitable charm at full stretch and the young woman's response was all he could have wished.

'Let's go down to the kitchen and have some coffee. It's warmer in there.'

The half-dozen or so steps leading down towards the back of the building, which was evidently built on a sloping site, were almost the full width of the hallway and the doorway they led to was set in a wooden screen that had been constructed to fill in a much wider opening. They passed through into a huge sunny room that was what would now be called a family kitchen. It was three times the size of any family kitchen Fizz had ever seen and, in spite of the modern appliances and the bright red Aga, you could still imagine it with a sheep turning on a spit in the fireplace.

'And in that case,' the young woman said, continuing her conversation with Giles, 'you didn't even know my name! It's Charlotte McIntosh, by the way. So, how did you track me down?'

Giles was doing fine with the social side of the business, so Fizz let him get on with it while she took stock of Vanessa Grassick's friend. She was much the same age as Vanessa had been, maybe a little nearer thirty: a big woman, a good two stone overweight, broad hipped and generously bosomed. She was cleverly dressed in a pair of well tailored trousers and a drapey sort of blouse with a knee-length cardigan on top but she couldn't hide the excess fat on a face that would otherwise have been quite lovely. She had huge dark eyes thickly fringed with curling lashes and wonderfully transparent, creamy skin.

She sat them down at the massive table in the centre of the room and spooned coffee into a cafetière while she listened to Giles's pitch, then she grabbed a handful of mugs and came over to sit beside them.

'Vanessa always stayed with us when she came north,' she said, using both hands to swoosh back her long scarf of hair. 'Not that we saw a great deal of her – once or twice a year if we were lucky – and she rarely stayed more than a couple of days.' She laid a palm on the cafetière and watched it thoughtfully as she pressed down the strainer. 'She wasn't a country girl, you see. She had to be doing something every minute of the day and there was too much going on in her life for her to waste a minute of it.'

She swallowed a couple of times, tears welling in her eyes, and blinked out at the walled garden beyond the windows. For a minute, it was so quiet that Fizz could hear the fridge humming. Then Charlotte sniffed and smiled and reached for the coffee mugs. 'I just can't believe she's not around any more.'

'It seems very possible,' Giles said, kindly keeping his gaze averted to give her time to get a grip on herself, 'that you and your husband were the last people to see Vanessa . . . um . . . um . . . before the accident. Obviously, I don't want to upset you more than—'

'No, no. I'm just being silly. It's not as if Vanessa and I were so very close. It's just so tragic to see a promising life cut short. Please . . . do ask me anything you like.'

Giles wasted a minute or two while they all fiddled around with their coffee, during which Fizz lost patience and said, 'We really need to know if Vanessa said or did anything, the evening she stayed with you, that might have led you to believe she was under some sort of strain.'

Charlotte's already wide eyes widened still further as she swung them from Fizz to Giles and back again. 'You're wondering if she . . . surely not!'

'It's a possibility we have to eliminate,' Fizz told her, sounding, to her own ears, quite official. 'It would also be a help if we knew, for instance, if she was worried or afraid.'

'What are you saying?' Charlotte was openly horrified.

'That it wasn't an accident? But, that's . . . Good heavens! Suicide? Vanessa? No! Absolutely not! Vanessa would never do a thing like that. If you knew her – no, I don't believe that for a second. Vanessa wasn't the kind to give up. Never!'

Fizz nodded as though she accepted this opinion without question. 'So, how was she that evening? Quiet? Happy? Tense? Relaxed?'

Giles made an uneasy movement with his hand, just as Buchanan would have done if he thought she was being too pushy but, hell, it was five o'clock and they didn't have all night.

Charlotte looked at her, but didn't say anything. Fizz could see her brain ticking away in there as she thought about it and she saw the uncertainty creep into her expression a little at a time. When she could see that Charlotte was becoming just a tad uneasy at the pictures her memory was flashing up she asked her, 'There was something strange about her, wasn't there?'

Charlotte frowned at the table top, not wanting to admit it. 'Perhaps she was a little more . . . excitable than usual. A little hyper. She drank more than usual . . . a large whisky when she arrived, wine at dinner, and more whisky in the evening.'

'Did she appear worried or angry about anything?' Giles asked.

'I can't believe this.' Charlotte put her elbows on the table and covered her face with her hands. 'Vanessa wasn't *like* that,' she said through her fingers. 'But, there it is, she *was* odd that evening. I thought nothing of it. People aren't always the same. They have moods. You don't immediately assume they're going to commit suicide.'

'But she didn't appear unhappy?' Fizz prodded.

'Why didn't she tell me?' Charlotte sat up, ignoring the question, her face haunted. 'Why didn't she talk to me about it instead of . . . surely she knew I'd have done anything . . .'

Fizz thought she was going to cry again but Giles reached across and put a hand on her arm and she satisfied herself with a few gulps.

'Tell me what you remember,' Giles said, almost tenderly, his voice carrying soothing undertones comparable to Buchanan at his best.

Charlotte took a minute or two for some deep breathing and tucked her hair back behind her ears. 'She was hyper when she came in. Very talkative. Dashing upstairs to her room, out to the garden. Couldn't sit down for a minute.'

'Did she seem afraid?' Fizz asked.

Charlotte pressed her lips together and nodded. 'Yes. I see now that she was afraid of something but she was trying to hide it from me. Oh, my God, why didn't she tell us? Hugh would have done something . . . called the police . . . At the very least, we could have prevented her from dashing back to Edinburgh like that . . .'

'What reason did she give you for suddenly cutting short her visit?' Giles prompted gently.

'She gave us no reason at all. She just went. While we were asleep. Not a word to either of us.'

Fizz exchanged an astounded glance with Giles who, for once, had no ready reply, and took it upon herself to reiterate, 'She left, without warning, in the middle of the night?'

'Not in the middle of the night,' Charlotte said. 'Otherwise how could she have been in Chirnside at two-thirty? It must have been just after we went to bed.'

'And what time was that?'

'About eleven.' Answering Fizz's question, she addressed her remarks to Giles, probably because he was encouraging her with an expression of tender concern. 'Hugh, my husband, has to be up at crack of dawn but usually Vanessa and I would sit chatting till the wee small hours. But that night she was exhausted . . . she *said* she was exhausted . . . so we all turned in at the same time. I . . . I think she must have left virtually right away.'

'You heard nothing? Not even the car starting?' Giles asked.

She shook her head. 'Nothing. We park our cars round at the old byre so we wouldn't have heard her leave. We knew nothing about it till the next morning when she didn't come down. Her bed hadn't been slept in. Of course, I phoned her Edinburgh number right away and . . . that's when Lawrence told me what had happened.'

'And you told Lawrence that she had left in a hurry?' Fizz said, and got a nod in reply. 'Had he any explanation for that?'

'No. He was as baffled as Hugh and I were. All we could suppose was that Vanessa had remembered something important . . .' She waved a hand vaguely. 'I don't know, something to do with her business, perhaps. You don't think that's possible?'

'Perfectly possible, Mrs McIntosh,' Giles said confidently, holding her eyes. 'Perfectly possible, believe me. I'm really sorry to have caused you distress, but I'm afraid these questions have to be answered. We have to examine every possibility until we establish the true cause of Mrs Grassick's death. I'm sure you understand that?'

Charlotte was happy to agree that you couldn't make omelettes without breaking eggs and invited them to stay and meet her husband who was due back from the fields in less than an hour. However, neither Fizz nor, apparently, Giles were desperate to hear Hugh's testimony. It was unlikely to differ in any important facet from his wife's and, furthermore, an hour was rather long to wait for him considering they still had a two-and-a-half-hour drive ahead of them.

'Quit while you're winning', Fizz suspected would be found engraved on her heart when she finally fell off her twig.

Fleming had decided that it would be unwise to meet at the Pear Tree too often, just in case somebody got suspicious.

185

That wasn't, in Buchanan's opinion, the least bit likely to happen but he was happy to go along with his choice of the Canny Man at Morningside. It was smokier and noisier than his regular pub but the beer was good.

Fleming, for a change, got in the first round. 'Right,' he said, wiping away his foam moustache with the heel of his hand. 'I had another look at the accidental death report and, between you and me, Tam, it's pretty hazy in places. It wouldn't have got past me, I can tell you.'

'Uh-huh?' Buchanan tried to look interested in the standards maintained by Hawick police station. 'What about Lawrence Grassick? Did it establish where he was on the night of the explosion?'

'Not too bloody specifically. That's what I'm saying. The whole report was badly written. It says that Vanessa's husband was contacted immediately and informed of his wife's death but it doesn't specify where and it doesn't specify precisely when. "Immediately" could mean within a couple of hours.' Fleming got out his cigarettes and stuck one between his lips, letting it wag up and down as he said, 'We can probably assume that he was at home, otherwise that fact would have to be made clear on the report. If he wasn't at home when contacted, somebody's going to be demoted to a sleeping policeman when I've finished with them.'

Buchanan had a momentary picture of Virgo lying in the middle of the road with cars bumping over him and the thought was not without its appeal. He said, 'No confirmation of his whereabouts? Nothing approaching an alibi?'

'Let's say, if I'd been in charge of the inquiry I'm pretty damn sure I'd have been looking for something a lot more specific. Frankly,' he paused for a gulp of beer and a drag at his cigarette, 'I wouldn't like to be in Lawrence Grassick's shoes right now. I do not like the way things are shaping up for him. Unless he has proof to the contrary, it looks like he had the means, he had the opportunity, and after ten years of marriage, I'd be surprised if he didn't have a choice of motives. And if it comes out that some silly bastard down in Hawick took a kickback to cover up for him, by Christ, you'll see Hell's foundations quiver all right. It'll be a whole sewage plant hitting the fan.'

Buchanan nodded. Everything Fleming said was true but, of course, Grassick had been the prime suspect from the beginning, simply by virtue of the fact that he was the victim's husband. He might not be able to prove his innocence, but that didn't make him guilty. It didn't make him innocent either, Buchanan reflected, and reached for the solace of his pint.

His concentration, this evening, was inclined to wander. Half his mind, since eleven o'clock this morning, had been dwelling on Fizz and on how, in God's name, he could have stopped her from going off with Giles. Her time was her own. If she wanted to earn a couple of hours' wages she turned up; if she had something better to do, she didn't. There was simply no way he could have pretended to have an urgent job for her to do and, the way things had been between them at that point, she'd have told him to get lost if he'd tried it.

That was the bitter bit. She'd been so mad at him – and probably with reason – that it would be no surprise at all to him if she had fallen straight into Giles's arms, just to spite him. Because, obviously, she had to know that Giles irritated him, with that sexy come-to-bed look and that cheesy grin and the oily way he buttered her up. Probably even she wouldn't be silly enough to suspect Buchanan of being jealous but she knew how to annoy him just the same.

She should have been back in Edinburgh by eight-thirty, at which time Buchanan had left home to meet Fleming, yet she hadn't phoned, as she would normally have done. What did this mean? Had she gone to dinner with Giles? Had they stayed over in Inverness? And what the hell were they doing now?

'I also looked into the ownership of the house next door. The one Jamie Ford lived in,' Fleming was saying when Buchanan re-focused on him. 'I don't know if you're interested, but it's a rented property. He'd only been living there since last November. The girl at the agency tells me he had a six-month let.'

'Last November?' So, if he was Vanessa Grassick's lover he hadn't taken long to seduce her. Maybe it had been love at first sight. 'What significance does it have whether his house was rented or not?'

Fleming folded his arms on the table and leaned forward so that he could drop his voice. 'I've had someone asking questions around the village – a pal, a guy I can trust. I wanted information about Vanessa Grassick's neighbours, about the Grassicks themselves, any scraps of gossip that might be useful. When you don't have recourse to official sources you have to scrape around for crumbs.'

Buchanan told him he knew all about that side of the business.

'Yes, well, there are no secrets in that village, I can tell you. Everyone you speak to could tell you all about Pringle's first wife's mother, the Armstrongs' visit to a marriage guidance counsellor, Lawrence Grassick's average catch of sea trout over the past year and a half – you name it, they know all the details. But, Jamie and Poppy Ford? Zilch.'

'But he has only lived there since last November,' Buchanan protested.

'Listen, Tam. When I say "zilch" I mean *nothing*. They know when he arrived down to the day and the hour, they know how many cases they carried into the house with them, they know he drinks Guinness but never more than two, but ask any of them where he came from, what he did for a living before going on the dole, or anything at all about his wife, and you hit a brick wall.'

Buchanan looked at his watch and wondered if there might be a message from Fizz waiting for him on his ansaphone. He said, 'Is that necessarily suspicious? D'you think Ford was some kind of crook?'

Fleming finished his pint and set down the empty glass with a click. Buchanan took the hint and got in two more beers and some packets of nuts.

'Well, what about it, Ian? What're your thoughts on Jamie Ford? Is there something fishy about him or not?'

'If I knew that, mate, I'd be head of the bloody CID.' Fleming lit another cigarette and screwed his eyes up to look at Buchanan through the smoke. 'I don't know why, but my good old bullshit detector snapped into action when I heard what the locals were saying – or rather, *not* saying – about him. I thought, Ian my old chum, there's a smell of the Bar-L about this laddie.'

'Barlinnie?' Buchanan said, recognising the nickname of Glasgow's prison. 'You think he's been doing time?'

'It would fit into the puzzle, Tam.' Fleming leaned back in the chair and waved his cigarette in a confident circle. 'People who are secretive about their past have invariably got something to hide and that's the usual skeleton in the cupboard.'

Buchanan's brain flagged. The thought of yet another strand that would have to be teased out of this complicated knot weighed on him like a concrete overcoat. He wanted to go home, kick his shoes off and watch something mindless on TV. 'You've Been Framed', 'Family Fortunes', he didn't care. He needed to relax. He needed to forget the Grassick case. He needed to stop thinking about Fizz.

Chapter Sixteen

It was a profound relief to Buchanan to see Fizz come storming down George Street as usual the following morning. It meant not only that she had not been accosted by her centurion since he last saw her, but that she had spent the night in her own little eyrie in the Royal Mile and not in some Highland hotel with Giles. Admittedly, it didn't follow that Giles had not been in the flat *with* her, but that, somehow, seemed less likely. Fizz's flat was . . . well, basic, to say the least and was seriously lacking in the sort of ambience necessary to a night of tender passion.

He got back behind his desk before Fizz spotted him watching for her and when she slammed into his office a few minutes later, ionising the atmosphere like ozone, he was immersed in a complicated contract.

'Well,' she said, flopping into the persecuted chair, 'what do you want first, the good news or the bad news?'

Buchanan already had the good news – at least, some of it. Apart from being unscathed and (hopefully) unadulterated, she had also forgotten to be angry with him, which meant that she hadn't spotted the plain clothes man watching her flat. This made him exuberant enough to say, 'Hit me with the bad news.'

'Okay. Giles saw a guy looking for Poppy's cat yesterday morning.'

Buchanan's heart gave a flutter of optimism. 'And?'

'And nothing. For some reason we'd both omitted to tell him that Poppy's cat was missing, presumed dead – in fact,

191

he didn't even know that Poppy ever *had* a cat. If we *had* mentioned it, he'd have known the guy would lead him to Poppy.' She put a disgusted hand on each cheek, dragging down the flesh so that her eyes looked like a St Bernard's. 'Giles was gutted. He was sizzling like something in a microwave for the rest of the day. So was I, to be honest. I mean, to think we were so close to . . . oh, well, sod it.'

Buchanan couldn't believe their lousy luck. 'Can Giles remember anything about the guy?' he said, clutching at straws. 'His car? Anything Fleming might be able to use to track him down?'

'Nope. Not a damn thing. Just that he was in his thirties and wore a Barbour jacket.' She removed an invisible speck of something from the sleeve of her sweater. 'Giles says he'll have to wind up his investigation today and get back to Manchester, but he plans to have a look around the village before he goes, just in case he spots the guy again.'

'He's packing in?' Buchanan said, absolutely unmoved by the news. 'Really? That must be a disappointment to you.'

'Yeah,' she said with an unconvincing sigh. 'I may weave wild flowers in my hair and go for a swim in the Forth.'

'What about the good news, then – or did you just put that bit in to make it more interesting?'

'The good news is that we managed to track down the friend Vanessa stayed with the evening before the explosion.' Fizz opened her eyes at him, inviting his applause. 'A woman called Charlotte McIntosh. And, guess what? Vanessa arrived at her place as planned but then scarpered without saying she was going, probably right after they'd all gone to bed.'

'Left? Without anyone knowing about it?' Buchanan asked, getting it straight in his head. He couldn't begin to make sense of this piece of information and a single glance at Fizz's expectant face was enough to quell any hope that she would be much assistance. Quite manifestly, *she* was hoping he was going to enlighten *her*. Speaking as much to himself as to Fizz, he muttered, 'Why on earth would she do that?'

'Search me, muchacho,' Fizz offered, swinging her feet up on to the desk. 'It's been doing my head in all night. She must have realised something at the last minute, when it was too late to tell her friend she was leaving. Or maybe someone phoned her on her mobile. Maybe she saw something or heard something that . . . I don't know . . . something that aroused her suspicions . . . something that jogged her memory . . .'

Buchanan didn't feel comfortable with that. 'No. I think she was spooked. She left there in a big hurry, otherwise she'd have left a note for her hosts – not necessarily a truthful one but at least an attempt to make some kind of an excuse. I reckon something must have made her realise that someone was out to kill her,' Buchanan suggested. 'Or she may have known that already but realised that she'd been followed to her friend's house and had to make a run for it at a moment's notice.'

'Charlotte McIntosh thought she was probably afraid of something,' Fizz said, nodding in agreement. 'She may have known she was in danger from the minute she got there – or before – but hoped she'd be safe for the night.'

'So she made a bolt to Brora Lodge where she would have her husband's protection – only he wasn't there.'

'We don't know that,' Fizz objected.

'Not for sure but I'd be surprised if he was there,' Buchanan said. 'Fleming says the police phoned him almost immediately to inform him of the accident, so he must have been at home. Vanessa *expected* him to be there but it begins to look like he must have changed his plans and she ran into Jamie Ford instead.'

'Bloody hell.' Fizz ran the fingers of both hands into her hair, destroying its morning neatness. 'Does that mean Jamie Ford had followed her to Inverness and back again?'

Buchanan didn't know what it meant. He felt he didn't

know what *any*thing meant. He said, 'Was her friend aware of any incident . . . maybe a phone message . . . that might have changed Vanessa's mind about staying over-night? Did she make any phone calls? Did she show any signs of having received a sudden shock?'

'I didn't think to ask,' Fizz admitted, clearly annoyed with herself. 'I hadn't got that far in my thinking.'

Given the unpredictability of hitting on the right question, Buchanan wasn't about to blame her. He slid the phone across to her and returned to his doodling while she dialled Directory Inquiries and then the number. The sub-sequent conversation, which lasted about ten minutes, was reasonably easy to follow, so he wasn't too disappointed when Fizz rang off and gave him a synopsis.

'She doesn't think anything happened to alarm Vanessa during the course of the evening. They had a quiet meal, a few drinks, and then went to bed. There were no visitors and, as far as she knows, no phone calls for Vanessa. However, Vanessa had her mobile phone, so anyone could have called her after eleven p.m. when she was in her room.'

'Or, conversely, she could have made a phone call.' Buchanan scratched his head with his pen. 'So, whatever happened to spook her, the chances are it must have happened immediately after she went to her room.'

Fizz focused on the toes of her boots and let her imagination roll. 'She phoned somebody. Somebody phoned her. She saw someone or something from her window. She put two and two together and realised she was in danger. She panicked.'

Buchanan flipped open his scribbling pad. 'Right. Let's get organised. Who do you have on your suspects list?'

'Lawrence,' Fizz said in a weary voice, holding up her left thumb and allocating a finger to each subsequent name. 'Ford. Rudyard. Poppy. Niall Menzies. Mrs Menzies – by proxy. Maybe that centurion who's been watching me. And a person or persons unknown. I don't think Mr

Menzies senior is the sort to put out a contract on someone but I guess we ought to include him just in case.'

Buchanan looked at the list he had jotted down. Sometimes just staring at a name on a piece of paper was enough to set his mind working but this time he was stumped. He could give most of the suspects a tick for means, motive and opportunity; some of them appeared barely feasible, but he had no information that would eliminate any of them.

'This isn't working, Fizz,' he told her, throwing his pen on the notepad. 'I don't know what we're doing wrong this time but we're not getting ahead.'

'Well, you know why that is, don't you?' Fizz threw wide her arms with an energy that made her chair creak dangerously. 'Genghis Grassick is working against us, isn't he? He's having us watched, he knows our every move, and every time we get too close to the truth he spirits away the evidence. We might as well throw in the towel.'

This was merely a figure of speech, of course. She had no intention of throwing in the towel but nor, apparently, did she have any alternative suggestions as to how they should move forward.

He picked up his pen and doodled a question mark beside his list of suspects. 'Where do we go from here?' he asked Fizz, or himself, or maybe the ghost of Sherlock Holmes, but got no reply. 'Fleming hasn't made much headway either. All he had to report when I spoke to him last night was that Lawrence was apparently at home in Edinburgh when the explosion occurred. Oh . . . and the Fords had only a six-month let on their house. They'd only been there for about four and a half months so Jamie can't have known Vanessa long.'

'Ah,' said Fizz vaguely, toying with her bootlaces. 'Giles did mention he'd looked through a crack in the window boards and thought it looked suspiciously tidy. No doubt it's been cleaned ready for the next tenant.'

'It's been cleaned? That's interesting,' Buchanan said. 'It

follows that Poppy must have given up her tenancy so, wherever she is, she's still alive, still making decisions and still has no intention of returning home.'

'Big deal,' Fizz returned. 'It doesn't put us all that much further forward, though, does it?'

Buchanan had to agree. 'We're in the doldrums,' he muttered, chewing his pen. 'There doesn't seem to be a single lead open to us.'

Fizz slid her feet off the desk and let them thud to the floor. 'Well, you know what they always say, snookums: if you don't have any leads you have to make 'em.'

Buchanan eyed her without enthusiasm. His respect for Fizz's flat-pack philosophy did not extend to accepting it as gospel. 'Oh yes? And you have some constructive ideas along those lines?'

'Maybe. They're still simmering but I have hopes.'

Buchanan shivered. 'Fizz . . .'

'Yeah, I know. Don't act on them without discussing it with yer holiness.' She sat up and stretched. 'Meanwhile I think we have to keep up the pressure on Old Man Menzies. I reckon he's a decent old bird and, in spite of what his wife says, he could still put his foot down if he chose to stop the sale of Lammerburn House. Of course, if the sale doesn't go through it would mean we'd lose the commission, but still—'

'But still we'd get our regular fees for administering the estate, which we'd probably miss out on if it went to a new owner.' Buchanan was, in any case, not at all convinced that she had any grounds for optimism and, furthermore, he didn't feel he could pester the Menzies clan any more than he had already done. However, he was willing to go as far as he could to straighten things out. Inquiries about the sale of Lammerburn Estate were already coming in and if the sale went to a quick completion the matter would be out of his hands.

It was excruciatingly tempting to let Fizz have one more go. She had an undeniable talent for persuasion. She could also – despite the fact that she had every fault observed in *Homo sapiens*, plus a few assimilated from the lower orders of the animal kingdom – make people trust her, if only for short periods. Buchanan trusted her only as far as he could spit her but he was unwilling to abandon the people of Lammerburn village without doing his utmost for them.

'I'll talk to him myself,' Fizz bargained, putting on her prettiest face. 'I reckon I could drop in on a casual visit, not as an employee of Buchanan and Stewart. He's stuck in the house so he'll be glad of a visitor – and I think he likes me.'

Buchanan thought so too, and that was enough to sway him. 'Just . . . don't do anything I'll have to sack you for, okay, Fizz?'

And, oh boy, that really gave her cause for concern, he congratulated himself. As well it might, since he had already sacked her at least twice with no observable effect.

Fizz hadn't really expected Buchanan to give her a lift over to the Menzies' residence. He made the excuse that he wanted to be on hand in case she felt she needed his input, but that excuse was thin to the point of anorexia compared to the much more likely reason: that he was ashamed of treating her like a wimp and wanted to show it without actually apologising. This suspicion was only confirmed by his willingness to wait outside in the ear while she tackled the Menzies family on her own; something he would never have done if he hadn't been trying to mollify her.

That was OK. She had forgiven him anyway. After all, Buchanan couldn't help but be overprotective. That was never going to change so you had to either ignore it or walk away, and after all the work she'd put in wangling her way into his employment, she wasn't going to take the second option. Quite apart from that, she could see that rain was on the way and she was wearing only a short jacket.

She could have done without the company of the stag's antlers, which had now managed to curl so far round her

headrest that she had to hold a prong away from her
jugular vein every time they took a left. However, mentioning this fact to Buchanan only brought on a fit of the
vapours because it was going to take three people and a
hand-saw to remove the damn thing without ripping his
car's pristine upholstery to shreds, so she had to bite the
bullet.

As she had predicted, Mr Menzies was openly delighted
to see her, a good deal more delighted than his wife, who
had just returned from Lammerburn. Fizz, herself, was
not exactly thrilled to find the old woman ensconced in
front of the television, watching a programme on how to
survive in the jungle without support, a situation in which
she was, Fizz felt, unlikely to find herself in the near
future.

'She's that little office girl of Tam Buchanan's,' the crone
was thinking, scarcely taking her eyes off the screen to
acknowledge her visitor before returning to her programme. 'What's she doing here?'

Mr Menzies scowled across at his wife's profile and tried
to speak over her. 'Well now, this is nice. Sit yourself
down, Miss Fitzpatrick.'

'Fizz. Everybody calls me Fizz.'

'Cheeze!' muttered Mrs Menzies, but whether she was
commenting on the nickname or on the TV presenter's
recipe for stewed bugs, was anybody's guess.

'Well, Fizz,' said her husband. 'You haven't come to tell
me you've sold my house already, have you?'

'Unfortunately not,' Fizz admitted with a smile. She slid
her chair closer to him, putting an extra two or three feet
between herself and the TV set which was evidently not
going to be turned off. 'But we have had a couple of
inquiries so it looks like we'll be starting to show the
property pretty soon. I thought, if you could spare me the
time, it would be helpful if we could discuss some of its
selling points in more depth than the prospectus goes into.'

'Happy to. It'll make a pleasant change.' Mr Menzies'

eyes darted briefly towards his wife, inadvertently hinting that not only had age withered her but custom had staled her infinite variety.

'I usually assist Dennis Whittaker in showing properties to clients and it makes it very much more effective if I can give advice as to possible changes the purchasers might wish to make. What snags they might come up against, such as dodgy terrain, local bye-laws—'

'That's the bloody rain started again,' Mrs Menzies thought, just as Fizz's inventive powers let her down. 'I told Shaw not to wash the windows but now look at them. He'll have it all to do again.'

'It occurred to me, for instance,' Fizz plodded on, pretending she didn't notice the mumbling, 'that if a new buyer considered the house a little on the small side – which it could be for some people – we could suggest extending it towards the rear. You hadn't considered that yourself at any time, I don't suppose?'

'What? Building on at the back?' Menzies said in a staccato bark, and his brows came down like stormclouds. 'What about the terrace? The dining room opens out on to that. We have breakfast out there in the summertime. You'd ruin the whole rear aspect of the place.'

'Yes, I'm afraid you would, Mr Menzies.' Fizz agreed sympathetically. 'But the extra room would probably be more important nowadays, particularly to the type of customer we'd expect. It's unlikely to be sold to a private owner, you know. More likely it'll end up as a country house hotel or a nursing home. That is, if it's not bought by a developer who'll want to demolish the house and cover the grounds with residential property.'

'Demolish the house?' Menzies glared around him as though he felt himself attacked on all fronts. 'No, I'll not have that. You hear that, missy? You tell your Mr Whittaker – aye, and Tam Buchanan too – that the house is not to be demolished. I don't want anybody smashing up the dining room terrace either. It's to be left the way it is.'

199

Joyce Holms

'Silly old fool,' said Mrs Menzies, apparently to the bronzed young man who was now showing her how to build a lean-to shelter out of tree branches.

Fizz clasped her hands earnestly. 'With the best will in the world, Mr Menzies, I don't see how we can do that. If somebody buys your estate they can do what they like with it – subject to the planning regulations. We can, of course, ask them their intentions but they are not bound to disclose them and, in my experience, if they suspect we might not approve of them they are quite likely to lie.'

Menzies chewed on that for a minute or two, during which his good lady told herself that she'd have to go, but she didn't specify where and she didn't move from her chair. Fizz gave Menzies time to think over what she'd told him and then twisted the knife.

'There doesn't appear to be any reason to suppose that planning permission, even for a development of residential property, would not be forthcoming. The property market in the Borders is on the up, and your land is close enough to Berwick to make it a viable proposition for a developer. I think you'd have to live with that scenario.'

'I have to admit it,' he said, massaging his shiny knuckles distractedly. 'I never pictured that sort of vandalism. I know . . . yes, yes, of course I know, my dear, that I've no right to put restrictions on the sale, but it's hard to think of Lammerburn going to the dogs like that. I think I told you when you were last here that I always had a soft spot—'

'I'll really have to go,' thought Mrs Menzies in an irritable murmur.

'Well, bloody *go* then, woman!' quoth the patriarch, unexpectedly allowing his irritation to surface and surprising himself as well as Fizz.

Mrs Menzies heaved herself to the edge of her seat and got organised with her Zimmer frame while Fizz, perceiving that speed was of the essence, opened the door for her.

'Sorry, my dear girl. Do forgive me, but one has to be quick.' Mr Menzies' craggy face creased in a smile. 'She

200

doesn't always register her thoughts, you see.'

Fizz, still on her feet, glanced at the rows of books on the shelves beside him and noticed a bunch of what could only be photograph albums. She nodded her head at them and asked, 'Do you have any old photographs of Lammerburn?'

He followed her eyes. 'These are full of Lammerburn snaps. Take a look, if you care to.'

Fizz lifted down the albums and sat down again to leaf through them. Every page was covered with carefully mounted black-and-white photographs showing baggy-trousered young men and short-skirted women, ghillies in plus-fours and maids in severe black dresses and white caps. There were several pictures of a ruggedly handsome Mr Menzies and his petite wife in a huge black car that might have been borrowed from Al Capone, and several of them were set against the luxurious background of Lammerburn House and its environs. Those were the days, was the message: the halcyon summers of youth and optimism when everyone was happy to have survived the second world war and was looking forward to living in a land fit for heroes.

'That was my first car,' Mr Menzies said, touching the page with a crooked forefinger and smiling with remembered pride. 'And that's my sister June who died in ninety-eight. And, look, that's the family having breakfast on the terrace like I was saying. And there, see that? Know what that is above the doorway?'

'Yes. I do know what it is, actually.' Fizz nodded, smiling at his surprise. 'It's the antlers of a twelve pointer. The only stag you ever shot.'

He blinked at her disbelievingly. 'Now, how on earth would you have known that?'

'Because I saw them when I was at Lammerburn last week. Niall said you were very fond of them.'

'Ah yes.' As a squall of rain lashed the windows he took the book on to his own knee and smoothed a hand over the faded image. 'The only stag I ever shot. Old Rusty, we used to call him. I loved watching him every year, guarding his hinds, roaring away like billy-o in the rutting season. He was a great old character. He was a good age when he finally broke his foreleg in a fight and I wouldn't trust anybody else to put him out of his misery.' He closed the book quietly. 'He went down with one bullet in the head, grand old beast that he was. God, it broke my heart to do it to him, but I promised the old fellow a place on my wall as long as I lived. And didn't he look magnificent?'

'Yes, he certainly did and I know exactly how you feel,' Fizz said, trying to ignore Buchanan's warning voice whispering in her ear. It was impossible to predict how the news she was about to deliver would hit Mr Menzies, but the chances were that it would be more likely to affect her cause favourably than otherwise. 'I knew a stag like that once, when I was growing up. A real character. You never forget them, do you? Which is a pity, because I have to tell you: Mrs Menzies disposed of that head with the rest of the furnishings she didn't want.'

'What? Not Old Rusty? She wouldn't do a thing like that! She knew how I felt about him.' He reared back his head as though he were in real pain, then sagged. 'Yes, she would,' he admitted. 'She would. It's a sad thing, my dear, but some people simply cannot accept that some objects are beyond price. My wife is a fine woman, but she never did share my love of Old Rusty. Dear, dear me. I wouldn't have had that happen for the world.'

He seemed to have slipped down in his chair and, to Fizz's somewhat contrite eyes, the spirit seemed to have gone out of him. He sat for a moment, looking at his useless hands, a sad old man, accepting that he was subject to the will of insensitive people, then he glanced up. 'The head went to the sale room last week with all the other stuff, I suppose?'

'Actually,' Fizz said, with downcast eyes, 'I may be able to locate it for you.'

Menzies made a sudden uncontrolled movement that made him wince. 'My dear . . . are you serious? You might be able to get it back?'

Fizz couldn't resist beaming like a game show host. 'I might,' she said pertly, and he laughed with delight. 'But, in return, I want you to do something for me. I want you to think, very very carefully – just think, that's all – whether you might not be happier living at Lammerburn for a few years. You'd be able to enjoy life so much more. With a little estate truck you could be driven around the grounds, and even when you were stuck indoors you'd have something more pleasant to look out at.'

He drew down his thick eyebrows in a frown but his eyes were twinkling underneath. 'And, quite incidentally, the staff could still go on living in the cottages, eh? Well, well, I won't say it hasn't crossed my mind these last few days, but I'm not going to promise anything.'

'Just think about it, okay?'

'I'll think about it.'

'Right,' Fizz stood up, and said, not unlike the Fairy Godmother in Cinderella, 'I'm going to need two extra pairs of hands and a thick blanket.'

This request presented no difficulty to Mr Menzies and in a couple of minutes the nurse and a gangly youth called Shaw met Fizz in the hallway with a choice of travelling rugs. It was, by that time, lashing with rain but the adjacent cloakroom held raincoats for them all and at least half a dozen to spare. Fizz was allocated the plastic mac she'd seen the nurse wearing at her last visit – a tatty-looking object, but with a hood which would keep her hair dry.

Buchanan's face, as he observed the advance of her little army, was rigid with trepidation and the idea of letting her perform an immediate antlerectomy did not grab him at all. It took all Fizz's invective, plus many soothing assurances from the nurse, to persuade him to allow them access. It was very obvious that he'd have preferred to see

Old Rusty's last remains hacked into manageable pieces but in the end, between the four of them, the removal was effected without doing any damage.

Fizz was tempted to leave Shaw and the nurse to restore the antlers to their owner but she couldn't resist going back with them to see the old boy's delight. He was waiting in the hallway to meet them, grinning like a boy, the cockles of his heart not just warmed but done to a turn. Behind him, Mrs Menzies watched the return of Old Rusty with baleful eyes.

'We'll have them up there, Shaw,' said the old man, waving one of his two sticks at the space above the front door. 'I don't want them down low where folks will be hanging their hats on them. Away and get your step ladder, laddie, and do it now.'

'Ugly, flea-bitten old eyesore,' thought his wife, referring no doubt to Old Rusty but glaring at Mr Menzies, so it was impossible to be certain.

Fizz said she had to be on her way and started to remove the borrowed coat but Mr Menzies waved a hand at her. 'You'll need that to get back to the car. Throw it in the bin when you've done with it.' He shuffled towards her and dropped a kiss on her cheek. 'You'll drop in again when you're passing, I hope?'

Fizz said she would, knowing she probably wouldn't, and headed for the door.

'The world would be a better place,' she heard Mrs Menzies muttering, 'if people would just mind their own business.'

Fizz had to smile. How often had she heard that before?

Chapter Seventeen

The morning went well for Buchanan, partly because Fizz was not in the office to keep him off his work and partly because he was motivated to get his In-tray emptied in time for him to squeeze in a fast nine holes before it got too dark. The rain had stopped some time through the night and by early afternoon the clouds were beginning to break up, predicting a reasonable start to the weekend.

About three o'clock he was just beginning to see some light at the end of the tunnel when Ian Fleming phoned.

'Have you time for a pint tonight?' he said, wasting no breath on formalities.

'Tonight?' Buchanan couldn't pretend that the idea grabbed him with any kind of compulsion. He'd be pushed to fit in some golf before his regular Friday night dinner and theatre date and he didn't fancy meeting Ian at eleven o'clock at night. 'Is it important?'

Fleming sniffed irritably. 'Maybe yes, maybe no,' he said. 'It depends on what you make of it.'

'Can't you tell me over the phone?'

'Sure. If all you want is the bare facts. I thought you'd want to discuss things, bounce some ideas off each other.'

'Well, yes, sure.' Buchanan found himself doodling a putter on the cover of his notepad and sighed. 'Maybe you could fill me in briefly just now and we can meet for a drink some time over the weekend. Tomorrow evening, say. I've turned up a few interesting facts over the last couple of days – at least, Fizz has – that I should pass on to you, but nothing of immediate importance.'

'Hang on,' said Fleming. Buchanan heard the sound of the receiver being put down on a hard surface followed by the slam of a door. 'That's better. Too many ears and eyes in this place. Right. There's a couple of things I've cleared up that you can cross off your list, the rest can wait. Firstly, the heater was probably bought from a house clearance that was advertised in the local paper about a month ago. We can't get a definite identification from the woman who handled the sale – she was doing it for a friend whose marriage had just collapsed – but she can confirm that the convector heater mentioned in the advertisement was the model in the catalogue we showed her. There can't be many of that particular model around nowadays, so I think we can assume it to be the same one.'

'Can't she remember anything about the guy she sold it to?' Buchanan said. 'You showed her a photograph of Grassick, I suppose?'

'I did, Tam. At least my pal did, but the woman didn't remember him and she hasn't a clue who bought what. The house was full of people, she says, and she was only interested in taking the money and getting shot of the obligation. That's how it goes, in this business. You win some, you lose some.'

Buchanan couldn't remember when he last won some but he made assenting noises anyway.

'OK. Next thing,' Fleming said. 'It looks like Lawrence Grassick has an alibi for the night his wife copped it. He was definitely at his Edinburgh address when he was informed of his wife's death. I spoke to his housekeeper and she confirms that the phone call came at seven a.m. on the Saturday morning.'

'That doesn't alibi Grassick,' Buchanan objected. 'That's more than four hours after the explosion: plenty of time for him to have driven up from Chirnside.'

'Yes,' Fleming agreed. 'It took time to establish that Mrs Grassick was definitely *in* the house when it went up.

However, Mrs Hewlett, the housekeeper, swears that he was at home all Friday night.'

'You believe her?' Buchanan had to say.

'She's very convincing, Tam, and also, I have confirmation that Grassick's car was in the local garage overnight having a minor ignition fault attended to – had been since late Friday afternoon. That's why he postponed his visit to Brora Lodge at the last minute.'

Buchanan was inclined to feel that this went a long way towards letting Grassick off the hook. Of course, it didn't necessarily follow, just because the man's car was off the road, that he couldn't have used some other means of transport to get to Chirnside. The housekeeper had not, presumably, been sharing his bed so she could hardly swear to the fact that he had not left the house in the six or seven hours between retiring and taking the phone call at seven a.m. All the same, Buchanan was inclined to believe the alibi was genuine. Maybe because, deep down, that was what he wanted to believe.

'Anything else?' he said.

'Nothing important. Lots of statistics but nothing that won't wait till tomorrow. What's new at your end?'

Buchanan gave him a two-minute briefing that covered Vanessa's sudden departure from her friend's house and the missing cat, and promised a fuller report at their next meeting. He had to agree to a pie and a pint at lunch time tomorrow, which broke up his weekend a bit, but Fleming clearly wanted a brainstorming session and – who could tell? – maybe it would bear fruit.

It was weighing on his conscience a little that he had left so much of the Chirnside aspect of the investigation to Giles. The temptation to keep both Fizz and himself as much in the shadows as possible had made him lax and he was already beginning to wish he had taken the trouble to speak to some of Giles's informants himself. He hadn't even met the Armstrong neighbours, which was nothing short of shameful.

This reflection whizzed through his mind in the second
he dropped the phone back in its cradle, and in the same
instant Fizz burst in like a hurricane and threw herself
into the spare chair. One day, Buchanan promised himself,
that chair would disintegrate beneath her and it would
serve her right.

'What are you doing here?' he said, refusing to be
pleased to see her. 'Just a quick answer, please, because I'm
going out.'

'Where?'

Buchanan gave her a hard stare, which amused her still
further.

'What an old grouch you are, Buchanan. And here I am,
thinking about you stuck in this gloomy old office with the
sun shining out there and the birds singing and spring
springing and—'

'Okay. Cut to the chase. You want a lift somewhere.'

'How sweet of you to offer, O pearl beyond price!'

'The answer's no. I'm going to play golf and then I have
plans for the evening.'

Her elfin smile vanished and she glared at him as though
she were about to buy the firm and sack him on the spot.
'Golf! Is that all you have to do with your time, Buchanan?
Are you really happy to let this Grassick thing drag on and
on while you play silly games half the working day?'

'My God, Fizz,' Buchanan responded in exasperation.
'We're talking about an hour's relaxation. You are the
most talented person I know at making mountains out of
molehills!'

'Yeah. Maybe I should have been a cosmetic surgeon.'
She bounced to her feet and strode to the window, hands
in the back pockets of her jeans. 'We should be out there
making things happen, not sitting around waiting for leads
to come to *us*.'

Buchanan could see his quick nine holes disappearing
down a long dark tunnel until it was a mere speck of hope
in the vast blackness of improbability. 'Do you have some

specific source you wish to explore?' he asked politely.

'Dozens,' she said bitterly. 'I want to explore Vanessa Grassick properly, for a start, but we can't go through her belongings without breaking into Grassick's house. We hardly know what sort of woman she was – everyone who knew her tells us something different: she was an iron lady, she was a neurotic, she was a city type, she was a stay-at-home who liked gardening and peace and quiet. I can't get a grip on her at all.'

Buchanan had no trouble in reconciling all of these different aspects of Vanessa Grassick's persona but he had to agree, she was still a shadowy character. Latching on to the most worrying piece of Fizz's speech, he said, 'Speaking of breaking into Grassick's house, Fizz, let's not—'

'Oh, behave yourself, Buchanan! I'm not desperate enough to try something like that – not yet, anyway,' she jabbed, stealing a gleeful look at his face. 'But I do think we should have another poke around Chirnside and have a closer look at the bomb site. If the gods are on our side we might even run into the cat hunter.'

Had Buchanan's thoughts not been running along these lines he might have told her to make her own arrangements, since she was so keen to go, but as things were he knew that his conscience would nag him if he didn't make the effort. Besides, spending a more or less spare couple of hours on the case this afternoon might save him a whole morning or afternoon next week.

They reached Chirnside at twenty-to-four and went into the village for a walkabout in the hope of finding the postman. Not surprisingly, no-one in Royal Mail uniform was in evidence but the pillar box informed them that he would be there to collect the mail at half-past-four, which was not long to wait. Buchanan, in the hope of finding someone who would gossip to them, suggested a cup off coffee to pass the time but Fizz refused – probably a first for her – on the grounds that she wanted to sift the ashes of Brora Lodge while there was still sufficient light to see what she was doing.

It was a silly idea because, not only had she no idea of what she might find, but if she subtracted the ten minutes it would take to drive there and the ten minutes for the return journey, she would have barely a quarter of an hour to search. Buchanan made bold to ask her what she would think of a return trip at the beginning of next week and had to listen to her telling him what she thought of it with appalling fluency and in no uncertain terms.

He was glad to leave her to scrabble about while he took a stroll down the side road for a fresh look at the other houses. The Pringles were still not in residence. He walked up the driveway and rang the front door bell, not expecting an answer but using the action as an excuse for a closer look through the windows. It was quite obvious that the old couple had departed in some haste: he could see the barely started jigsaw puzzle Giles had mentioned, plus a couple of vases of daffodils drooping in stagnant water.

The Fords' house was still untenanted and, like the people who'd lived in it, was giving little away. Apart from the few pieces of rubbish that had blown over from the remains of the house next door, the garden was devoid of colour. The little of it that wasn't flagged over was devoted to two rectangular strips of lawn and a small bed of shrubs, an easily maintained design that was probably convenient in a rented property. Buchanan was standing at the gate looking at the boarded windows when he sensed he was being watched.

He had expected the Armstrong house to be as empty as the others at this hour on a weekday but there was, unmistakably, someone observing his movements from the side of the lounge window. He took a look at his watch and found it was ten-past-four, which left him no time for an in-depth interview with whichever of the Armstrongs was hovering there, but he decided to ring the bell, in any case, and hopefully make an appointment for a later date.

He didn't have to ring the bell. The woman who had

been watching him must have realised she'd been rumbled because, as he reached the end of her driveway, the door opened and she emerged on to the threshold. Perhaps fortunately, the orientation of the house was such that Fizz could not see her from where she was still poking at things with a bit of curtain rail.

Mrs Armstrong, if it were indeed she, was little more than a girl, which was enough of a surprise to Buchanan, since he had classed her in his imagination as roughly a contemporary of the Pringles. But what was more of a surprise was that she was drop-dead gorgeous and sexy enough to knock a guy's eye out at twenty paces.

Her straight caramel-coloured hair lay over her shoulders like a stole and her eyes were brooding and weary as they swept Buchanan from head to toe. She was wearing a lot of shiny eye shadow and her fat lips glittered with what looked like blood red Vaseline, making her look like a lascivious vampire in low-slung jeans. Her cropped top, Buchanan noticed, was so tight he could hardly breathe.

He introduced himself, and inquired if, perchance, he was addressing Mrs Armstrong.

'Yes,' husked the vision, sticking her hands in her pockets, a movement which drew back her shoulders and made two very prominent nipples appear under the thin wool of her mini sweater.

'I . . . I, er, hadn't expected to find you at home today, Mrs Armstrong,' Buchanan told her. 'I understood that both you and Mr Armstrong were out at work.'

'Yes,' she said again, leaving it at that, without embarrassment, as though she felt that the monosyllable was all she need proffer to keep up her end of the conversation.

'I should have called on you earlier to ascertain whether you could help me with the inquiries I'm making into Mrs Grassick's death. I believe you already spoke to Mr Cambridge, the insurance investigator?'

'Yes.'

'Yes, well . . .' Buchanan found himself contemplating her navel and ripped his eyes away. 'I don't want to go over the same ground as Mr Cambridge, but I wondered if I might arrange a time when it would be convenient for you to answer a few of my own questions.'

'Like what?' asked Mrs Armstrong, waxing loquacious.

'Ah . . . well, for instance . . . I would like to know when you last saw either of the Grassicks.'

She leaned a hip against the door jamb and thought about that. 'Mr Grassick was staying down here the weekend before the accident.'

'Just Mr Grassick? His wife wasn't with him?'

'No. She doesn't come down much this time of year.' She straightened suddenly and pushed open the door behind her. 'You'd better come in.'

Buchanan hesitated for less than a millisecond. The postman would be there again on Monday, after all.

Mrs Armstrong took him into the sun room at the side of the house and, unfortunately, he was unable to signal to Fizz from there. However, he didn't plan to be more than two or three minutes so that didn't bother him unduly. He sat down on the end of a cane chaise-longue and carried on from where he had left off. 'And neither of the Grassicks ever came down midweek, I presume.'

'Now and then,' she said, perching opposite him and wriggling her way backwards into the bosomy cushions as hedonistically as a cat. 'But, because our house faces the other way, I didn't always notice they were there. Sometimes I'd see them drive by when I was in Chirnside and think, oh they must be at the cottage today.' She lit a cigarette, making it a performance that wouldn't have got an under-fifteen certificate. 'Like the day of the accident.'

'You saw one of them in Chirnside on the day of the accident?' Buchanan slid to the edge of his seat, knocking a pile of magazines off the cushions beside him.

'No,' she said. 'I told you, I hadn't seen either of them since the weekend before, but I saw the car that day, so one of them must have been at Brora Lodge – or was on the way there.'

'Which way was it headed?' Buchanan asked.

'It wasn't going anywhere,' said Mrs Armstrong, extending the tip of a red tongue to moisten her lower lip. 'I got away from work early, like I did today, because business is so slack at this time of year. I'm a hairdresser, and the boss says it looks bad to have three of us sitting around the salon filing our nails. Anyway, I was driving home along the back road and I saw the car parked in the entrance to a field, up the road there.'

'What time was that?'

'About one o'clock. Maybe a little before that. Twelve-thirty, probably.'

'You didn't mention this to Mr Cambridge?'

'No.' She raised her perfectly shaped eyebrows. 'Should I have?'

Buchanan could scarcely believe it. 'You're quite sure it was Lawrence Grassick's car?'

'Oh, no,' she said blithely, tapping the ash from her cigarette. 'It wasn't *his* car. It was Vanessa's.'

Fizz had started her analysis of the fallout secure in the expectation that it would prove worthwhile. The certainty that the police and the fire brigade had removed everything of interest – a fact that was central to Buchanan's opposition – really didn't count for a great deal. She might find something the original searchers – who had had a different objective – had ignored. It would be great if she did but she was also hoping for something that would be of assistance on a more subliminal level. The largely mindless task concentrated her thoughts – or rather, it disengaged them like transcendental meditation while, at the same time, keeping them focused on Vanessa Grassick. It wasn't the sort of thing you could explain to a man – certainly not a man like Buchanan who was a Martian to his toenails.

She could have done with a lot longer than fifteen minutes, of course. Five minutes into her search she was still thinking of other things while she rifled the shrubbery, raked under bushes, read scraps of paper, hunted down anything that might give her a name or a lead, however tenuous, to follow.

Buchanan had disappeared from her consciousness as though he had never been, leaving only the ghost of an expectation that he would tell her when it was time to go. That was probably why, when the sound of a car engine penetrated her engrossment, she filed it under 'Buchanan' instead of 'run for it'.

She was still making the most of the last few seconds of scrutiny remaining to her when a pair of very shiny black shoes appeared at the corner of her vision. This was totally in keeping with her expectations so she sat back, clawed her hair out of her eyes and looked up, with a horrible jolt, at Lawrence Grassick.

At the debate, where she had been enthralled by his rationalism, she had found him almost handsome but there was nothing appealing in the face that glared furiously down at her, nor did there remain a trace of his persuasive reasoning in the voice that barked, 'What are *you* looking for?'

Fizz was struck dumb with shock, her mind scrolling fast through a list of possible answers to his question: a contact lens, a four-leafed clover, frog spawn, mushrooms, fossils, flatworms, badger tracks . . .

Feeling at a serious disadvantage, she stood up but even then he seemed to tower over her, blotting out the light. His eyes narrowed on her face.

'I've seen you before,' he said. 'That's right. You were in the audience last week when I was speaking . . . I saw you jumping up and down in your seat as if you were about to start throwing something at the panel, but you never opened your mouth.'

'Yes, that was me,' Fizz exclaimed, light-headed with

relief, and started gabbling nineteen to the dozen, steering him off down this unexpected avenue of escape. 'What a wonderful debate. I really really enjoyed it. And you spoke so compellingly that you totally changed my mind about the issue. In fact, I've decided I really must get more actively involved in social issues like that. If more people—'

He was only half listening to her and, as she twittered on, his eyes did a quick recce of the street. Luckily Buchanan's Saab was out of sight in the turning bay beyond the Armstrong house.

'Ah, yes,' he interrupted, in a swift return to the harsh voice he had used for his first remark. 'You're Tam Buchanan's little girl, the one Niall Menzies mentioned. Helping your boss snuffle around in my private affairs, are you? Rooting for something to get his face in the papers again, eh? What d'you call that – work experience?'

'I'm not Tam Buchanan's little girl,' Fizz said, with a rush of blood to the head. She could see nothing of Buchanan and concluded that he was keeping a low profile. Lower than the nearest garden hedge, probably, and damn right too. 'I'm nobody's "little girl". I'm—'

'Right,' Grassick snarled, supremely uninterested in who she claimed to be. 'Then I'll tell you what I told Buchanan: mind your own business! If I see you snooping around my property again I'll call the police and have you charged.'

Fizz threw her useful piece of curtain rod into the bushes and backed off a step, but she couldn't bear to let him push her around without getting something out of it. Without a preamble, which he would have cut off in its prime, she asked, 'Are you having me followed?'

'Eh?' He was visibly caught off balance. 'Followed? What's this? No, I have not damn well had you followed! You have an inflated sense of your own importance – you and that idiot boss of yours both!'

'Tam Buchanan is no idiot,' Fizz said, hating him as much as she had bothered to hate anyone for years. 'And not only is he smart, Mr Grassick, he's honest, which is a combination that ought to worry a man like you.'

Grassick immediately went apeshit and started bellowing in a voice that must have carried clearly to Tam, wherever he was hiding.

'What d'you mean, "a man like me", you insolent wee smout? You'd better watch your tongue or you'll find yourself in serious trouble, and that's a warning! Dammit, I'm not having this. There will be a stop put to it first thing Monday morning, and that's the end of it.'

He had a lot more to say, along these general lines, but he suddenly appeared to realise that he was wasting his breath on the monkey when he really wanted to berate the organ-grinder and, with a last and most insulting 'Tcha!', he turned on his heel and marched away, breaking his stride only once, to yell back at her, 'Now get the hell off my land, y'hear me?'

Fizz was only too happy to comply. In truth, she had to force herself to keep to a steady pace as she stumbled out on to the roadway and headed for the main road. She had to assume that Buchanan could see where she was going but she had to get out of sight of Grassick who was now loading garden urns into the boot of his car.

A few paces along the road she found a small wood where she could hide till the coast was clear and it was only when she stopped to sit down that she realised how traumatised she was by her encounter – not by Grassick's aggression so much as by the loss of her prospects of an illustrious career, at least as far as Edinburgh was concerned. Her legs were shaking and something akin to a sob escaped her, bubbling up through her chest like a cross between a hiccup and a gasp. Sod the bastard, she told herself, looking for something not too lethal to punch.

She didn't give a hoot what Buchanan thought about Grassick's alibi. She'd see him pronounced guilty even if she had to frame the bastard.

Chapter Eighteen

Buchanan could not understand how Fizz could accept the disaster so calmly. Either she was putting a brave face on it – which would surely have been beyond even Fizz – or she didn't care.

If you can keep your head when all about you are losing theirs, he thought, as they headed back to Edinburgh, maybe you haven't fully grasped the situation.

'Hey, shit happens,' was her response to his primary reaction of mild hysteria. 'And, anyway, it hasn't happened. *Yet*. He can't take out an injunction against us till after the weekend, and as far as ruining my career goes, I'll worry about that when I'm waiting in the queue at the Job Centre, not before. That's the trouble with you, Buchanan, you worry about things before you have to and half the time they turn out to be not worth worrying about. Lighten up.'

Buchanan made an effort to embrace this theory, in which he could discern a certain logic, but he couldn't even start to deal with the crushing weight of guilt that was his and his alone. Not only had he allowed Fizz to be identified as his accessary but he had abandoned her, at the critical moment, for a voluptuous bimbo when he might have spotted Grassick's approach and warned her to get lost.

'So, what did Mrs Armstrong tell you?' Fizz chirped, putting a firm end to his self-castigation. 'Nothing of interest, I suppose?'

Buchanan's optimism on hearing about Mrs Armstrong's sighting of Vanessa's car had by now, like every other ray of hope in his immediate future, evaporated. It didn't offer any fast solution to the mystery surrounding the explosion; in fact, it only increased the confusion. He told Fizz about it anyway and she was as puzzled as he.

'Why park the car so far from the house?' Fizz asked herself and then answered her own question. 'Because she didn't want the neighbours to know she was there. All the neighbours? Or just the Pringles? Or just Jamie Ford's wife? Huh?' She turned her head to check if Buchanan was listening to her. 'Was it, in fact, really Vanessa who was driving the car at that point, or could Lawrence have borrowed it because his own was acting up?'

'We have confirmation that Vanessa was in Inverness, presumably in her own car – check that, will you? – by five-ish. Mrs Armstrong saw the car at twelve-thirty, which gives Vanessa a clear four and a half hours to get to her first appointment in Inverness. Ample time. She could do it in three if she really put her foot down.'

'But if Lawrence had been driving her car earlier he'd still have had time to get it back to her before she left home, right?'

'I suppose so,' Buchanan agreed, perceiving that she now had it in for Grassick in a big way. God help the man.

'You see?' Fizz beat a clenched fist on her knee. 'We're hamstrung because we don't know anything about Vanessa. We don't even have a photograph of her so how can we begin to tell what sort of person she really was? People tell us that she wouldn't have looked twice at Jamie Ford. "She was too posh", right? But was she? And if it wasn't sex that brought the two of them together, what was it?'

'The only two people who might have the answer to that, Fizz, are her husband and Poppy Ford, and there's not much chance of either of them inviting us over for a cosy chat.'

Fizz looked out her window at a distant oil tanker making its way up the Forth to Grangemouth. 'No,' she said, thoughtfully, 'but it's just occurred to me that Vanessa must have had office space at work and I'll lay you seven to four that lazy sod Rudyard hasn't cleared her desk yet. I wouldn't mind a look-see.'

Buchanan was immediately against the idea, and said so, but in the absence of any better leads he eventually allowed himself to be talked round to it. He was persuaded as much by the knowledge of his own guilt as by Fizz. After dropping her into this mess, the least he could do was to get her out of it by any means possible, and before Grassick could stop him.

'But, bear in mind, Fizz, that we don't have any business to be raking through Vanessa's effects,' he warned her, for all the good it would do him. 'If Rudyard is willing to help us go through her papers, that's fine, but we tell him up front what we want and give him the option to tell us to go to hell.'

'He won't tell us to go to hell,' Fizz stated positively. 'He's too bloody lethargic to care.'

Buchanan had serious doubts about that, but they proved to be unfounded. Rudyard was not even roused to asperity by the arrival of two visitors just as he was about to lock up shop for the weekend. The last of the staff were on their way out as he led Buchanan and Fizz into his office and cleared spaces for them to sit down.

'We've been badly held up in the processing of Mrs Grassick's will,' Fizz told him as she wiped something off the seat and fell into it with her usual delicacy. 'But with any luck – and a little help from our friends,' she added with a twinkly smile for the bemused Rudyard, 'we're hoping to get everything wound up by the beginning of next week. That's why we thought we'd try to catch you today before you disappeared for the weekend. I know we're a nuisance but a few minutes at this point would be well spent.'

Rudyard was clearly at a loss to know what he'd done to bring on such chumminess in one who had barely looked in his direction at the time of her last visit. He watched closely as Fizz loosened her jacket and fluffed up her hair and it took him a moment or two to formulate the sentence, 'Uh ... no problem. I'm not in any hurry tonight.'

'That's good,' Fizz said, 'because it would be nice just to have a quiet chat.'

Rudyard glanced at Buchanan but, receiving no elucidation of this remark, he returned his attention to Fizz. 'What about?' he said.

'Oh, just about Vanessa,' Fizz assured him, as though that were the most natural thing in the world and, such was her serenity, he didn't make any protest.

He must surely, Buchanan thought, have already told them everything he knew about his former business partner, and anyone else would have jibbed at the idea of being questioned for the third time about the circumstances surrounding her death. Rudyard, however, didn't give a damn about anything and was no more miserable undergoing questioning than he would have been had they left him alone.

Fizz put an elbow on the desk and cupped her chin in her hand. 'We were wondering about Vanessa's car,' she said lazily. 'Did her husband ever borrow it – in emergencies, for instance, like when his own was off the road?'

A small puzzled frown came and went between Rudyard's eyebrows. 'I wouldn't know,' he said vaguely. 'I suppose he might borrow it if Vanessa didn't need it but I don't remember Vanessa ever saying as much to me. Why do you ask that?'

'Because, Lawrence's car was off the road for the afternoon and evening of the day before Vanessa was killed.' Fizz smiled faintly. 'Would it be likely, do you think, for Vanessa to let Lawrence have the car and, perhaps, to have flown up to Inverness instead?'

Rudyard sighed and slumped lower in his seat, his expression as well as his body language indicating that he couldn't see why he should be expected to know what Vanessa might have done. Buchanan could sympathise with him but realised that Fizz was merely softening him up for the question she really wanted to ask.

'She might have gone by air,' Rudyard admitted. 'She took a plane once or twice before but she preferred to take her car so that she could nip around Inverness between customers. She definitely planned to go by car that last time.'

'I don't suppose you'd have any idea when her car was last serviced?' Fizz asked next, surprising both of her listeners.

Buchanan couldn't see the point of such a line of inquiry but Fizz clearly had some idea of where she was heading so he decided to preserve his observer status.

'No, I haven't a clue.' Rudyard muttered.

'There wouldn't be any documentation around the office, would there?'

Rudyard's mournful eyes drifted momentarily to his computer, but then he shook his head. 'No. I wouldn't have any of that stuff. It wasn't a firm's car, you see; she just claimed mileage. Does it matter?'

'That's a pity,' Fizz's forefinger touched her lip in a fair assumption of consternation. 'Would that sort of thing be on her own computer, I wonder?'

'Maybe,' he said. 'Want me to look?'

'Would you?' Fizz lavished a smile on him and stood up. 'You're very kind.'

Buchanan got his feet under him to follow them from the room but Fizz, in passing his chair, put a hand on his shoulder and pressed him back down. At the door, she paused and, in a complicated mime, instructed him either to lie on the floor and eat something, or to stay where he was and keep talking, neither of which seemed to make any sense.

However, he had underestimated her talent for manipulation. Rudyard returned to his seat behind the desk within a couple of minutes, so Buchanan went for the second option, asking every question he could think of that would keep him out of Fizz's hair. There came a time, however, when neither of them could pretend not to notice that Fizz was taking an eternity. Finally, Rudyard looked, for the third time, at his watch and said he really ought to be moving along, leaving Buchanan with no option but to agree.

As they stepped out into the corridor he could see Fizz, through an open doorway, still frowning at a computer. 'Sorry . . . am I holding you back? Only, I'm not very good at spreadsheets and I kept on getting shunted back to the desktop. I guess I'll have to leave it for now.'

She hitched her jacket closed and slung her bag over her shoulder while Rudyard sped them on their way with woebegone predictions of traffic jams all his way home.

Buchanan was never so glad to get out of anywhere. Bad enough to be stuck in a small dirty room with a crime against society like Rudyard, without knowing, beyond a shadow of doubt, that Fizz was doing something grossly immoral, if not illegal, a matter of feet away. The fact that Rudyard had given her permission to look at a specific spreadsheet was small comfort to anyone who knew Fizz, and there was something in the way she had slung that bag over her shoulder that had turned Buchanan's blood to ice.

'You went through the desk drawers,' he said to her as they emerged into Nicholson Street, and she laughed like an innocent child.

'Yer on to me, guv. It's a fair cop. I won't give yer no trouble.'

'For God's sake, Fizz. Don't you ever worry that you might get caught? If I'd guessed you'd do a thing like that I'd never have come with you.'

Fizz grabbed his arm and dragged him to a halt, standing in the middle of the pavement with a solid flow of people swirling by on each side of them. 'Listen, Buchanan. In a couple of days we'll both be dead, as far as our careers are concerned, and I've no intention of sitting around on my tush waiting for Grassick to do a hatchet job on us. Over this weekend I'll be fighting for my life. It's our last chance and I don't want any interference from you, okay? If you can't stand the heat, stay out of the kitchen.'

And off she went, striding down the hill towards the High Street like an invading horde of one. Buchanan followed her and caught her up. He had little option because, whatever she did, he wanted to know about it. Even if his role was merely that of damage limitation, he had no intention of letting her go it alone.

'So, what's in the shoulder bag?' he asked, taking her arm to slow her down.

'I don't know. I didn't have time to look. It's only the rubbish that was in her waste-paper basket.' She glanced up at him with her eyes full of mischief. 'The place was practically unlived-in. Obviously, she spent most of her working day on the road and only used the office as a way station. There was nothing in the desk drawers except business stuff and the computer was just as sterile so, when I heard you coming, I just tipped the rubbish into my bag. Rubbish can be very illuminating, you know. I'll sort through it when I get home. Want to help me?'

Her flat was only a couple of blocks away so they left the car round the corner from Rudyard's studio, where Buchanan had managed to find a parking place, and walked.

Buchanan had been in Fizz's flat on only half a dozen occasions in the two years he'd known her and he still felt inexplicably flattered to be allowed to cross her threshold. As far as he knew, he was the only person she had invited in, with the single exception of his cousin, Mark, who had stitched up her eyebrow last summer.

Fizz didn't like just anyone to know too much about her, and her flat, basic as it was, told Buchanan quite a lot, and possibly more than he wanted to know. There was little comfort in the two rooms that she rented: a bed, a built-in wardrobe and dressing-table, a kitchen table and three chairs and a few kitchen appliances like a fridge and cooker. Of Fizz herself there was virtually nothing, and what there was – her course books, an irreducible amount of clothing, and the scatter of photographs on the mantelpiece – could, at the drop of a hat, either be thrown away or packed into a rucksack should she decide to return to her roving ways. The place was, as ever, scrupulously neat, but then, how could she make a mess from so few ingredients?

She threw off her jacket and made a couple of mugs of coffee before she did anything else and Buchanan took the opportunity to look at her gallery of snapshots in case there were any of Giles. There weren't: just the usual selection of Grampa and Auntie Duff, one of her pal, Rowena, with her husband and baby, and a couple of views of Loch Tay showing Am Bealach's five houses and the inn. He wondered if there were other photographs somewhere that showed scenes from her life abroad and whether, if there were, he would ever be allowed to see them.

'OK, compadre, let's get on with it.'

Fizz handed him his coffee and tipped out her bag on the kitchen table, displaying such interesting objects as a toothbrush, a diary, a pair of socks, a neatly coiled piece of string, a pair of sunglasses, a penknife, a silk scarf, a hair bobble, an Elastoplast dressing, a tassel of safety pins and a packet of tissues. These all went back into the bag leaving behind a good sized heap of scrap paper and other trash.

Fizz picked out a twisted-up sheet of foolscap, spread it out on the table, scanned it, and pushed it aside without comment. Buchanan, overcoming his shame and distaste, followed her example and, steadily, they worked through the heap.

No matter how you looked at it, there really was nothing worth a second glance. The sum total of Buchanan's findings at the end of his perusal amounted to little more than the discovery that Vanessa got through a lot of emery boards, was a member of the RSPB, ate Wispa bars and, judging by the postmarks on most of the discarded envelopes, didn't empty her waste-paper basket very often.

'Well, it was a long shot anyway,' Fizz admitted, scooping the junk into a plastic bin bag. 'But if we don't get a break in the next couple of days I wouldn't mind having a look at what's in Lawrence's wheelie bin.'

The idea of rummaging in someone else's garbage – even his own, for that matter – made Buchanan feel sick. But that was typical of Fizz, he thought. If she wanted something she went for it, straight on past where any sensible person would have had enough, no matter if her monumental effort gained her only half an inch of headway.

He said, 'We haven't had many breaks in the past two weeks. If we get one over the weekend it'll be a miracle.'

'From now on, like I said, we make our own breaks. I've got an idea that might work. First thing tomorrow we pay a visit to the . . .'

Buchanan looked up from the litter of paper clips and elastic bands which he was sweeping into the bin bag to see her examining a narrow strip of cardboard no more than a couple of inches long. 'What's that?'

She narrowed her eyes, scowling at the scrap as though commanding it to give up its secrets. 'I don't know . . . but I recognise those colours. That sickly pink and turquoise blue. I could be totally off beam on this, Buchanan. I mean it could be anything . . .'

'Yes?' said Buchanan, tiring of all this justification.

'I'm just saying . . . I'd have to check, of course, but . . . it reminds me of the packaging from a pregnancy test kit.'

Chapter Nineteen

It was impossible for Fizz to check out her pregnancy-test theory immediately because the chemists' shops were closed. She had to leave it till nine o'clock the following morning when Buchanan came to pick her up and drive her to their next nefarious project.

Luckily, there was a pharmacy right next door to her flat and it only took a moment to check it out while Buchanan sat, double-parked and choleric, outside.

'Well?' he asked, as he pulled away virtually under the nose of a traffic warden. 'Were you right?'

'Am I ever wrong, muchacho?'

Fizz really liked it when things went well first thing in the morning. You could be almost certain it would continue to be a good day: a day when everything you set your hand to would go the way you wanted it to and random chance would operate in your favour. A day that started off badly was doomed to be one in which even inanimate objects turned against you, but today she had a feeling that they were going to see some action.

'Does that mean . . .?' Buchanan asked, as they waited at the roundabout at Holyrood House. 'Does that mean we can be reasonably sure that the cardboard came from a pregnancy test kit, or are there other packages with the same colour scheme? You know . . . some pharmaceuticals have a livery of colours that all their products come in.'

'No, not this one,' Fizz assured him. 'I had a good look around the shelves for anything similar – and, anyway, no

227

two companies would pick such vile colours. I'd stake my ranch in Texas on it.'

God knows, she thought, I've seen enough of those packets to recognise one when I see it. She wondered briefly about the flatmate she'd lived with in Manchester. Linda Something. She used to make out that she was so cool, so streetwise, yet every other month there was a pink-and-turquoise packet in the bathroom bin. Poor fat-headed Linda. She'd probably have acquired six kids, chronic depression, and no future by this time.

'We don't even know when Vanessa bought the thing, do we?' Buchanan was saying. 'Could have been months ago.'

'No, I don't think so. None of her rubbish was that old. Didn't you look at the dates on the letters and the post-marks on the envelopes? They only went back to about six weeks before she died.' Fizz did a little mental arithmetic. 'I reckon she bought that test around about the last week in January at the earliest. Any earlier than that and it wouldn't have been in the bin.'

Buchanan slid her a funny look as one who would say, and anyway, how come you're such an expert on preg-nancy tests? but Fizz didn't feel she had to explain herself to him.

After a while he said, 'We're making rather a lot of unfounded assumptions, of course. The test may not have been Vanessa's, or it could have been left behind in the waste bin accidentally – maybe months ago – when she last emptied it, and anyway, we've no way of telling whether the actual test turned out positive or negative.'

Fizz was as certain as she could be that the test was positive. People like Vanessa didn't fool around with sex. If Rudyard was right in saying that she didn't want a family, there was no way she'd have been taking chances like some simple-minded schoolgirl. So, whatever means of contra-ception she'd been using, she must have had an accident – an accident she hadn't been aware of, otherwise she'd have rushed out for a morning-after pill. Forgetting to take a crucial contraceptive pill, or even a faulty condom, could have been sufficient to put her in the club.

'She was pregnant,' she said. 'If she'd been used to having irregular periods she wouldn't have worried. I reckon she was pretty well certain she was pregnant before she bought the test.'

'You can't possibly know that, Fizz,' Buchanan said, being congenitally unable to see anything but solid facts.

Fizz didn't bother to argue. Sooner or later he'd find she was right.

The Forth appeared in intermittent flashes between the warehouses and industrial premises along Seafield Road, slate grey and sluggish. On the far shore the Kingdom of Fife was masked by low cloud, making Fizz feel she was looking at a seascape.

'You do know where this place is?' Buchanan said.

'Not precisely, but it's on the shore side. I remember noticing the lines of kennels one time when I was taking people to view a house in Portobello. I'm sure we'll see the sign.'

'I hope you've thought this through, Fizz. I wouldn't like to see you being charged with wasting police time.' Buchanan leaned forward, peering through the streaming windscreen to scan the buildings on their left. 'And you could be, you know. Very easily.'

'No chance,' Fizz claimed, with partly feigned confidence. 'I've brought my disguise with me.'

She heaved her bag over from the back seat and produced a pair of glasses and a ski cap with a broad skip. 'See?' she said, when she had tucked all her hair out of view. 'Admit it – you couldn't tell me from Schwarzenegger.'

Buchanan rolled his eyes but was prevented from saying something sarcastic by the appearance of the sign advertising the dog and cat home.

The place looked like a miniature POW camp. The main construction material appeared to be chain-link fencing, which surrounded the long rows of whitewashed kennels with their cramped runs, the administrative buildings and the exercise areas. Inside, however, the place was spotlessly clean and, Fizz was glad to note, smelled of neither disinfectant nor doggy poo.

There was a small reception area, well stocked with leads, dog food, cat toys, baskets, and books about how to discipline your dog or carry out your cat's wishes to its satisfaction. Fizz waited her turn at the desk, identified herself as a potential customer, and was told to follow a white line to the waiting room. Buchanan tagged along uneasily, out into the yard, past a couple of low buildings, and into a room containing a few chairs and a wall of kids' drawings. Bereft of any other amusement, they studied the artwork until a young girl arrived to attend to them.

'Looking for a cat?' she inquired, chewing vigorously on a large wad of gum. 'Follow me.'

The cattery was only a few paces away: more chain-link fencing inside a long, not unpleasant building still lit by fugitive shafts of low morning sunlight. Only a dozen or so of the cages were occupied.

'Is this the lot?' Fizz asked.

'Yep. Some days we don't have a spare cage,' the girl said, 'other days we've hardly any cats at all. Just depends. Cats go fast, you see. Not like dogs.'

Each cage bore a card giving the particulars of the occupant and contained a comfortable basket with woolly rugs and a couple of cat toys. Opposite the main battery of temporary accommodation there were a couple of chain-link 'playrooms' that someone had designed with love and intelligence so that the cats had things to climb and chase and explore.

Buchanan was immediately importuned by a big ginger and white tom who rushed to the front of his cage and started stropping himself up and down the links till his mark was forced to insert a finger and scratch his cheek. Fizz, knowing Buchanan for a sucker, was on to him right away.

'Let's not cuddle them all, Buchanan, huh? We don't want to waste too much time.'

Buchanan swept an eye over the cages. 'What about that one?'

'Too much white on him.'

'Is white a no-no?'

Fizz sighed. 'Buchanan,' she muttered in an undertone, 'you wouldn't call a cat "Jet" if it wasn't totally black, now would you? Like that one there.'

She indicated a motionless object in one of the playrooms. Surrounded by what amounted to a feline Disneyland, it was lying on its side on a piece of rug in an attitude of deepest unconcern, and looked like it had been filleted and left out in the sun to cure.

Fizz turned to their assistant. 'Can you tell me about this one?'

The girl heaved herself off the door post and wandered over to an empty cage to read the card. 'Male, two years old, his name's Pooky and he was handed in the day before yesterday by his owner who was going abroad. Thirty pounds.'

Fizz was somewhat taken aback by the price. She had more or less assumed that they'd be giving cats away with a packet of tea but, since it was totally dependent on charity, the home, she supposed, would need to get some money from somewhere to support the long-stay animals. She risked a glance at Buchanan's face and discovered him looking a trifle pained but, what the hell? He'd spend that much on a decent meal without thinking twice about it.

'I'd like that one,' she said, making a unilateral decision to save time. 'We have a cat basket in the car.'

Pooky barely woke up as the girl picked him up and carried him back to the reception desk. Nor did he make any objection when, presently, he was transferred into Buchanan's arms and carried out to the Saab. Actually, he was a very attractive cat, if you liked that sort of thing, with huge green eyes and a purr that clearly stole Buchanan's heart.

'What are they going to think when you take him back tomorrow,' he asked as he tenderly laid the inert bundle in Selina's travelling basket.

Fizz was not at all worried about that. If it actually came to pass, which she doubted, she'd be surprised if the people at the home would mind being able to sell Pooky for another thirty pounds.

Unlike Selina, who hated the sight of her travelling basket and demanded the freedom of the whole car on a journey of any length, Pooky was tickled pink with the mohair lap rug with which it was padded and fell asleep almost right away. Every time Buchanan stopped the car to check that he was still content and in perfect health his reports were heart-gladdeningly optimistic and they reached Hawick without incident.

'We'd better eat first,' Fizz said, spotting a promising restaurant in the main street and simultaneously experiencing a strong spasm of hunger.

'What about Pooky?'

'Look at him. He's unconscious.'

'Yes, but what if he wakes up and finds us gone?'

'Buchanan, he's a cat.' Fizz gave him a warning look. 'It won't mark him for life. And I'm hungry.'

He took a further careful look at the inert moggy and reluctantly abandoned it to its fate for all of twenty minutes. Fortunately, Fizz could eat quite a lot in twenty minutes and, seeing that they had no idea when they'd next get a decent meal, she forced Buchanan not only to do the same, but to buy a stock of Yorkie bars and canned drinks sufficient to sustain them for an indefinite period.

'Okay, mon capitaine,' Fizz said, as she sampled one of the Yorkie bars, 'let's do it.'

They couldn't miss the police station: it was an impressive three-storey building, as befitted the main office for the Borders district, standing on its own in the main street and only a few yards from where they'd parked the car. Pooky, as far as Fizz could tell, didn't even wake up as she carried the basket into the foyer and laid it on the counter of the inquiry desk.

'Help you, miss?'

The desk sergeant was no rookie. He had one of those middle-aged faces that has seen human nature at its worst and would slap the cuffs on you as soon as look at you. Not the ideal sucker for any sort of scam.

Fizz gave him a nervous smile which was only partly counterfeit. 'I'm staying up at Chirnside and I've been looking after this cat for a couple of weeks. It was starving. I'd really like to keep it but a neighbour told me she'd seen a guy looking for a black cat.'

'Yes, well we don't take in lost animals, miss. You'd have to take it to the council offices. They have a system for dealing with them there.'

This was news to Fizz and it didn't fit in at all well with her plans. In fact, it looked like she'd made a complete pig's arse of things. 'But the council offices aren't open on a Saturday, are they?' she complained, hanging on in the belief that if you kept on talking you'd say the right thing sooner or later or, alternatively, you'd at least give the guy time to change his mind. 'See . . . I remember when our cat wandered away. I was only five and it really upset me. I cried myself to sleep every night till it came back. I'd really love to keep . . . er . . . Sooty, but I'd just hate it if I was upsetting another kid like that.'

'Yes, well you see, miss,' the sergeant said, with a now-I've-seen-everything look directed at his buddy who'd been reading a bunch of forms behind him, 'we don't have any place to keep a cat in the station here. Why don't you wait till Monday and—'

'Er . . . hang on a minute.' The guy behind him came forward to the counter and gave his partner a lingering sort of glance that conveyed nothing to Fizz but caused the sergeant to narrow his eyes a trifle. 'Let's have a look.'

He brought his eye close to the openweave panel on top of the basket and examined the soporific Pooky. 'Uh-huh. Would you mind holding on a minute, miss?'

Both he and his buddy walked to the back of the office and, after a brief exchange of mutters, the sergeant made a phone call. It took him about five minutes, which Fizz passed in fingering an unfamiliar object in her coat pocket, and then he came back to the counter and picked up the basket. 'That's all right, miss. We can take care of this for you. Just leave your phone number and if we can't find the owner we'll see the cat is returned to you.'

Fizz was flushed with success. It looked as if she had managed to snatch a bull's-eye from the jaws of a pig's arse. She wasn't up for identifying herself too precisely but she gave a false name and the phone number of her next door neighbour, Mrs Auld, claiming it was her work number in case they recognised the code.

Outside, she found Buchanan awaiting her reappearance with a set face.

'That took a long time,' he said tensely. 'I thought you'd be just in and out again.'

'Kemo Sabe, Rome was not built in a day.'

Buchanan studied her expression. 'You look extraordinarily pleased with yourself. I take it this means you have reason to believe—'

'God! You sound like you're dictating your words to a stonemason sometimes, you know that, Buchanan? Yes! I am pleased with myself. I reckon they'd been told to keep an eye out for a black cat. What am I – a genius or what? I'm telling you, rosebud, this is going to be our lucky, lucky day. We simply cannot lose. There is a phalanx of angels at our shoulder. Our strength is as the strength of ten because our hearts are pure.'

'God,' Buchanan said widening his hot blue eyes in awe. 'Is it really going to work?'

'Can't fail,' Fizz assured him, awarding herself another Yorkie bar. 'All we have to do is wait.'

They pulled across the road and parked close to the start of a side street from where they could observe both the main entrance and the side door of the police station and there they waited and watched. Three hours, four Yorkie bars and two cans of Sprite later they were still waiting and watching. Nobody with a cat basket went either in or out.

It wasn't too tedious because they took turns to walk up and down the street, a few paces one way and a few paces the other. Fizz did a bit of window-shopping, phoned Mrs Auld to let her know to expect a phone call from the Hawick police, and visited the public loo. Buchanan jogged down their side street and back again, replenished their food supply, and bought a newspaper.

'She won't come herself for the cat,' Buchanan said, on his return from his third period of R&R. 'She'll send the chap that Giles spotted at Chirnside, or somebody else. And anyway, whoever comes for the cat, if they know it by sight they'll take one look at Pooky and realise he's not Jet. They could have been and gone hours ago.'

'That's true,' Fizz admitted, having worked that out way back when the plan had first occurred to her. But she'd done a lot of thinking since then. 'Poppy won't come, I'm with you on that, but I reckon nobody but the owner could be sure that Pooky isn't Jet, not after Jet had presumably put in a week or two living rough and probably starving most of the time. They'd have to take him for Poppy to identify before they could be sure. I reckon the only thing we have to worry about is that Jet may have had some identifying mark, like a torn ear or something obvious like that. Otherwise, we're in with a shout. And I still feel lucky.'

'Good for you,' Buchanan said, clicking back his seat a couple of notches. 'Keep it up, then, and give me a nudge if anything happens. I'm going to grab a little shut-eye in case this takes all night.'

Fizz, who had been about to commandeer that privilege for herself, could only resolve not to underestimate him in future and console herself with the last Yorkie bar. It was deadly boring just sitting there without even Buchanan to talk to. She couldn't go for a walk to ease the monotony, she was fed up listening to the radio, and by the time things started to move she was beginning to feel herself in imminent danger of getting deep-vein thrombosis.

The first thing she noticed was a black car that pulled into the restricted parking slots just outside the side door of the station. The driver was tall and slim, about thirty-five, and knew where he was going. Fizz nudged Buchanan.

'What?'

'See that black car?'

'Where?'

'At the side door. Is it a Ford?'

'Why?'

Fizz scowled at him. 'If you say "When?" next, Buchanan, I'll sock you in the mouth. The word we got at the hospital, Giles and I, was that Poppy had been picked up there by a guy in a black Ford Ka. They said he was in his thirties, which isn't a bad description of the guy who just marched in at the side door like he owned the place.'

Buchanan yawned. 'Likely to be a policeman, then,' he said. 'Were you expecting a policeman to come and identify Poppy's cat?'

'No, I can't say I was.' Fizz was staring so unblinkingly at the side door that her eyes were starting to water. 'But it doesn't throw me. Anything's possible. Just as long as he's not shacking up with her twenty-four hours a day, otherwise it'll be the devil's own job to get near enough to her for a chat.'

It was about ten minutes before the guy reappeared and the sight of the cat basket he was carrying made Fizz want to dance a salsa. He slid it into the back, with less gentleness than Buchanan felt should go unremarked, and started to back out.

'Okay, genius, here we go,' Buchanan said and slotted the Saab, as to the manner born, into the stream of traffic three cars behind what was now identifiable as a Ford Ka.

Fizz was on a real high. She was convinced she was on a run. She felt so empowered she could probably heal scrofula with her touch. They were on their way to Poppy's hideaway and Poppy had to be the person who knew what was what. Obviously. Otherwise, why was it so important to keep her hidden away?

Chapter Twenty

The rain had started again with a vengeance, and Buchanan had great difficulty keeping the Ford in sight while, at the same time, keeping at least two cars between it and himself.

He hadn't driven through Hawick before and the driver of the Ford Ka was either just as unfamiliar with the traffic systems as he, or he was taking a circuitous route to his destination in the hope of throwing off any pursuit. This uncertainty made Buchanan even more jittery than he already was and, in spite of Fizz's stream of helpful suggestions, he took every precaution he could against being spotted, even to the point of losing sight of his quarry for harrowing minutes at a time while traversing a parallel route.

He had ground his teeth to stubs – so Fizz assured him – by the time they saw the Ford stop at a terrace house on the outskirts of Greenlaw. They had to drive straight past the end of the road but Buchanan swung a U-turn and zapped back again in time to see the cat basket and its lanky custodian moving up the path towards the door.

There was only about thirty or forty feet between the doorway and the hedge that Fizz, having leapt out on their first pass, was peering through, and as Buchanan joined her the caller lifted a fist and rapped on the window beside the door. Two soft raps, three sharp, and one soft.

'Did you see that?' Fizz said, with a giggle, when the door had closed behind the guy. 'A coded knock! You wouldn't believe it if you read it in a book, would you?'

Fizz wasn't given to giggling but Buchanan suspected she was, if not hysterical, a fraction over-excited. 'A sensible precaution, I'd call it,' he whispered. 'Did you see who opened the door to him?'

'No. But I thought I heard a woman's voice – kind of high-pitched. I imagine that's what Poppy would sound like if she thought she was getting her cat back.'

Buchanan hoped she was right. The whole escapade had progressed much further that he had ever anticipated. From the outset, he had rated their hopes of success somewhere between point one per cent and zero, but he had felt obliged, out of sheer culpability, to give Fizz all the help she needed, no matter what. And now, in spite of all the pitfalls they could have encountered, here they were on Poppy Ford's doorstep. Fizz had to be right: there were angels at their shoulders.

When the guy emerged from the doorway, some fifteen minutes later, he was still carrying the cat basket. Pooky was off on another adventure and Buchanan's heart bled to see him go.

They waited till the policeman's car was out of sight and then zapped round the corner and up Poppy's garden path. Fizz, who was ahead by a couple of paces, tapped on the window: two soft, three sharp, one soft, and then ducked down below the level of the window.

'You didn't need to do that, surely?' Buchanan said, and had to bend down to catch her reply which was, in any case, inaudible behind the clatter of the downpour.

The curtain moved briefly, as he stood up, but in a manner so cursory that it would have been impossible for the person inside to say whether the figure outside in the half darkness and the pouring rain was really the previous caller or not. A moment later, Buchanan heard the sound of a chain being disengaged and locks being unfastened.

'Did you forget—' said the pale face that floated out of the gloom, and then she screamed.

'Don't be afraid!' Buchanan cried, lacerated by the

sound, but Fizz stepped around him and stuck a boot in the door the woman was frantically trying to slam shut.

Suddenly all three of them were in a shadowy hallway, with the door closed behind them and Fizz holding Poppy firmly by the wrists as she said, 'It's all right, Poppy. We're lawyers. We're here to help you.'

Buchanan was adding his pleas to the babble of noise, apologising to Poppy over and over for frightening her. He wanted nothing more than to run away and shoot himself in the head, but Fizz was firmly in charge of the situation and was going nowhere.

In the end, it was obvious to both of them that it was Buchanan's distraught face that convinced Poppy of their *bona fides*. Gradually, her screaming and sobbing subsided and Fizz, who was roughly her height and weight, was able to release her.

'We really are no danger to you, Mrs Ford,' Buchanan said. 'Believe me, if I'd known how much our appearance would distress you I'd never have put you through it. I do hope you can forgive us.'

'Yes . . . if you'll just *go*!' she wailed through her tears. 'You're *still* frightening me! Please just *go away*!'

'I'm sorry, Poppy, but we can't go,' Fizz said, guiding her through a lamp-lit doorway into the living room. 'Not right away. My career hangs on getting to speak to you for a few minutes. Just ten minutes and then we'll leave. If you still want us to go.'

Poppy looked again at Buchanan, her brimming eyes reading his face as though she wanted to believe what she saw there. He gave her the hankie from his breast pocket and tentatively patted her shoulder.

'It's the truth, Mrs Ford. We've been investigating Mrs Grassick's death and we've got ourselves in a spot of trouble. We really need your help.' He found one of his business cards and, although he knew he should be keeping his identity a secret, handed it to her.

She afforded it barely a glance but it appeared, to some

degree, to put her mind at rest. She took a few unsteady steps towards a low overstuffed couch and sat down, covering her eyes with a clenched wad of Buchanan's hankie.

Buchanan could hardly bear to look at her. She was a skinny little thing, no taller than Fizz but, where Fizz appeared compact and healthy, Poppy's slimness spoke of junk food and an unhealthy lifestyle. Her blonde hair was stringy, and the pallid arms sticking out of her short-sleeved sweater were skin and bone. There were still two dressings covering what must have been deep cuts on her arms and her face was covered with lesser, half-healed lacerations.

It had never once occurred to Buchanan that her reaction to being found would be such a negative one, but now the pieces were fast falling into place and he could understand the alarm he must have caused her. The cat swindle had been cruel enough and only Fizz's desperate situation had persuaded him to go along with it, but to realise that he had added to the trauma this poor girl had already suffered was doing his head in.

Fizz stood in the middle of the floor, rain dripping off her borrowed mac on to the carpet, and emanated impatience like static electricity. She pointed at an invisible wristwatch and operated an imaginary starting handle while her eyes rolled to the door in a mime of shocked anticipation.

Buchanan doubted very much if they would be interrupted. If the policeman had spotted them, which he felt pretty sure was not the case, he'd have come back by now and, the way Buchanan was reading the signs, nobody else knew Poppy's current address. He frowned at Fizz and pointed firmly to a chair and, after a concise and insulting mime, she threw off her mac and settled down.

Buchanan took the low armchair that faced Poppy's couch across the fireplace and said, 'Would a cup of tea help, Mrs Ford?'

She shook her head, still hiding behind the hankie, but,

after a moment, she emerged, wiped her eyes and gave each of them a nervous appraisal. 'What do you want?' she said to Buchanan in a voice that twisted his guts. 'Who are you?'

Buchanan made a small gesture towards the card she had dropped on her lap. 'I'm a solicitor, Mrs Ford. I'm executor of Vanessa Grassick's will and my assistant, Fizz, and I have been trying to find out exactly what happened the night she died, and why.'

He glanced at Fizz but she was apparently disposed, for the present at least, to let him do the talking. Poppy, too, was willing him to go on so he did, keeping his voice as slow and gentle as he knew how, to avoid spooking her again.

'We've been blundering around in the dark for two weeks and getting nowhere. In fact it wasn't until I saw how frightened you were that I realised the truth – or, at least, part of the truth. And, please believe me, I'd never have put you through that if I'd known what we were doing.'

He shut his teeth together to stop himself from going on and on about how sorry he was and, in the pause, he could see Fizz staring at him, her whole face a question. Partly to keep her silent and partly to get it out of the way, he continued, 'You're being looked after through a Witness Protection Scheme, of course. I should have realised it when we saw the chap picking up the cat. We suspected that he was a policeman but things were happening so quickly I didn't think it through.'

'Fat lot of protection they're giving me!' she said violently, her breath still coming in dry sobs. 'If you can find me, so can they!'

'I think that's extremely unlikely,' Buchanan said, projecting a confidence he didn't feel.

'No it's not! I'm bloody sure they were on to us in the last house.'

'In Chirnside? What make you think that, Mrs Ford?'

'Someone had been asking in the pub about new residents in the village. Who had moved in within the last six

months? What age were they? What did they look like?'
She was spitting the words out, almost incoherent with
rage and despair. 'It got back to Jamie pretty quick and
they – the WPS department – said they'd move us on at the
weekend. Only they weren't bloody quick enough, were
they? And now *you've* found me and it'll be *them* next. Am
I going to have to live like this for the rest of my life?'

'Who are *they*?' Fizz asked, without giving the woman
time to wipe her eyes.

Poppy spared her barely a glance and shook her head
violently. 'I can't talk about it.'

'Why not?' Fizz persisted but Buchanan frowned her
down.

He said, 'That's all right, Mrs Ford. We won't pester you
to say anything that makes you feel threatened. That's the
last thing we want.'

Poppy nodded, almost imperceptibly. 'I wish you
wouldn't call me Mrs Ford. I'm not Mrs Ford any more.
That's all past. I'm myself again.'

'Will you be happier that way?' Buchanan said.

'You bet I will! It was no fun being married to a two-
faced liar . . . a drug-dealer . . . a thug . . . a rotten . . .'
Tears welled in her eyes and she brushed them away with an
angry sweep of her fist. 'If I can just disappear, like they
promised me . . .'

'You'll be able to put it all behind you and live your own
life,' Buchanan finished for her. 'And I'm sure you will,
Poppy. If they found you at Chirnside it must have been
through some very remote stroke of luck. Believe me, I've
been involved with WPS before and I've never heard of a
single instance of the protection being inadequate. If
neither you nor your husband told anyone that you weren't
who you appeared to be—'

'Yes, but he did,' Poppy said violently. She got up and
walked over to pick up a packet of cigarettes from the top
of the TV. 'Jamie told one of the local cops the night they
picked him up for drunk driving. Bloody fool! He'd have

been better to pay his fine, or whatever, and keep his mouth shut. But that was Jamie.' She stuck a cigarette between her lips and laughed bitterly as she lit it. 'That was my wonderful husband. Never faced up to anything in his bloody life. Everything was somebody else's fault: his mum's, his teacher's, his parole officer's – never Jamie Ford's. Had to wriggle out of everything, didn't he? Even if it meant giving away our past. I knew that bloody copper would let it slip. I told Jamie it was too juicy a piece of gossip for a local bobby to keep to himself. He might as well have put it in the local paper.'

She dragged in a lungful of nicotine and resumed her seat as she let the smoke drift out through her nose. Buchanan would have killed for a cup of tea but clearly she had no intention of making one, so he said, 'Do you feel able to tell us what happened that night, Poppy? The night Brora Lodge was demolished?'

She let out a puff of tobacco smoke in a single spurt as she raised her eyes to the ceiling and said, 'Huh!'

It looked like she was going to refuse but, after a minute, she started to talk like she needed to get it out.

'It was just a matter of hours after we'd requested a move so we were both pretty nervy and not sleeping too well. Jamie had got up to make us a cup of tea – must have been nearly two-thirty – and he saw someone in the Grassicks' garden, moving about with a torch.'

'You knew the house was empty?' Fizz asked.

'Yes, 'cause we'd thought that Lawrence might come down that weekend and he didn't. Nobody had arrived by the time we went to bed at one o'clock.' She drew on her cigarette and smoothed her skirt as though she had lost the thread of what she was saying.

'So,' Buchanan prompted tentatively, 'you must have wondered, given the situation, if someone had mistaken their house for yours.'

'Right. Either that or the place was being burgled, and nothing would stop Jamie from going to meet trouble halfway. I wanted him just to phone Dougie – he's our WPS contact and we have his mobile number so that we can speak to him right away, whatever the time of day or night.' She rubbed distractedly at a cigarette burn on the arm of her chair. 'Anyway, he got out his gun and crept out through the gardens. I begged him not to go in, but he said the best way would be to ring the doorbell and hide till he could see who came to the door. I know . . . in fact, I'm bloody sure he would have gone in anyway if nobody had appeared – that's how crazy he was – but he didn't get the chance. I could see him from the bedroom window as he crossed the gardens. He was very careful. Kept himself hidden all the way. He was just pressing the bell when – *woosh*! – like the whole world exploded!'

Her hands were shaking so much she could hardly handle her cigarette but the words kept tumbling out so urgently that Buchanan felt it better to let her run.

'I didn't really see what happened. The windows came in . . . and the *bang* . . . you wouldn't believe how loud . . . and everything was lit up, bright as day, by the flames . . .'

Buchanan, unable to prevent himself, crossed over to sit beside her and reached for her hand, whereupon she threw herself against his chest and burst into a storm of weeping. All he could think to do was wrap his arms round her and pat her back, neither action having the least therapeutic effect. After a couple of minutes of this he said, 'I think a cup of tea is called for. Fizz, maybe you could rustle up something?'

'Tcha!' Fizz returned, having clearly picked up this useful expression from Mrs Menzies, and came over to crouch beside Poppy. 'Where d'you keep your booze, kid?'

This allusion turned out to be something of a miracle cure. Poppy gave a few closing snorts, wiped her eyes and lurched across to a glass-topped cupboard and, minutes later, she and Fizz were getting outside a pair of titanic scotch and cokes, while Buchanan had to settle for neat soda.

'If you've already given your evidence,' Fizz asked, coming across to take Buchanan's abandoned armchair, 'surely the people you gave evidence against are behind bars? So, who's after you?'

'They banged up all the guys who were actively involved in the syndicate – that's what Jamie called the bunch of thugs he worked for – but the head honcho's son always had it in for Jamie. Jerry Kincaid. He never showed his face around his dad's operation but he had operations of his own – big business, like transporting illegal immigrants, drugs, money-laundering. The police won't ever get anything on him – his left hand doesn't know what his right hand's doing – but he's the only one who would be after us now. And he'll keep going till he finds me.'

Her fingers tightened on Buchanan's hand, which she was still, apparently, unable to dispense with. The cushions of the couch being what they were, both she and Buchanan had sunk down into a half crouch that felt, to one of them at least, a damn sight too cosy.

Buchanan did his best to achieve a slightly more upright posture as he said, 'So, you both gave evidence? Not just Jamie?'

She nodded, looking thoughtfully into her whisky. 'Jamie never tried to keep me out of things. I knew right from the off that he was into something and, of course, I wasn't supposed to know the details, but Jamie never could keep anything to himself. Kincaid – Jerry's dad, like – enjoyed flaunting his "family", as he called us. He thought he was untouchable and he loved rubbing people's noses in it – the police and everybody else. He'd take us all out for flashy dinners every week, the boys and their wives or girlfriends – or girls hired for the evening. We all had to be done up to the nines, wearing bags of jewellery and fancy evening dresses – the works. Fifteen or twenty of us sometimes.'

She concentrated on her drink and a second cigarette for a few moments, smiling to herself with bitter rancour.

'It was all so silly and childish, but at the time I thought I was living high, living life the smart way. Then Kincaid started giving me little jobs to do. Just once in a while. Just on the fringes of the operation. You know – taking stuff through customs, driving a van load somewhere, stuff that it's easier for a woman to get away with. I never got stopped. Maybe I looked too young and innocent. Being quite small, you know?'

Buchanan knew all right. He didn't look at Fizz as he asked, 'Jamie didn't mind you being involved?'

'No. Why should he? The money was good and Kincaid always said that if we got nabbed he'd get us off. He had contacts. That's what he told us anyway.' She leaned forward to stub out her cigarette. 'But then he started asking me to do other things, like luring a mark into a taxi and then buggering off. I never asked why I was doing it but it eventually sunk in that I never saw that mark again.'

'You mean, Kincaid was bumping them off?' Fizz wanted to know.

'That's what I believed, even though Jamie tried to tell me they'd just been told to leave town. Either way, I wasn't too happy about it and I told Jamie I wasn't doing it any more, but he wouldn't listen to me.' She twisted her lips nastily. 'Jamie had a way of making you listen to his opinion that had me in stitches – literally. More than once. And Kincaid was another one who got ugly with people who didn't do what they were told. The way he put it, if you weren't with him you were against him.'

Fizz was about to start prompting as soon as Poppy stopped for breath but Buchanan sent her a warning look and waited. Poppy hauled herself up out of the sofa's close embrace and refilled their glasses. Both she and Fizz had already sunk more spirits than it would have taken to slow Buchanan's reflexes quite considerably, but only Poppy was showing it.

'Anyway,' she said, coming back to her seat and reclaiming Buchanan's hand, 'Jamie started to want out as well, after a while. I think he was doing things for Kincaid, by that time, that were a bit much even for him. He never said, but I could tell he was getting scared. Then, this guy came along. I think they called him "Bats". He had a friend in the force – that's what he told Jamie, but we suspected he was really a police nark – and he put it to Jamie, bit by bit – you know? – that if he grassed on Kincaid's operation he'd do pretty well out of it: no charges against him, a new house as good as the one we were staying in, a complete new identity and all the rest of it.'

'So you went along with it?' Fizz got in.

Poppy nodded, guzzling her drink. 'You know,' she said, manifestly voicing the thought as it occurred to her, 'I'm really glad you two came in this evening. I needed a bit of company. I'm feeling better than I've felt since . . . it happened. You're awf'ly nice.'

Fizz took that compliment to herself, smiling chummily at Poppy as if she were succumbing as rapidly as Poppy was to a whisky-induced euphoria. 'And after the trial you were set up in a rented house in Chirnside, right?'

'Just temporarily. They'd promised us a nice place like the house we'd left – not tucked away in the back of beyond like that one. It was driving me nuts, that place, with no-one to talk to but Liza Armstrong and the *Pringles*, for God's sake – Bonnie and Clyde with wrinkles, Jamie used to call them. I wish those two nosy old buggers had got blown up into the bargain.'

Buchanan would have liked to free his hand. Hers was uncomfortably hot, suddenly, and a bit sweaty and besides, he had a suspicion that she was actually pushing her luck a bit. Whether it was due to his comforting presence or the result of getting her story off her chest or, more likely, the whisky, she was undoubtedly on the mend. Her head was lolling on the back of the couch but she was, to his eyes, more elated than sleepy.

'So, how does Vanessa Grassick come into the story?' Fizz said, still as razor sharp as ever, which was, to

Buchanan's mind, yet another sign of a mis-spent youth.

Poppy lifted her head a fraction but the effort was too much for her and she let it bounce back again. 'Vanessa? Has she got something to do with it? How do you mean?'

'What was she doing in Brora Lodge?'

'She lives there.'

'Yes, but how come she was arriving at two-thirty in the morning?'

'How would I know?' Poppy retorted, with a certain lack of clarity and a happy giggle. 'I didn't ev'n know she was *in* there till they tol' me.'

That was not the answer Fizz had been hoping for. She said, 'You and Jamie – you weren't involved with the Grassicks?'

'You kidding? They didn't even wave to us over the hedge. Very pally with the Pringles, though. Old man Pringle looked after their house for them. Had done for years.'

'Yes, we know all about that,' Fizz said with a hint of impatience, and spent a little time tapping her glass irritably against her teeth. Then she said, 'But Vanessa didn't usually visit Brora Lodge on her own, did she? If she came at all she came with her husband, right?'

'Not always,' Poppy said, sounding a fraction defensive. 'She w's there 'lone one mornin' quite early, not that long ago. Just for 'bout five minutes. I saw her go in with a heater.'

Fizz's face froze in an expression of shocked disbelief and, since he was currently questioning the efficacy of his own hearing, Buchanan had to assume that he looked much the same. Nobody said a word.

Then the door crashed open, rebounding off the wall and sending the smashed handle flying across the room.

250

Chapter Twenty-One

Fizz was stone-cold sober. If she hadn't been a moment ago she sure as hell was now.

Even before the door had hit the wall, or so it seemed to her, she had dived over the arm of her hugely overstuffed chair and was now crouched on her knees beside it making herself invisible. Only not invisible enough.

'You!' roared an unfamiliar voice. 'Out of there and round here where I can see you!'

There wasn't much doubt who he was speaking to since both Poppy and Buchanan were trapped in the embrace of the couch and staring past her with their eyes on a level with their kneecaps. She stood up and moved, as if someone new at the job was operating her with strings, into the middle of the carpet, discovering as she did so that the intruder was the centurion-type she'd suspected of tailing her. He was streaming wet, throbbing with potential violence, and waving a massive gun that would have made Dirty Harry's look like a cigarette lighter.

'Over there.' He waved the pistol and Fizz made haste to obey, flattening herself against the wall facing the fireplace.

Buchanan and Poppy were roughly the same shade of pale blue; Buchanan rigidly unmoving, Poppy gasping for air and clinging to him like a condom.

The centurion gave a chuckle, deep in his chest, which did all sorts of unpleasant things to Fizz's sphincter muscles.

'Well, well, well. Now this *is* a pleasant surprise. Three fish in the one net. That's something I *hadn't* expected.'

He stepped forward into the room and stood there, straddle-legged and grinning, while he looked them over with almost obscene rapacity.

No-one could have called him an attractive man, but Fizz had failed to register on their previous encounters just how ugly he was. His face was big and muscular, like his body, with a large, fleshy and discoloured nose like an aged scrotum, and his jaw alone was, to Fizz's inflamed senses, a weapon of mass destruction. It was heavily boned and too wide even for his big face, and it was set with big yellow teeth that leaned this way and that like old tombstones. Now that his hair was plastered to his head Fizz could see a square scar above one temple: probably the result of an operation or the repair of an old wound.

Moving crabwise and keeping them all covered with his cannon, he grabbed the open bottle of whisky and sunk a couple of large gulps.

'Right,' he said, allowing a trickle of amber liquid to run unchecked down his chin so that he could retain his grip on the bottle. 'Now let's not do this the hard way, folks. Nobody's going to get hurt. You're all going to stay very quiet. No talking. No fidgeting around. You're going to sit there and I'm going to sit here and we'll all get along like a house on fire.'

He lowered himself carefully to the seat Fizz had just vacated and, keeping the gun swinging backwards and forwards between all of them, he took a mobile phone out of his jerkin pocket and, using the same hand, thumbed in a number.

'It's me. I got good news for you.' He leaned back on the cushions and grinned all over his face. 'Yeah, but not just her, I got the other two here as well . . . the lawyers . . . Yeah. No, Curly didn't lead me anywhere, in the end. It was the copper you were talking to in the pub . . . Yeah, eventually . . . with a little persuasion. Sure. Had to, didn't

I? But don't worry, I tidied up real careful. The lawyers?
Yeah, sure they're alive. You said to . . . yeah, well I didn't
know that, did I? They was all sitting here, like Sunday
school, havin' a quiet drink. Well . . . Yeah sure. No prob-
lemo. How long . . .?' The grin withered abruptly and he
sat up, struggling against the pull of the fat cushions.
'You're bloody joking. Can't you make it before that? Why
can't I do it myself? Yeah, but the other two? Yeah, well
okay Jerry, but put your foot down, for fuck's sake. I've got
another migraine and it's fuckin' blinding me. Yeah, well
try.'

His good humour hadn't lasted long. He put the phone
down on the arm of his chair and, standing up, carefully
shrugged off his wet jerkin, one arm at a time, and threw it
on the floor. As he sat down again, Fizz could hear
Buchanan shhhhh-ing Poppy who was gargling like a
coffee percolator and trying to hide inside his jacket.

'That's right,' the centurion growled, pouring some more
whisky down his gullet. 'You just keep her quiet and we
won't have any trouble.'

Fizz's intellectual faculties were not operating on all
cylinders. In fact, she was in such a state of panic that her
brain had virtually shut down to permit all support systems
to be diverted to the primary task of keeping her conscious.
Had it not been for the proximity of the wall, she thought,
her legs would have given way minutes ago. Even as it was,
they were twitching so hard she was sure Buchanan could
see her jeans flapping, and the way he was looking at her,
she was afraid he'd do or say something and get himself
pistol-whipped at the very least. Hurriedly, she moved a
hand a little to attract the centurion's attention and said,
'I'm sorry, but I'm going to faint. Can I sit down?'

He took his time about answering her, letting his eyes
travel lazily over her face and body while he thought about
it. Then he said, 'Okay. Slowly. And keep your hands
where I can see them.'

Fizz slid down the wall. It felt infinitely better to be able

Joyce Holms

to wrap her arms around her shins and rest her head on her knees. After a minute, she had regained enough bottle to see if she could get the centurion talking. She hadn't a clue what good it might do but it certainly wasn't doing any good waiting here quietly till Jerry Kincaid arrived to top them all – and she was hideously convinced that something of that nature was on the agenda. The time limit was anybody's guess, but she reckoned they must have at least half an hour, otherwise the centurion wouldn't have complained so much. Taking a couple of deep breaths, she lifted her head.

'Thank you,' she whispered, as an opening gambit. She hadn't intended to whisper but that's how it came out. 'I feel better now.'

He looked at her without either sympathy or annoyance and returned to rubbing his temples, which he had been doing since he dropped the phone, alternating the massage with pinching the bridge of his nose between his eyes, and delicately fingering his closed lids – unfortunately one at a time.

Not that Fizz would have jumped him, even if he'd shut both eyes at once, but she wouldn't put it past Buchanan to do something so insanely suicidal. She knew him well enough to be able to see at a glance that he was trying to think of some way out and he was such a frigging hero that he was perfectly capable of throwing himself on the gun in the hope that Fizz and Poppy might somehow profit by his death. And *that* Fizz was determined to avoid.

She looked at the centurion and cleared her throat.

'You must have known about the cat, then.' She said it very quietly, as if that would make a blind bit of difference.

'Shut it!' He swung the gun round at her, making Buchanan twitch, and then added, with sullen reluctance, 'What cat?'

Fizz knew then that she'd hooked him and, if she could just play him for a while, she could at least divert some of his attention from Buchanan. She nodded her head at Poppy.

254

'Her cat.'

The centurion examined the sobbing Poppy for a minute, squinting his eyes as though he wasn't focusing too well. 'What about her cat?'

'That's how we found out where she had moved to. I thought you must have done the same. Or did you follow us?'

'Shut it!' he said again, evidently feeling that she was taking a mile. The words were delivered in a bark but it made him wince and when he spoke again he had turned down the volume. 'This isn't a fucking debating society. I asked you about the fucking cat. Don't make me ask you again.'

Fizz tried to look willing while still spinning out the story as much as she dared. 'We were told the cat was dead – and it looks like it probably is – but we heard that somebody was looking for it so we bought a cat and took it to the police station and said we'd found it at Chirnside. They took it in and I suppose they notified the guy from the Witness Protection Scheme. Anyway, we just waited outside till someone came out carrying the cat basket and then we followed him here. That's why I wondered if you'd followed us.'

He leered and moved the gun significantly. 'I have my own methods.' His scrunched up eyes swung round on Poppy. 'If your grovelling little bastard of a husband had kept his mouth shut, just once in his fucking life, you'd've been sitting pretty. Once a secret's out, it's out.' His smile was not a thing of beauty. He glanced again at his gun. 'But don't worry, kiddies. It's not going to go any further. I just sorted that out.'

If he was trying to frighten them he was doing a grand job, at least on Fizz and, quite manifestly, on Poppy. Buchanan had regained some colour and his eyes were moving carefully around the room as if he were looking for a weapon or some other aid to escape. Fizz was pretty sure he wouldn't find anything, because she'd been pursuing that line of thought herself, but she wished he'd stop thinking of a physical approach and start using his intellect.

The centurion was in an unassailable position and while he held that awesome firearm nobody was going anywhere. The WPS bloke was not going to return, the cavalry was not going to arrive, and a conveniently distracting shelf of pans in the kitchen was probably not going to collapse with a crash, diverting his attention while they all jumped on him. Their only hope was to keep on trying to distract him, watch out for a weakness, and pray for a lucky break.

The only weakness in his defence, as far as Fizz could see, was his migraine. It was, by now, quite apparent that he was in serious pain and might even, she thought, be showing signs of nausea. He had put aside the bottle of whisky, his expression betraying just a passing hint of distaste, and there were beads of sweat gathering on his brow. If only he would throw up maybe there would be a split second when they could try for the gun.

Struggling to think of some way of keeping him talking, she murmured, 'You mean, you shot a policeman?'

He didn't like her talking but he did like frightening her and, after a brief struggle with his higher consciousness, he decided to spoil himself. 'You can't make an omelette without breaking eggs, sweetheart. Couldn't very well leave him to tell his boss who he'd been blabbing to, could I? Not that he *wanted* to blab. No, no. Had to be persuaded a little, didn't he? Took a little time but he was happy enough to get it off his chest in the end.'

'What did you do to him?' Fizz asked. She positively did not want to know but she could see he was dying to tell her and if he was concentrating on enjoying himself he'd be that much more vulnerable.

'Are you sure you want to know, sweetheart?'

'Actually,' said Buchanan in a reasonable voice, 'I don't think it would be a good idea.'

The gun swept round to point at his chest.

'Who asked your opinion, Valentino?'

'Nobody,' said Buchanan mildly. 'But I don't really think you want to listen to a bout of hysterics and it's already taking me all my time to keep this lady from going completely off the rails. If you'll take my advice—'

'Shut it! Keep your fucking advice to yourself, you'll be needing it more than me.'

'Could Poppy at least have a glass of water?' Buchanan persisted, so hopelessly that Fizz knew he was deliberately taking over from her as interlocutor.

'No she fucking couldn't.' He made the mistake of shouting his reply and regretted it visibly. 'Fuck,' he said, and pointed the gun at Poppy. 'You, bitch. Get me some painkillers.'

Poppy burst into tears again and wailed that she didn't have any, she didn't use them, she had an ulcer, she'd just moved in, and a bunch of other extraneous information that only made the centurion all the madder. He told her to 'shut it' twice in a dampened tone but finally had to shout it, which was just about the last straw.

'Just shut it, the lot of you.' He leaned forward, his elbows on his knees and his big jaw hanging like a ham. He looked haggard but the gun was still pointed unwaveringly at Buchanan's chest.

Fizz felt the sweat break out of her the instant the brainwave hit her. She knew for a certainty that she would be up to her eyebrows in the shit if she tried and failed, and that scared the breath from her body. If she had not been totally certain that they were all about to die she wouldn't have had the audacity – the desperation – to grasp at what was only a single, very fragile straw.

She lifted an arm to wipe the sweat out of her eyes with her sleeve and the movement caught the centurion's eye. Wordlessly, she pointed at the plastic coat lying at his feet where it had fallen as she dived for cover.

He frowned down at it and then back at her face. 'What?'

'Aspirins,' Fizz croaked. She knew immediately that she'd said the wrong thing. If she'd said 'painkillers' she might have got away with it but now, if he noticed that they weren't aspirins, he'd realise what she was up to and there would be repercussions. Painful, if not fatal repercussions.

Her brain had already predicted every possible eventuality – including Buchanan getting himself shot trying to save her – in the few seconds it took for the centurion to slide the coat towards him with his foot. Luckily it was the right way up for him to see the aspirin bottle through the transparent plastic. Keeping the gun level he stooped down and closed his hand round it.

Fizz couldn't watch. She closed her eyes and leaned her head back against the wall, hugging her knees to her chest so that he wouldn't see her shivering. She heard the rattle of the tablets as they were tipped out of their container. She heard an unexpected gurgle of liquid, and then recognised it as coming from the whisky bottle. Her teeth started to chatter.

When she finally got her eyes open everything looked the same as when she had shut them except that Buchanan was now looking at her as if he was momentarily expecting her to pitch forward on her face. The fear of him doing something silly, at this stage in the game, forced her, while the centurion was pinching his nose, to give her head a tiny shake and look pointedly at the bottle of pills. It was lying on its side on the arm of the centurion's chair and he hadn't bothered to replace the cap, which implied he was intending to have more if he needed them.

Fizz wondered how many he had taken. She was pretty sure the nurse had said two would knock Mr Menzies out for twelve hours, but even if the centurion had taken just one there was a chance it would slow his reflexes a bit. Whatever happened, they were going to have to make their move against him soon since his boss was bound to arrive in the next few minutes.

After waiting a minute or two, she tried wiping her brow

with her sleeve again and, this time, he didn't swing round
to look at her. She couldn't see his eyes properly because
he held them slitted anyway and, in profile, she wasn't sure
how alert they were. But then, little by microscopic little,
he started to sag sideways against the arm of the chair
and, a moment later, the gun slid from his flaccid fingers.

In a blur of movement, Buchanan had it in his hand and
was standing over the centurion. He put a hand on the
man's shoulder and gave him a small shove and they all
watched, unbelievingly, as the big guy slouched back in his
little nest and let his jaw thud to his chest.

Buchanan came over to Fizz and picked her up by the
elbows and wiped the sweat – it must have been sweat –
from her eyes with his thumb.

'What were they?' he asked.

'The sleeping pills the nurse took away from Mr Menzies.
She left them in her coat pocket. I felt the bottle there but I
didn't register what it was till he asked for painkillers. How
many did he take?'

'At least four.' He looked at her carefully and then urged
her forward with an arm round her shoulders. 'OK. Get
the hell out of here. Here are the car keys. You and Poppy
can wait there while I immobilise this guy and phone the
police.'

'I'll help you,' Fizz said, not totally in favour of the
splitting-up scenario, but he just shook his head and got
Poppy on her feet.

'Get moving. Jerry Kincaid won't keep us waiting much
longer. And Fizz, stay in the car till I join you, right?'

Fizz would have loved to argue but it would have been a
waste of time and, if the truth were told, she didn't have
the bottle. She had expended every trace of adrenalin in
her entire glandular system and if Jerry Kincaid were to
pop up right now she knew she'd be nothing but a liability.
She grabbed up the plastic mac and a coat for Poppy and
the pair of them, tightly clasped like a couple of refugees,
staggered round the corner to the Saab.

★ ★ ★

Buchanan took off his tie and belt and immobilised the comatose centurion. He didn't look like he would be a nuisance to anybody for at least a couple of days but Buchanan wasn't taking any chances. That done, he phoned Hawick police station and told them what was happening and suggested that they inform the WPS plus the ambulance service in case a stomach pump was needed.

There was no movement to be seen outside yet but, regardless of who'd get here first, he knew he wouldn't have long to wait. He went into the hall and unlatched the front door, then he got his hands under the centurion's armpits and dragged him into the bedroom. It was icy cold in there because the window had been lying open since the centurion's felonious entry, but that wasn't a big worry. He stuffed a handful of Poppy's briefs into the guy's mouth – it took five to fill it – and lashed them in place with a pair of nylon tights. More nylon tights reinforced his makeshift fetters and attached the still snoring centurion to the radiator.

Back in the living room, he swung the smashed door back against the wall, kicked the centurion's black leather jerkin out of sight behind the couch, and sat down to wait. If Kincaid was the first to arrive, he was going to make bloody sure he stayed here till the police showed up.

And Kincaid did come first: moving almost soundlessly through the unlocked front door and along the passage-way to appear framed in the doorway with his hands casually in his coat pockets and his blond hair dark with rain.

'Hello Giles,' Buchanan said, understanding swamping his brief flash of surprise. 'Or do I call you Jerry now?'

'Jerry would be nice,' he said, grinning his white grin and swaggering forward to glance around the room. 'Am I too late for the party?'

'I fear so. But there's some booze left. Can I offer you a drink?'

Giles paused for a second as though he were listening for something and then said, 'Just a small one, I'm driving.'

Buchanan held out the whisky bottle and Jerry took his left hand out of his coat pocket to accept it. One didn't have to ask oneself what he held in his right.

'So let's talk, Tam,' he said, propping his behind against the edge of the drinks cupboard.

Buchanan himself had chosen the arm of the couch hoping that Jerry would fall for the charms of the over-stuffed armchair but Jerry had been too long at the game to fall for that one.

'Sure. What would you like to talk about, Jerry?'

'Sylvie Bennett, alias Poppy Ford. Where is she now?'

'Gone,' said Buchanan obtusely, playing for time. 'Didn't you know that already?'

Jerry narrowed his focus. 'You mean Bragg's taken her?'

'Bragg? I don't think I know anyone of that name.'

'Let's stop playing silly buggers, Tam,' Giles barked, suddenly losing his cool and whipping forth his pistol. 'You know damn well who Bragg is. Is Sylvie with him?'

'If you mean the chap you've had following Fizz – and no doubt myself – I'd be very surprised if Sylvie were with him.'

'So, where is she? And stop wasting time, Buchanan, or I'll put a bullet in your head.'

Buchanan, straining his ears for the arrival of the police, heard a faint sound from the hallway, and could have cheered with relief. 'That wouldn't be a good idea – would it? – since I'm the only person who knows where she is?'

Saying that turned out not to be such a good idea, either. Jerry's face suddenly contorted with fury and, before Buchanan could react, he brought up his pistol and pulled the trigger.

Buchanan went over backwards on to the fat cushions of the couch. For a couple of seconds shock and outrage blotted out the pain, and for the next couple of seconds real terror gripped him as he heard Fizz's voice yell, 'You bastard!'

As he clawed his way out of the clutch of the upholstery he saw Jerry swing the gun round on Fizz and, without wasting time on deliberation, he grabbed the centurion's cannot from where he'd concealed it between the cushions and shot Jerry, as luck would have it, in the buttock.

The impact threw Jerry forward at Fizz's feet and she promptly stood on his hand and snatched his gun. 'Bloody hell, Buchanan,' she said, above Jerry's agonised roars, 'I can't leave you alone for a minute.'

Buchanan was swamped by pain and wallowing in the blood that appeared to be gushing from the side of his chest.

'Fizz,' he got out between gritted teeth. 'You're sacked.'

Chapter Twenty-Two

Fizz decided against visiting Buchanan in hospital on Sunday. Admittedly, she would have liked to assure herself that his wound was not as serious as it had appeared to be the night before but this was well outweighed by three facts: (1) she hated hospitals, (2) she didn't feel all that good herself, and (3) a cooling-off period wouldn't do any harm.

Buchanan, when last seen, had been ready to make her his second victim and so potent had been his vituperation and abuse that she had begun to admit to herself that he might have a point. At the same time, it was all very well for Buchanan to yell, he wasn't the one who'd had to sit in that freezing car watching the arrival of sodding Jerry Kincaid and wondering what the hell was going on. And anyway, Kincaid wouldn't have stopped at one bullet. If she hadn't shown up when she did he'd have kept on shooting bits off Buchanan till he established Poppy's whereabouts. Which just showed what a thankless bastard Buchanan was. He didn't deserve a visit.

The shock of finding that Jerry Kincaid and Giles Cambridge were one and the same person had just about worn off but it galled her to think how easily he had won her confidence. It was the first time in many years that she'd been taken for a ride and, she had to admit, it stung. Which was another reason she was in no hurry to face Buchanan's pitying smile.

She spent the day alternately trying to study and thinking about Vanessa. Now that she had all the jigsaw pieces

that made up the picture of her demise, the only question
to be answered was how to make the best use of them.
And by Monday morning she had the answer to that.

She got up early and washed her hair and braided it
tightly while it was still wet, that being the only way she
could make it look businesslike. Then she dressed carefully
in her grey jacket, black skirt and tights, and buffed up her
solitary pair of heels. A touch of make-up, and she was
ready to go into battle.

Eleven-fifteen saw her breaching the outer defences of
Lawrence Grassick's retreat, buzzing all over with a not
entirely pleasant feeling of anticipation. She gave her
name, adding the clarification that Mr Grassick and she
had met at Brora Lodge on Friday, and wasn't surprised to
be admitted, presently, to the inner sanctum.

Grassick was seated behind a desk the size of a table for
eight and didn't rise when she came in.

'I won't ask you to sit down,' he said, with a cold stare.
'I'm sure your business won't take long.'

Fizz gave him her sweetest smile and took a chair. 'Well,
I hope you're right, Mr Grassick, but I'll take the weight
off my feet anyway.' She parked her bag on the floor and
plunged straight on without giving him time for any more
of his childish behaviour. 'I thought you should know
right away that Tam Buchanan and I have now completed
our investigation into your wife's death.'

'Oh, really?' he sneered, a layer of fake interest applied
to cover the very real curiosity that lit his eyes. 'You
wasted two weeks on proving the facts to be precisely what
I claimed them to be. Congratulations.'

'Yes,' Fizz said. 'You told us the truth, as far as it went.'

His black brows snapped down. 'What d'you mean, "as
far as it went"? I don't have time to listen to any of Tam
Buchanan's daft imaginings. You've told me all I need to
know; now you can take yourself off.'

Fizz crossed her legs and put on a look of profound
sympathy. She could already feel her hair wriggling its way

out of her braids but she resisted raising a hand to tidy it. 'There is just the question of what we should do with our information,' she said gently.

Grassick sat slowly back in his chair and returned her smile with suppressed venom. 'If you want my opinion on that, Miss Fitzpatrick, I'll have to know specifically what information you're referring to.'

'What I'm referring to,' Fizz said, with only the faintest tremor betraying the effect this was having on her nervous system, 'is attempted murder.'

Grassick didn't even blink. 'Attempted murder, eh? Well now, that's a serious charge. I do hope you have good grounds for laying it. Do tell me: whose attempted murder of whom?'

'Vanessa's attempted murder of you, Mr Grassick. Surely you were aware of what had happened?'

After a brief silence, Grassick shook his head and produced a bark of laughter. 'This is the result of Buchanan's inquiry, eh? Two weeks raking around and this is what he comes up with? You should take up fiction writing, the two of you.'

'Perhaps you'd allow me to run over our line of reasoning, sir, so that you can point out where we went wrong?'

Grassick made a show of looking at his watch. 'I can give you five minutes.'

'Thank you, sir.' Fizz felt she should have addressed him as 'm'lud'. Half of what she was about to hit him with was circumstantial evidence but, with a bit of luck, it would be enough to shut him up. 'To our way of thinking, the whole thing stemmed from the fact that Vanessa became accidentally pregnant. It must have come as a very nasty shock to her because, according to witnesses, she absolutely did not want a baby. But she was stuck with it, wasn't she? Your political career was built on your Pro Life stance and, if it emerged that your wife'd had an abortion, you'd be back to the drawing board. It would be hard for anyone to prove what you did to prevent her getting rid of the baby but, since it's your money behind her business, one could make an educated guess.'

Grassick didn't move but his face showed only a faint amusement as he waited for her to continue. Fizz hadn't expected him to break down in tears at her first salvo but, even though she knew his calm had to be faked, she still found it horribly unnerving to have to start insinuating that his marriage must have been on its last legs.

'In the end, I think her business meant more to Vanessa than you did. If she wasn't to be lumbered with an unwanted child, you had to go.' She caught sight of her hands shaking and knotted them in her lap. 'She was in no financial position to divorce you so she planned to make use of your visits to Brora Lodge to put an end to your relationship. Probably over a period of a couple of weeks at least, she topped up your store of gas cylinders in the basement, then she bought an old heater from a house sale, one that had a thermostat that would give off a spark when it switched off.'

'Most ingenious.' Grassick nodded condescendingly as if this was all new to him. 'Sounds like a nice little time-bomb.'

'I imagine it would have done the job,' Fizz agreed. 'All Vanessa had to do was turn on the gas cylinders. We have a witness who saw her at the cottage that Friday afternoon when she was doubtless doing just that. You yourself would have set things in motion when you turned on the electricity at the mains on your arrival, allowing the heater to slowly raise the temperature of the cellar till the thermostat switched off. No doubt, she'd set the thermostat to switch off quickly, but by then she would have been alibing herself in Inverness. Had your car not started to act up I suspect it would have been your grieving widow I'd have been talking to today.'

'My ex-wife would not have given you the time of day, miss! Nor would she have listened to a word of your complete drivel.'

'But *you* have, Mr Grassick,' Fizz dared to point out and paused to let the implication sink in. 'So, with your permission, I'll go on.'

He flushed ruby red but chose not to reply, which Fizz took as a good sign.

By the time Vanessa arrived at the home of her friend, Charlotte McIntosh, she was all hyped up. But some time during that evening you called her mobile phone and she learned that you had not gone to Brora Lodge after all. She must have seen, not only that her plan had failed, but that she was in danger of being found out. The gas would have leaked all through the house by the time you got there the following day. You'd smell it and check the cylinders . . . find them all open . . . find the heater . . .' She paused, giving Grassick the chance to comment, but he said nothing and his face remained unreadable. His stillness shook her confidence a little but she ploughed on. 'Vanessa had to do something. She must have reckoned that she could make it to Chirnside, perform a swift cover-up, and get back to Inverness before she was missed. Maybe she planned to abort the murder attempt for the time being. Maybe she thought she could get most of the gas out of the cellar and start again from scratch, so that there would be just enough leakage to cause the explosion some time after your arrival the following morning. It's impossible to know which was her intention, but that's when she was killed. She had been in the house only a few seconds – probably making a quick dash to turn off the gas cylinders. It was the doorbell being rung that provided the spark – it was battery operated, wasn't it?'

She took a long breath, trying to gather her thoughts, but Grassick gave another bark of laughter and pushed back his chair. 'Well, if that's the best you can come up with, Miss Fitzpatrick, I don't think the Procurator Fiscal will want anything to do with it. In fact, the standing of Buchanan and Stewart will be no higher than a snake's belly. And now, I'm afraid I have heard enough nonsense for one morning so if you would kindly—'

'Don't you want to know what Jamie Ford was doing there with your wife at two-thirty in the morning?'

Fizz had been sure all along that Grassick didn't know the answer to that one even before she had confirmed it with Dougie, the WPS copper, the night before. The police were so determined to keep Ford's story a secret that they had let Grassick stew over that and he'd have been pretty dumb not to wonder if his wife and Jamie were lovers and if, consequently, Vanessa's child was Jamie's. All the same, it pleased her to see Grassick sit back in his chair.

'I may as well hear the whole story, I suppose. But please make it brief.'

'According to Mrs Ford, who has been extremely difficult to locate,' Fizz said, 'Jamie Ford was a light sleeper. He heard the sound of a car, saw the reflection of a torch beam in the garden of Brora Lodge, and assumed that the place was being burgled. He went over and rang the bell, intending to hide till he saw who came to the door. However, with the gas already leaking up the basement steps to the hallway, the spark from the doorbell detonated the explosion.'

Grassick made a robust effort to hide his emotion. For a couple of seconds his face held on to his granite expression of neutrality and then began to slacken as though it were made of melting wax. His jowls sagged, the faint bags under his eyes deepened, and his eyelids drooped over his weary eyes. Fizz could almost have felt sorry for him. Almost.

'I'm sure that knowledge must set your mind at rest,' she said brazenly, before he could get back to throwing her out. 'Which is at least something you owe Tam Buchanan. I doubt very much if anyone else would have had the tenacity to pursue that piece of information.'

Grassick cleared his throat. 'He was never short of tenacity. Nobody could accuse him of that. Nor, I'm willing to admit, of downright, unnecessary nosiness.'

Fizz sat up and recrossed her legs. 'Well that's one thing we're *not* going to disagree about, sir,' she said, getting ready to go in for the kill with a bright and happy smile that would have cheered up Pagliacci. 'I've worked with Buchanan for more than two years and I'd have to say he's probably the most honourable man I've ever met in my life. I know for a fact how dearly he would have loved to turn his back on this inquiry, and I think the rest of the Edinburgh legal fraternity would agree with me when I say that if his determination to follow the dictates of his conscience were to damage his career it would be—'

'Oh, do you?' snarled Grassick, abruptly returning to his normal viperish persona. 'And you're an expert on such matters, I've no doubt. I suppose you think we'll all go weak at the knees under the effect of his bonnie blue eyes, is that it? Away home to your romantic novels and your soap operas, lassie, and give me peace.'

'My intention was merely to assure you, Mr Grassick, that Tam Buchanan would not dream of taking what he knows to the police or, indeed, to the newspapers.'

He had done very well, up to this point, to have kept his temper under control but now Fizz guessed she was about to witness the fabled holocaust of his rage. Exactly why he held back was something of a mystery: either Buchanan's warning had rung true or he was muzzled by the perceived threat in her defence of Tam's morals.

'He wouldn't, eh?' he said nastily. 'But *you* would, is that right?'

'Of course I wouldn't,' Fizz assured him. 'Not intentionally. All I meant to imply was that Buchanan is a man you can trust.'

'I understand perfectly what you intended to imply, Miss Fitzpatrick.' He spat out the words as if they were poison. 'I take it that your purpose in invading my chambers today has something to do with striking a bargain.'

'If you are insinuating something as degrading as blackmail,' Fizz declared, putting on an Oscar-deserving performance of outrage, 'I have to protest. My purpose was to invite your admiration for a brilliant, highly qualified, and dedicated lawyer who deserves your patronage rather than your knife in his back. Admittedly, he has dealt with some high-profile cases over the past few years, but I can assure you that he did not seek them out, quite the reverse.' She found herself standing up and put her fists on the edge of the desk to steady herself. 'Mr Grassick, that man is wasted behind a solicitor's desk. He is being stultified. He needs – and deserves – a job where he can use his talents to their full extent – for instance, as an advocate.'

Grassick stared at her with his lips apart for several seconds as if he doubted the evidence of his ears. Then a wide grin broke across his face and he gave vent to a quickly smothered spurt of laughter.

'Miss Fitzpatrick, you are full of surprises. Please sit down.' He folded his arms on the desk and hunched his shoulders as he watched her drop into her chair. 'Yes indeed. You are a most surprising – and, if I may say so – enterprising young lady. You're in your third year, I understand, and widely expected to get a first, if you keep on the way you're doing. Oh, yes, er . . . Fizz . . . I was interested enough to ask a mutual friend about you over the weekend. He thought you were star material, you'll be happy to hear.'

Fizz couldn't imagine where this was likely to lead but she wasn't about to drop her guard just yet. She kept her mouth shut.

'A survivor, he called you, and tough as old boots. Well, that's no bad thing for a lawyer. You'll need all the toughness you can get.' He narrowed his eyes to look closely at her face. 'And you have carved yourself a little niche in Buchanan and Stewart already, eh? Good proactive thinking that, and I've no doubt that's the reason you decided to champion young Buchanan, eh? Safeguarding your own future, am I right?'

Fizz moistened dry lips and decided that candour was her best option at this delicate stage in the proceedings. 'Only partly. I do want to make sure I have a firm to work for when I qualify but, more importantly, I think Buchanan is one of the straightest guys in the profession and I think he deserves to get ahead.'

He clasped his hands and confined a smile to one corner of his mouth. 'And how do you know that he'd welcome being called to the bar? Have you spoken to him about this little ploy of yours?'

'No, I haven't. And if I did he'd probably sack me for interfering,' she said. The fact that he had sacked her already was, she felt, irrelevant since she'd be back doing business at the old stand before he was fit again and by then his annoyance would have evaporated. 'But I know he'd jump at the chance. It's what he should have gone for in the first place if he hadn't been bulldozed by his parents.'

Grassick nodded and regarded his clasped hands in silence for a few moments. 'I have to say, Fizz, that I like your style and, to tell the truth, I can't help liking Tam's style as well – even without your unsolicited testimonial. Honesty is not a quality that one meets up with every day – not the kind of honesty that outweighs self-interest, and I hear nothing but good about the lad.' He smiled wryly. 'He's not short of confidence, I'll say that for him.'

Fizz wanted to take a deep breath but couldn't quite make it. She had a suspicion that he was ready to cut a deal but it wasn't easy to be certain. She still had plenty to hit him with. Interfering with the course of justice, for a start. It was perfectly obvious that he had pulled strings to have some aspects of the case suppressed. At another time even he would probably have found that difficult but, given the involvement of the WPS, the Procurator Fiscal would, in any case, have been bending over backwards to hush up the whole business. She was also totally convinced that it was Grassick who had funded the Pringles' disappearance.

It would have been well worth his while to offer them a cruise in the Med or at least a fortnight in a swish hotel to put them beyond Buchanan's reach, and it was clear that nobody else was likely to have profited by their disappearance. She'd have loved to see his reaction to both of these accusations but they could wait till she saw which way the wind was blowing. It was never a good idea to expend ammunition which could be used another time. However, she did feel able to increase the pressure a little.

'Unfortunately, we turned up more than we expected to during the course of our investigations,' she said. 'I think I can tell you, in strictest confidence, that Jamie Ford was under the Witness Protection Scheme and in investigating him we accidentally crossed swords with the villains who were trying to kill him. I really can't go into any details, as you'll understand, sir, but during the arrest of the villains on Saturday night Buchanan was shot in the chest. Just a flesh wound, fortunately, but the A&E unit at the Royal decided he had to stay in for observation.'

Grassick put a hand to his forehead and closed his eyes for a second. 'And you tell me he doesn't seek out these confrontations?'

'I have to confess,' Fizz admitted, 'he's inclined to blame it on me.'

'Now, why doesn't that surprise me?' He stood up and walked around his desk and, cupping her elbow, escorted her to the door. 'My dear, you must excuse me now. Will you let me think this matter over and get back to you?'

'Of course,' Fizz said and shook the hand he held out to her. OK, she should have said something real tough about not taking too long about it, but if ever there was a time to quit when she was winning, this was it.

It was still raining outside as she headed down the Mound towards the office, but she scarcely noticed it as the mental tape of her interview with Grassick replayed itself in her head. She'd been moderately optimistic when she left Grassick's chambers but already her mind was filled with doubt. Had he been stringing her along? Keeping her sweet and playing for time so that he could pull some legal manoeuvre and have her silenced? That would, of course, be the smart thing to do and she had no idea whether he could get away with it or not. Sod it! She should have demanded immediate action on the bargain while she held the high ground.

All afternoon, as she worked her way through her In-tray, it preyed on her mind and by five o'clock she knew, beyond any doubt, that Grassick was such a snake in the grass he'd see both herself and Buchanan obliterated before he knuckled down to blackmail.

She took the long way home, marching briskly through the rain in the hope of working some endorphins into her system, but she was still in need of some TLC when she got there. She had plenty of studying to do to keep her mind occupied but, tonight, she couldn't settle to it and when six-thirty came she gave up the pretence and went to visit Buchanan.

The Royal Infirmary was only a ten-minute walk away, which was fortunate because, when she got there, she was informed that Buchanan had been released an hour ago, so she had to backtrack down the Mound to the New Town. She'd have been soaked to the skin by the time she got there without the protection of the plastic coat. It wasn't what the in-crowd were wearing but it had won a place in her wardrobe and in her heart and, on top of that, it kept her extremely dry.

Buchanan tried to look unwelcoming, but she could see he was only kidding.

'I was about to have an early night,' he said, kicking the door shut behind her with delight.

'Not at seven o'clock, surely?'

He followed her into the living room, cradling the arm closest to the wound at the side of his ribs, and sank gingerly into an armchair. 'In case you've forgotten, I have

273

a hole in my chest. That red stuff all over me on Saturday was blood.'

'Oh come on,' Fizz said bracingly. 'I've seen worse at a circumcision. I can't see why they had to keep you in so long.'

She got rid of her mac and boots and then became aware of something different. Selina had missed out on her Kamikaze welcome tonight. She was sitting on top of the TV, still as a sphinx, her eyes fixed on something beyond the tip of Fizz's right elbow. Fizz followed her stare and saw a shiny black shadow lying across the row of books at the back of Buchanan's desk. One elegant leg dangled down limply across the spines and a steady, low-pitched purring identified the alien.

'Buchanan! You didn't!' Fizz tried not to laugh but couldn't repress a grin.

'What did you expect?' He glowered at her, clutching his phony peevishness to him tenaciously. 'That I'd send him back to the cattery?'

Fizz didn't really want to go into what she'd expected so she said, 'What about Selina? How's she taking it?'

'The jury's still out.' Buchanan nodded towards the still life atop the TV. 'She's been like that since Dougie dropped Pooky off about an hour ago. She hasn't so much as blinked.'

'Dougie? The WPS guy? That was nice of him.'

Buchanan's glower lightened a shade. 'He and his mates are apparently pretty chuffed to have Jerry and Bragg under lock and key – which makes us the good guys for a change. I'm trying not to think about what Ian Fleming's going to say when he discovers we sent him on a wild goose chase. He was quite looking forward to proving that Virgo was on the take.'

'That was the royal "we" you used just there, I take it? I don't think I actually spoke to Ian at all, this time, did I?'

There was a sour edge to Buchanan's smile. 'I don't believe you did, Fizz. Looks like you're smelling of violets after all.'

'Not in *your* nostrils. I suspect,' Fizz returned, bored with ignoring his gloomy face. 'Or am I just imagining the antagonism smouldering under your teddy-bear surface? No doubt you're still piqued because I saved your life?'

Buchanan shifted his position in his chair, pretending to be in great pain. 'My life was not in danger, Fizz. It was your life that was in danger – leaping into the room like a mad thing just when the bullets were about to start flying. You were that close – *that* close,' he stressed, brandishing his thumb and forefinger, 'to being killed. How do you expect me to feel? How would I have felt if you'd been fatally wounded, or crippled, or scarred for life?'

'What did I tell you, Buchanan? You're always worrying about things that never happen. And anyway – how do you think I'd have felt if he'd killed you?' Suddenly hearing what she was saying, Fizz backtracked in a big hurry. 'Actually, I thought he *had* killed you and I was about to leg it when the sweary words popped out, and then it was too late.'

'Fizz, I *told* you to stay in the car where you'd be safe and not cause complications.'

'Oh, pooh! I don't have to do everything you tell me.' Fizz sure as hell wasn't going to tell him she'd seen that two-faced rat Kincaid drive up and had decided the portents warranted a speedy gallop to the rescue. She could just imagine what nonsense he would read into that. He appeared, however, to be slightly mollified, having got his grievances off his chest, so she tried changing the subject.

'Did you tell your folks what happened?'

'Just Dad. He'd been leaving excitable messages on the answering-machine since Friday afternoon so I had to tell him where I'd been. He promised he wouldn't tell Mum I'd been in hospital but I suspect he'll be over here first thing in the morning to view the corpse.'

'What was he so excitable about?' Fizz asked, this not being an epithet one would normally apply to Big Daddy.

The last shreds of Buchanan's grouchiness disappeared

behind a smug grin. 'He'd had Mr Menzies senior on the telephone insisting that Lammerburn Estate was to be taken off the market as of that minute and he wanted to know who or what had got the old guy so worked up.'

'To which you said . . .?'

'To which I said that it was none of our business. I said I had spoken to Mr Menzies in person and found him wholly able to conduct his own affairs without the help of either his son or his wife. So the matter is closed. Thank God.'

'Thank God,' Fizz echoed. 'Shall we have a cup of coffee to celebrate?'

Buchanan blinked pathetically. 'If you're sure you have the time.'

She went through to the kitchen and made two mugs of instant and, finding a packet of chocolate chip cookies tucked away, for some reason, in the fridge, added that to the tray. When she got back neither Selina nor Pooky had moved a whisker and Buchanan was dozing peacefully on his cushions.

'So,' she said, poking him to make him sit up and take his mug, 'did they allocate you an ambulance to drive you home?'

'Fat chance,' he said, yawning. 'You have to have had at least one leg amputated before they send you home by ambulance these days.'

'Who ran you home, then? Did you get a taxi?'

'No,' he said, and for all his endeavours couldn't stop his face from lighting up. 'You'll never guess who ran me home!'

'Surprise me.'

'Lawrence Grassick.'

'*Oof!*' Fizz didn't have to fake her surprise. Lawrence Grassick hadn't wasted any time and, judging by the exultant grin, he must have made an offer Buchanan couldn't refuse. 'You're having me on,' she said, wiping spilled coffee off her jeans and starting to hyperventilate.

'I'm not. I swear to God, Fizz. He strolled in just after I'd been given the okay to get dressed – not even visiting hour – all smiles and commiserations, bunch of magazines and what have you, like he was my father.'

'I can't believe it,' Fizz gasped, amazed at the potency of her persuasive talents. Had she really been responsible for changing Grassick's mind, or had he merely found it impossible to put a legal gag on her?

'Neither can I. I've been sitting here wondering if I was delirious this afternoon or if I really heard him offer me a job.'

'He offered you a *job*?'

'He asked if I'd ever considered advocacy.' Buchanan hugged his coffee mug and tried to contain his euphoria but a sound escaped him which, in anyone else, would have been a snigger. 'I couldn't understand why he'd offer to take me on to his staff, but he made it clear that he really wanted me to accept. He said he'd been impressed with my moral stance and my intelligence – would you believe? – and admitted that everyone he spoke to in legal circles had only good to say about me. He thought I was wasting my talents as a solicitor.'

It occurred to Fizz that if Grassick had been discussing Buchanan so much recently his intentions hadn't been all that good. Perhaps he'd tried to blacken Buchanan's name and met with a resistance that made him think again. No matter, this was not the time to say so.

'And have you decided whether to accept or not?' she queried.

'Are you kidding?' He looked so boyish when he grinned like that – which was something like twice a year – that Fizz was in danger of forgetting what a trial he was most of the time. 'Are you kidding? How simple would I have to be?'

Lucky that he was in a fragile condition, otherwise she'd have had to hug him. 'I'll miss you,' she heard herself say – not only out loud, which was naff enough, but in a voice that sounded totally pathetic.

'You should be so lucky,' he returned, looking at her in a way that made her go hot and cold. 'I'll be in and out of the office till we get a new partner – just a temporary one, to tide us over till you get your degree.'

Fizz had to swallow a couple of times before she could say, 'You mean that, Buchanan? You'll take me on?'

'Sure I mean it. I never expected to get out of it.' He laughed softly, his blue, blue eyes on her face, and slid forward in his chair to lay his free hand on her arm. 'You're the best I could get, Fizz. I'm not in any doubt about that and anyway, I like having you around. What you've done for me over the past two weeks, the risks you've taken with your own career – I don't know anyone else who'd do that for me. Good friends are worth keeping.'

Now, Fizz realised, was the time to make a swift exit. When things moved so fast down an unexplored route the smart thing to do was to play for time to think. She grabbed her coat.

'Gotta go. I've got to finish an essay for tomorrow morning. Besides, you'd be better off in bed.'

Buchanan smiled at her fondly. 'What would I do without you to look after me, Fizz?'

As she passed behind his chair she bent down, gave his cheek a quick pinch, and murmured, 'Stick with me, baby, and you'll go places.'

Skinner's Trail

Quintin Jardine

First the joyous birth of Skinner's son . . .

Then the grim reality of murder in one of Edinburgh's prosperous suburbs. A man has been found knifed in a luxury villa.

The victim had run a chain of laundrettes, saunas and pubs throughout the city, but for some time the police suspected these to be the front for a drug-distribution network. As the murder investigation continues without result, it seems the killer was particularly cunning in covering his tracks – leaving no clues or leads to pursue.

But then another, seemingly minor, crime – involving property fraud – takes Assistant Chief Constable Bob Skinner in a new direction. Moving from Scotland to northern Spain, then back to a chilling climax in Edinburgh, this complex and suspenseful thriller follows a tortuous and bloodsoaked trail involving vice, corruption and the merchants of death.

0 7472 4141 4

headline

Now you can buy any of these other bestselling Headline books from your bookshop or *direct from the publisher*.

A Place of Safety	Caroline Graham	£6.99
Running Scared	Ann Granger	£5.99
Shades of Murder	Ann Granger	£5.99
Biting the Moon	Martha Grimes	£5.99
The Lamorna Wink	Martha Grimes	£5.99
Tip Off	John Francome	£6.99
The Cat Who Robbed a Bank	Lilian Jackson Braun	£5.99
Screen Savers	Quintin Jardine	£5.99
Thursday Legends	Quintin Jardine	£5.99
A Chemical Prison	Barbara Nadel	£5.99
Stronger Than Death	Manda Scott	£5.99
Oxford Shift	Veronica Stallwood	£5.99
Fleeced	Georgina Wroe	£6.99

TO ORDER SIMPLY CALL THIS NUMBER

01235 400 414

or e-mail <u>orders@bookpoint.co.uk</u>

Prices and availability subject to change without notice.